THE
QUANTUM
BREACH

DENVER ACEY

PRAISE FOR *THE QUANTUM BREACH*

"*The Quantum Breach* will change your life. It is an exciting espionage story, a page-turner rivaling the books of Tom Clancy and John LeCarre. . . . Denver Acey recognizes the great weaknesses of our culture, a culture that purposely isolates us from each other. He understands that the tighter we embrace our culture the lonelier we become. The answer is not the digital communities we invent to allay our emptiness. They are illusions never replacing the soul-satisfying unity found in true spiritual communion. It is this realization Acey convincingly develops in *The Quantum Breach*. And it is this realization that will change your life."

—JOHN GUBBINS, author of *Profound River* and *Raven's Fire*

"Technically accurate, realistic, and compelling. An eye-opening look into modern hacking techniques."

—ROGER CRIDDLE, professional systems analyst

THE QUANTUM BREACH

DENVER ACEY

BONNEVILLE BOOKS ™

An Imprint of Cedar Fort, Inc.
Springville, Utah

This is a work of fiction. The characters, names, incidents, places, and dialogue are products of the author's imagination and are not to be construed as real. The opinions and views expressed herein belong solely to the author and do not necessarily represent the opinions or views of Cedar Fort, Inc. Permission for the use of sources, graphics, and photos is also solely the responsibility of the author.

ISBN 13: 978-1-4621-1434-4

Published by Bonneville Books, an imprint of Cedar Fort, Inc.
2373 W. 700 S., Springville, UT 84663
Distributed by Cedar Fort, Inc., www.cedarfort.com

LIBRARY OF CONGRESS CATALOGING-IN-PUBLICATION DATA

Acey, Denver.
  The Quantum Breach / Denver Acey.
    pages cm
  ISBN 978-1-4621-1434-4 (pbk. : acid-free paper)
  1. Computer hackers--Fiction. 2. Mormons--Fiction. 3. Kidnapping--Fiction. 4. Suspense fiction.
  I. Title.
  PS3601.C488Q36 2014
  813'.6--dc23
                              2013050769

Cover design by Kristen Reeves
Cover design © 2014 by Lyle Mortimer
Typeset and edited by Melissa J. Caldwell

Printed in the United States of America

10 9 8 7 6 5 4 3 2 1

PROLOGUE

AUGUST 10, TIJUANA, MEXICO

Jeff Kessler was a desperate man.

The stench of sweat and blood filled the air of the dusty, dilapidated building. He was in an abandoned warehouse somewhere on the outskirts of Tijuana. Jeff sat at the edge of a makeshift cockfighting arena, anxiously sipping a cold *cerveza*, while a hundred men watched two roosters fighting to the death. *Surely this is no place for a gringo,* Jeff thought, cursing the fact that his contact had insisted on meeting in this inauspicious location. Jeff checked his watch again, scanning the raucous crowd for a man in a green John Deere hat. *Still not here.*

Jeff restlessly pondered his financial predicament as he waited. His risky business investments had all failed, leaving him few options to pacify his demanding creditors. Unfortunately, the thirty-two-year-old couldn't seek financial refuge in bankruptcy or liquidation, because his debt was linked to embezzlement and money laundering. In his now-frantic attempt to acquire ten million dollars, Jeff had foolishly agreed to complete an unusual job for a Chinese spy organization. He now had just one hundred days to deliver classified documents to the Chinese or face a certain and tortuous death.

"You want another, *amigo*?" asked the old bartender in broken English as he approached Jeff.

"No, *gracias*," Jeff answered, shifting his focus away from the balding

1

man with a gold front tooth. Jeff wanted to remain anonymous, and he hoped to blend in to the frenzied environment with his blue T-shirt and San Diego Padres baseball hat. Seeing that the foreigner was in no mood to talk, the proprietor reluctantly walked off to wait on his other patrons.

A few moments later, a Latino man in a green John Deere hat appeared at Jeff's side.

"Hello," Juan said cheerfully. Taking a seat at the cheap card table, he motioned for the bartender to return with a beverage. He paused a moment to enjoy his drink before discussing business.

"I'm sorry I'm late, *amigo*. I hope I didn't keep you waiting." Juan's English was fluent, but he still spoke with an obvious Spanish accent.

"I'm fine," was Jeff's curt reply. "Did you bring the gear?"

"*¡Claro que sí!*" Juan answered enthusiastically as he removed a faded backpack from his shoulder. He opened up the bag, revealing six state-of-the-art satellite phones (satphones)—unique mobile devices that communicated using low-orbit satellites instead of regular cell phone towers.

"Are they activated and ready to go?"

"Yes, with full encryption. They even work with normal phones, but it was hard to get these without raising any suspicion," Juan replied, hinting that his fee had just gone up.

"What about Tanner Zane? Did you find him?" Jeff asked as he examined one of the satphones in his hand. In many ways it looked and felt like a typical cell phone, only slightly bigger.

"He's still in Albuquerque, just as you suspected. All of the information is in here," Juan said. He removed a manila folder from his backpack.

"Excellent. What's the price?" Jeff asked.

"Sixty thousand."

"That's ten more than we agreed," Jeff said. He put the satphone down on the table and quickly thumbed through the folder.

"Yes, but these phones are made exclusively for the military. I had to steal them from the manufacturer," Juan said.

"I can give you fifty-five," Jeff countered, pretending that he was yielding to the other criminal's demands. In reality, Jeff would have paid much more. Obtaining these prototype satphones was the final step before starting his espionage operation.

"Okay, *amigo*. It's a deal," Juan said with a large smile.

"The money is out in my car. I didn't dare bring it in here," Jeff said. He quickly finished his drink and dropped a ten-dollar bill on the table.

"Yes, this is a wild place," Juan observed as a brawl suddenly erupted between two men betting on the cockfight. "Let's go."

Jeff and Juan stepped out into the hot August night, leaving behind the shouts and smells of the gutted warehouse. Jeff led Juan down a dark alley toward his rental car.

"The money is in the spare tire compartment," Jeff said, opening the trunk of the Chevy Impala. "Can you give me a hand?"

Eager to get his reward, Juan set down the backpack and reached in, extending his torso over the edge of the car. Without warning, Jeff turned rapidly and smashed the tire iron into the back of Juan's skull, knocking him unconscious. Jeff quickly hoisted up the limp body and stuffed it into the trunk. Then, grabbing the backpack, Jeff drove to the US border, where he abandoned the rental car, leaving himself just enough time to catch the last trolley back to San Diego.

His plan was in motion.

< 1 >

SEPTEMBER 3, ALBUQUERQUE, NEW MEXICO

The alarm clock buzzed the same annoying way it had each morning for the past seven years, but today the sound was more tolerable. Tanner Zane didn't loathe waking up at the early hour. In fact, he was thrilled to start the day. After years of diligent work as a computer programmer, he was ready to take his long-awaited vacation.

Shaking the sleep from his head, Tanner got out of bed and walked toward the kitchen in an early morning daze. He opened the empty refrigerator, looking for a can of soda. Soda was, perhaps, an odd choice for a morning drink, but Tanner didn't drink coffee, instead opting for the sweet taste of Mountain Dew. He often heard that Silicon Valley ran on Mountain Dew. *Maybe it's the same thing here in the Rio Grande Valley*, Tanner speculated. Reluctantly, though, he realized he was out of his favorite drink.

Despite the lack of Mountain Dew, today was a momentous day. Tanner glanced at his packed bags by the door. He had finally made it to his sabbatical, the reward his employer gave him after seven years of faithful work. Most of his coworkers fell off the face of the earth during their two-month sabbatical, and Tanner intended to do the same. He planned to be a rested, carefree employee when he returned back to work after Halloween.

Tanner headed into the bathroom, pausing for a moment in front of the mirror. His brown hair was getting a little long. He should have gotten it cut before taking his trip, but he had been preoccupied with some last-minute details at work. Even though he had earned the right to have his sabbatical, Tanner didn't want to dump everything on his remaining coworkers who had to pick up his project load while he was gone.

Tanner vigorously rubbed his blue eyes before splashing hot water on his face. It was time for his daily shaving ritual. As he lathered up his face, he listened to the news coming from the TV in his bedroom.

"Today's headline comes from California," the reporter started. "Another major retailer is the victim of a hacking incident. Initial estimates say that nearly twenty million credit card numbers were stolen over the past two weeks. The hackers appear to have gained access to the private information by exploiting an unknown security flaw in the corporation's point-of-sale network."

Tanner shook his head as he listened to the report. The cyber-attacks were becoming more frequent and more public. He understood firsthand the damage a cyber-criminal could do to an unsuspecting corporation.

After all, he'd done it himself once.

Tanner finished shaving and took a brief shower. He quickly got dressed and packed his SUV with two suitcases and his prized possession—a Fender bass guitar. He wasn't sure if he'd get a chance to play his guitar during his sabbatical, but he decided to bring it anyway. His last task before leaving was to take out the trash.

"Hey, Tanner," his next-door neighbor shouted as Tanner walked outside into the cool September morning.

"Morning, Doc," Tanner said. Larry Killpack was a dentist who had moved in last month.

"Anything planned for this weekend?" Larry asked. He put his garbage can on the curb next to Tanner's.

"As a matter of fact, there is. I'm leaving on my sabbatical today."

"Sabbatical? I thought those were just for professors. Don't you work at a microchip company?" Larry asked.

"That's right, but everyone at my company gets a paid sabbatical after seven years of employment," Tanner explained.

"That's a nice benefit. I should get a job like that."

"Hey, you're a dentist," Tanner joked. "You don't even work a full five days a week."

"That's a good point," Larry said before changing the subject. "Do you need me to get your mail while you're gone?"

"No thanks. I've got the post office keeping it." Tanner liked his new neighbor, but he was paranoid about anyone holding his mail. The majority of people received credit card statements and other private information in the mail, and Tanner knew that it didn't take much effort to steal an envelope and assume a new identity.

"Maybe there is something you can do," Tanner said, deciding to take his neighbor up on his offer to help. "Would you mind putting my trash can back? I'll be gone for a while."

"No problem. Have a good trip," Larry said as Tanner turned and walked back to his garage.

"Enjoy pulling teeth," Tanner responded before climbing into his Toyota 4Runner.

Despite having ample money in the bank, Tanner lived a modest lifestyle. Being a millionaire wasn't one of his dreams. Technically, he had already "been there, done that," and the lifestyle wasn't as wonderful as most people anticipated. That had been four years ago. Tanner had abandoned his lavish lifestyle when he found religion and joined The Church of Jesus Christ of Latter-day Saints, informally known as the Mormon Church. However, he had kept one item from his time of affluence—his forest-green Toyota 4Runner. It wasn't the best vehicle for gas mileage, but it was perfect for his occasional weekend trip to the Jemez Mountains.

Driving out of his neighborhood, Tanner glanced east toward Sandia Peak. It was the highest mountain around and had a tram going from the eastern edge of town to a fancy restaurant on top. Tanner had never eaten up there, but he had taken the tram to the summit many times to watch the spectacular sunset. With his focus on Sandia Peak in the distance, Tanner failed to notice the black Suburban following nonchalantly behind his 4Runner.

Three miles down the road, Tanner made a quick stop at a convenience store. Grabbing a forty-four-ounce cup, he filled it with Mountain Dew. Choosing a donut from the counter, Tanner willfully surrendered $2.36 for his unhealthy breakfast before calling his parents on his cell phone.

"Hello," Tanner's father, Gordon Zane, answered.

"Gordo!" Tanner said as he walked out to his SUV. Tanner knew it rubbed his dad the wrong way when he called him Gordo, and that was the exact reason why Tanner playfully continued doing it.

"Where are you?" his dad asked.

"I'm just heading out. I should be there by dinner." Tanner was taking his mom and dad on a leisurely tour of the Pacific Coast during his two-month sabbatical. It was something he had wanted to do for years. He planned on picking up his parents in Arizona before heading over to Southern California.

"We're really excited for this trip," his dad said. "We're all set to go."

"Remember, I'm paying for everything. I won't let you buy a single piece of gum," Tanner reminded him.

"I know, I know. You've already made that perfectly clear."

Gordon and Carla Zane were well into their sixties, and Tanner had decided it was the perfect time for an extended trip with his parents before health issues might prevent them from such an adventure in the future.

"I'll call you when I get to Phoenix," Tanner said, preparing to end the phone call.

"Wait, Mom wants to say hi," Gordon countered. Tanner endured the awkwardly long pause before his mom finally got on the phone. It always seemed like she was preoccupied with something else.

"Are you bringing anyone on the trip with you?" Carla Zane asked.

Here we go again. "I'm not seeing anyone right now." Tanner braced himself for the inevitable conversation that always followed when talking about his love life.

"Don't you think it's about time for you to bring someone home to meet your parents?" Carla pressed. "You're thirty years old now. A nice young man your age should have settled down and started a family already."

Tanner winced at his mother's comment. He wondered if she knew that being single at thirty wasn't all that uncommon anymore. "Don't worry, Mom. I'll let you know when I have a serious prospect."

Carla softened her tone. "We just don't want you to be lonely your whole life. That's all."

"I know, but don't worry about me. I'm still waiting for the right person to come along," Tanner assured.

"Okay. We'll see you tonight," Carla said. "I love you."

"Love ya too, Mom."

As an only child, Tanner often copped grief from his parents about still being single. Tanner knew his parents tolerated his conversion to Mormonism in hopes that he might get married sooner and introduce grandchildren to the family. Unfortunately, Albuquerque wasn't exactly overflowing with single Mormon females his age. Of course, the LDS faith didn't prohibit Tanner from marrying outside his religion, but he felt it was best to find a spouse who shared his newly embraced beliefs.

Over the years, Tanner had dated a variety of different women. Ironically, the closest he ever got to marriage was before his religious conversion, back when he'd dated Megan Holland during his junior year in college. Unfortunately, a misunderstanding had soured their relationship, and they separated instead of working things out. Tanner slightly shook his head in frustration. He had acted foolishly, handling the breakup like a pimple-faced teenager instead of a young adult. He wished he had spent more time making the relationship work instead of pulling out after a heated argument. As he accelerated his SUV onto the interstate, Tanner thought about Megan and where she might have ended up in life.

Tanner reached the outskirts of Phoenix just as the sun completed its descent over the White Tank Mountains. He called his parents' home but hung up when the answering machine started. Tanner tried his dad's cell number next, but it also went unanswered, something that frequently happened.

The Valley of the Sun had changed a lot since Tanner had grown up there. Old cow towns, like Gilbert and Chandler that he remembered from his youth, were now huge cities themselves. It seemed the city had doubled in size since he'd accepted a scholarship to the University of New Mexico almost twelve years ago.

Pulling into his parents' neighborhood, Tanner recognized the familiar saguaros welcoming him back. Tanner never lived at this particular address because his parents had moved twice since he'd moved out. Nevertheless, visiting his mom and dad in Arizona still had the feeling of coming home.

Parking his 4Runner in the driveway, Tanner took a moment for an elongated stretch in the cool evening air before heading up to the porch. He rang the doorbell, but nobody answered. Usually Angie, the family's cocker spaniel, barked anytime the doorbell chimed, but tonight her yapping was noticeably absent. Tanner checked the front door and found that it was unlocked. Something wasn't right.

Letting himself in, Tanner shouted "I'm home." All he heard in reply was a muffled cry. Looking toward the kitchen, Tanner stopped in astonishment. His mom and dad were blindfolded, gagged, and bound to dining room chairs. Shocked, Tanner quickly moved to help his restrained parents. He started to undo the ropes binding his mother's hands to the chair but suddenly felt himself lurching backward as he was forcefully grabbed from behind.

Tanner tried to scream for help but couldn't. A hand covered his entire mouth while a large and powerful arm compressed his carotid artery in a sleeper hold. Tanner vainly fought against the unseen assailant, but it was no use. The room went black.

September 3, Los Alamos, New Mexico

One hundred miles northwest of Albuquerque sits the quiet town of Los Alamos, New Mexico. With a population near 12,000 people, this city on a remote mountain plateau is anything but typical. Los Alamos happens to be home to Los Alamos National Laboratory, or LANL, making it the city with the highest concentration of PhDs in the world. The laboratory is one of the largest science and technology institutions on earth. Over eight thousand physicists, chemists, engineers, and other scientists work at the thirty-six-square-mile facility, conducting multidisciplinary research in areas as varied as national security, renewable energy, nanotechnology, and supercomputing. Despite these current areas of focus, LANL's notoriety comes from the super-secret Manhattan Project of World War II.

Before 1943, Los Alamos was a private boys' ranch on the Pajarito Plateau in northern New Mexico. Looking for a secret and secure location to develop the first atomic bomb, the United States government purchased the ranch and replaced the adventurous boys with the most brilliant scientific minds of the time. From universities all over the country, hundreds of scientists and their families disappeared into the desert to develop the atomic bomb before Nazi Germany could. Under the direction of J. Robert Oppenheimer, the scientists of Site Y achieved their goal and proved it by detonating the world's first nuclear weapon on July 16, 1945.

While nuclear weapon stewardship was still a primary focus at Los Alamos, the laboratory had since branched out into other fields, searching for the next scientific breakthrough. Such an event was unfolding in Technical Area Six, where Dr. Jodi McDonald and her team of scientists watched in amazement. For three years they had anticipated this moment. Battling through numerous budget cuts and congressional oversight committees, some of them wondered if their hours of work would pay off. They had. Gathered in the dark in a secure room in Building 72, the scientists created history as they started up the world's first operational quantum computer.

Dozens of green lasers sparkled spectacularly off a 500-carat diamond surrounded by wires and other optical components. This was no ordinary diamond—it was a man-made quantum diamond intentionally filled with imperfections. Throughout the diamond's crystal lattice structure were thousands of nitrogen vacancy centers, where a nitrogen atom was embedded instead of a normal carbon atom. By adjusting the frequency of the green laser, Dr. McDonald and her team of eight scientists had managed to control the magnetic spin of the nitrogen atom, creating a qubit, the fundamental component of quantum computing.

Quantum computers differ significantly from their traditional counterparts, which have been around since the 1970s. In essence, a traditional computer can only perform one computation at a time, but with qubit manipulation, a quantum computer can work on billions of computations simultaneously. All over the world, scientists were racing toward quantum computing with limited success. Recently, a Canadian start-up company showcased their prototype quantum computer using just a half-dozen qubits. Pursuing a different concept using nitrogen vacancy centers, the scientists at Los Alamos National Labs were able to manipulate 128 different qubits at once. This allowed their quantum computer to perform 2^{128} or 340 trillion, trillion, trillion simultaneous calculations—more processing power than every computer on the planet combined.

• ———— •

Jodi McDonald stood off to one side in the dark room, watching the high-fives and hugs among her team. With her arms folded across her white lab coat, she quietly embraced the euphoria of the moment. Even she, as the leading scientist on the project, had trouble wrapping her mind around the momentous occasion. A junior physicist who had noticed his boss quietly watching the rest of the group left the impromptu celebration and approached Jodi.

"Don't you want to join us?"

"I'm just savoring the moment. I can't believe we did it," Jodi said.

"It's history in the making," her coworker observed.

Jodi's smile faded. "Unfortunately, we're still several weeks away from going public with our breakthrough. We've got to test everything again and validate our findings. We can't afford to be off on anything."

"Always the skeptical one, eh?"

"I've been burned by hasty conclusions more than once in my tenure. We have to be absolutely sure about the processing power. I don't want any doubt when I present our findings next month."

Jodi tensed as she thought about the upcoming International Conference on Quantum Information and Computation. She was a keynote speaker, promising to wow the conference attendees with "unprecedented research in quantum computing."

"It's not just about the conference, is it?" the other scientist playfully prodded.

Jodi glared at her junior teammate. Then an enormous grin broke out across her face. The upcoming conference was important, but everyone on the team knew that wasn't the real prize Jodi wanted. If her presentation at the conference was successful, it would pave the way for her nomination for the Nobel Prize next year.

SEPTEMBER 3, CHANDLER, ARIZONA

Everything was dark. Tanner's mind spun in frantic circles, trying to make sense of his current situation. He forced his eyes open and stared blankly at a single lightbulb overhead. It took him a moment to recognize his surroundings. He was sitting on a dining room chair in his parents' garage.

"I imagine you're shocked," a man's voice said from the shadows. Turning toward the mysterious voice, Tanner realized his wrists were duct-taped together and bound behind his back. Trying to use his legs as leverage, Tanner realized they too were bound together.

"What's going on?" Tanner demanded, working to regain his composure and annoyed that his voice sounded so feeble. Off to the side of the garage, he noticed lifeless carcass of the family pet discarded in a cruel manner. A sickening feeling washed over him. What had he gotten himself into?

"Let's start with what you know," the voice said. Slowly, a bearded man in his early fifties moved out of the shadows and into Tanner's view. While the man's voice had been intimidating, it was his size that truly struck fear into Tanner now—his assailant had to be at least six feet six inches tall and 240 pounds.

The attacker smiled brazenly at Tanner's fear, staring penetratingly into his eyes. "We are in control. Cooperation is your only option. Do you understand?"

"What are you talking about?" Tanner asked, fear gripping his emotions.

"You'll have to wait another seven years for your sabbatical," the tall man said. "You're going to spend the next two months working on a special project for us. There's no negotiation. If you cooperate, your parents will live to see their next wedding anniversary."

"What do you want?" Tanner asked, feeling more desperate. His wrists were beginning to throb, and his bladder was about to explode from too much Mountain Dew.

Leaning toward Tanner's right ear, the attacker whispered, "We need you to do some computer hacking for us."

Tanner's back stiffened, and he held his breath. The revelation that someone had found out about his secret hacking past was frightening. Tanner's fear turned to panic. He started to tremble and a wet spot appeared on his jeans. "Tall" smirked as he watched Tanner looking like a little puppy that had just wet itself after being scolded by its master.

Desperate to get some control over the situation, Tanner tried to reason with his unknown captor. "Okay, let my parents go, and we can talk."

"It's not going to work that way," Tall said. He nodded curtly his head, and an unseen conspirator standing directly behind Tanner went to work.

Someone behind Tanner held him in place as Tall put two strips of duct tape over Tanner's mouth. Then Tall placed a dark canvas bag over Tanner's head, completely blinding him. There was a brief pause, and then Tanner jolted as water from a garden hose washed away his urine. Cold and wet, with no ability to speak or see, Tanner only had his sense of hearing to predict what was coming next. He heard the garage door open and a large car or truck backed into the entrance. The vehicle turned off, and the garage door closed.

"We're going for a little ride," Tall said as he and the other captor lifted Tanner, still bound to his chair, and tossed him through the open hatch of a Suburban. Landing painfully on his left shoulder, Tanner felt like a discarded bag of trash left on the curb.

Tanner wasn't sure where he was going or how long he would remain in this precarious state, but he didn't have much time to speculate. Someone grabbed his right forearm, and Tanner recognized the cool tingle of evaporating rubbing alcohol. He knew what was coming next. He jerked involuntarily at the sharp prick of a needle. Fighting ineffectively against his restraints, Tanner realized he was being drugged. As his heart pumped what was probably Propofol throughout his body, Tanner's mind relaxed into a passive stupor. He was now heavily sedated, but not unconscious. He would remain coherent for the next several hours, but the milk of amnesia would effectively prevent him from remembering anything that had just happened.

●———————●

Seeing that Tanner was prepped and ready for his long trip back to New Mexico, the mysterious men went to work on his parents. Gordon and Carla Zane wouldn't get the luxury of being drugged to forget the next part of their arduous journey. Still gagged and bound to their dining room chairs, Mr. and Mrs. Zane were covered with a blanket and wheeled out the back door of their home on a moving dolly. Using the cover of darkness to their advantage, the captors transported the couple across the quiet backyard to a U-Haul truck waiting in an adjacent alley. The kidnappers went about their duties nonchalantly, appearing to the casual observer to be legitimate moving men. The husband and wife were pushed up the ramp and into the moving truck. Quickly securing the chairs into place with moving straps, the men threw in the four suitcases that the couple had conveniently packed for their tour of the West Coast. With their passengers and luggage ready to go, the kidnappers started up the U-Haul and discreetly followed the black Suburban out of the quiet neighborhood.

FALL SEMESTER, UNIVERSITY OF NEW MEXICO
TEN YEARS AGO

C"ome on, I need your help," Jeff Kessler pleaded. "It's not that I can't do it. It's just that I'm not sure it's worth it," Tanner responded to his twenty-two-year-old roommate.

"There's no way I'm going to pass that class. If you don't change my grade, I might not graduate next year," Jeff said.

Tanner thought about his roommate's predicament. Jeff was failing chemistry, badly. Even if he studied day and night, Tanner knew that Jeff still wouldn't learn enough about chemical reactions and covalent bonds to ever pass. In his desperation, Jeff had begged Tanner to hack into the campus computer network and alter his grade.

"What's in it for me?" Tanner asked.

"I'll buy you a pizza."

"I could get into a lot of trouble. That's a lot of risk for just a pizza," Tanner said.

"Then consider this the ultimate challenge," Jeff said. "We'll see who's smarter. You or the campus IT department."

Tanner laughed out loud. Jeff knew how to push a deal. He should have been a used-car salesman. "Okay, I'll try it. Just to see if it can be done. But if it gets too messy, I'm out."

"Just see what you can do. That's all I ask," Jeff said. "But I know you're a computer nerd, so I doubt you'll have any trouble."

16

Tanner hadn't realized it at the time, but he had just crossed the blurry line of ethics and entered into the world of computer hacking. Ironically, it wasn't the promise of wealth or fame that made Tanner commit his first cyber-crime. It was the thrill of trying something that hadn't been done before.

It didn't take long for Tanner to accomplish his hacking job because computer security was not a high priority at the time. The university used standardized computer accounts for everyone, consisting of a combination of a person's last and first names. From that information, Tanner quickly determined that the chemistry professor's login was "dixonbar." Discovering her password was almost as simple. All he had to do was go to the chemistry department.

"Hi, I'm Tanner Zane. Is Dr. Dixon here?" Tanner asked the part-time student receptionist.

"No, she's out for the rest of the day. Can I take a message?" the young woman asked.

Tanner flashed the receptionist an easy smile. Turn on the charm. "It's nothing really. I just brought her a little gift, seeing that the term is almost done." He held up a box of chocolates covered with wrapping paper.

"Are you trying to buy a good grade?"

"That's not necessary. I already have an A in her class," Tanner said with a tiny bit of arrogance. "But she's the best professor I've ever had, so I wanted to get her something to show my appreciation."

The receptionist studied Tanner and apparently decided that he seemed harmless "Her office door is open. It's the last one on the left. You can just put the gift in there," she offered.

Tanner gave the young woman a friendly wave before walking down the hall. Once inside Professor Dixon's office, he set down the gift and got to work. First he checked the professor's computer screen to see if she was logged in. She was, but the terminal was locked. He glanced around the desk and then lifted up the keyboard. He found what he was looking for, a yellow sticky note with "Whiskers" written on it.

Probably the name of her pet.

Tanner quickly logged in to the professor's computer with her password. It worked, but he didn't change Jeff's grade. Instead, Tanner locked the screen and left the office. If he spent too much time in here, it would raise suspicion. There were hundreds of terminals across campus where he could change the grade shortly.

"Anything else?" the receptionist asked as Tanner came back down the hall.

"No, you've been very helpful. Thank you," Tanner said,

It was just that easy.

Later that night, Jeff and Tanner celebrated his success over pizza.

"Did you give me an A?" Jeff asked.

"No way. That would be too obvious. I gave you a C." Tanner said as he took another bite of pizza. They were at their favorite pizza joint—Dion's.

Jeff leaned in over the table. "You know, I've been thinking. We might be able to turn this into a profit," he whispered. Jeff was always looking to make a quick buck.

"Changing grades for money?"

"Exactly. We could set up a little business. I'd be the front man and recruit all our customers, while you'd do the computer stuff. We'd charge people a hundred bucks to change their grade or get other valuable information," Jeff said.

The thought had also crossed Tanner's mind, but it was more than just the money. Tanner was hooked on the rush of doing something illegal. He wanted more, and with youthful invincibility unrestricted by moral values, Tanner quickly agreed to Jeff's scheme.

"We'd have to keep it simple. If we go too big, we'll get caught," Tanner said.

"Agreed," Jeff said. "I'll do all the leg work to find clients."

"And I'll do the hacking." Tanner chuckled.

The next day, the duo embarked on their new business venture. Changing grades or finding out a girl's class schedule would soon become some of their more popular requests. Since the chemistry professor didn't have the sense to change her password frequently, they had unlimited access to the university's mainframe to pilfer all sorts of information. Tanner didn't know it at the time, but their little business venture would earn them almost $10,000 over the next two years.

———•———

The black Suburban bumped wildly as it turned onto a dirt road, jarring Tanner out of his drug-induced sleep. Where was he?

Tanner felt horrible—like he was experiencing one of the hangovers he'd frequently had before swearing off alcohol. Trying to clear his mind, he blinked a few times until he realized that a bag over his head, not blindness, was the reason he couldn't see.

Listening carefully, he searched for some sort of clue to his whereabouts. He could hear the faint sound of the car engine and feel the rhythmic movement of the vehicle as it bounced over a dirt road. Tanner's entire body was immobilized, and he couldn't open his mouth to speak. Making grunting noises, he tried to signal anyone who might hear him. Suddenly, the cloth sack covering his head was rapidly jerked away.

"Good morning, beauty," Tall said, slapping Tanner hard across the face. "How'd you sleep?" Tanner winced from the blow, and Tall laughed before crawling back to the passenger seat.

Tanner tried to get his bearings. His internal clock told him it was morning, and looking out the rear window to see faint pink light on scattered clouds above, Tanner figured he was correct. He tried to put the facts together from the previous night. He remembered arriving at his parents' home and finding them tied up, but after that he drew a blank. He couldn't remember anything else. It was as if time had skipped from last night to right now.

Tanner willed himself to relax and think. Observing and analyzing were some of his best strengths. Like his dad often said when he was younger, Tanner was full of street smarts. He knew he'd have to get his emotional mind in check. Only rational and deliberate decisions would help him survive.

The vehicle came to a sudden halt. With the Suburban motionless now, Tanner's mind quickly focused on the aches and pains in his body. From what he could determine, he had been tied to the chair all night. His back hurt terribly, and his legs were numb. Trying to swallow the pasty saliva in his mouth, Tanner wished for a cold drink of water and a Tylenol.

The tailgate of the Suburban quickly opened as Tall and another kidnapper lifted Tanner out of the back and set him upright on the ground. Tanner got a head rush as the blood flowed down to his legs. Tall reached out and ripped the duct tape off Tanner's mouth. Tanner howled in response due to a day's worth of stubble being ripped out by the roots. He wanted to swear at his kidnappers, but suddenly he remembered more pressing matters.

"I gotta go to the bathroom," he said rapidly.

"Well, go then," Tall responded unsympathetically. Unable to control his natural functions, Tanner wet his pants for the second time in twelve hours.

"Welcome to your new home," Tall announced, stepping back from the mess Tanner had created on the gravel driveway. "This is where you'll live and work for the next two months."

Tanner glanced around and got his first good look of the area. He was in a high mountain meadow. Large pine trees lined the edge of the clearing and seemed to spread out in every direction. A cabin stood off about ten yards from Tanner—really more of a mountain home than a cabin, with a log façade and a green steel roof. A spacious wooden deck came out the front door and wrapped around the entire ground level, with another deck extending out of a master bedroom on the second floor.

Tall spoke again. "As you can see, we are completely isolated here. That dirt road is the only way in or out," he said, motioning to the path they had just traveled. "It's a four-mile hike in any direction until you see another sign of life. That's plenty of time for us to track you down and kill you, just like hunting a deer. Our best marksman can easily hit a target at five hundred yards with his sniper rifle. You'd be foolish to even attempt an escape."

Tanner studied the other kidnapper. A little shorter and skinnier than the leader, this man had blond hair and glasses. He too looked ordinary and had no tattoos or other identifiable marks. Chances are Tanner would walk right past this man on the street and not even give him a second glance.

The shorter man reached into his coat pocket and took out a switchblade. Flipping the knife out, he cut the duct tape off Tanner's arms, wrists, and legs. Tanner momentarily thought he might be free, but before he could do anything, Tall lunged forward and smashed his fist into Tanner's gut. Tanner fell to the ground, gasping in pain. The two kidnappers then grabbed Tanner by his arms and dragged him onto the porch. Opening the front door, they shoved him through the entrance and threw him onto the floor. Tanner lay motionless for a moment, clenching his stomach.

The two men again lifted Tanner to his feet. "Don't!" he gasped. "I won't run. Just stop it, okay?" Satisfied he wasn't going to flee, the two men took a passive, but watchful, step back.

"Take off your clothes. You stink," Tall said.

Tanner did as he was told and was escorted by Tall to a small bathroom down the hall.

"Take a shower and clean up, but don't do anything stupid," Tall ordered. Tanner turned on the water and stepped into the shower, feeling uncomfortable that another man was watching him just three feet away. But the warm water soon soaked Tanner's head and helped clear his mind. Glancing around, Tanner noticed that he was in a typical bathroom complete with soap, shampoo, towels, and … his electric razor on the counter.

Tall noticed Tanner's longer than usual gaze at the counter and responded, "Yes, that's your razor. You'll also find your other personal items here. This is your bathroom. Across the hall is a closet with all the stuff that you conveniently packed for your sabbatical. But you don't get your own bedroom," he warned. "You'll sleep on the couch."

Finished with his shower, Tanner grabbed a brown towel and dried off before walking over to the hall closet. Someone had neatly unpacked his clothes and hung everything up. At the bottom of the closet was a small dresser that contained his socks and underwear. He even had an extra pair of tennis shoes waiting for him. Tanner slowly got dressed, favoring his stomach, which was still sore from the sucker punch. With a fresh pair of clothes on, Tanner turned toward Tall.

"Well, what do I do now?"

September 4, Outside Las Vegas, New Mexico

Approximately 150 miles to the east was another cabin. Located in the pine-covered hills outside the quiet town of Las Vegas, New Mexico, Gordon and Carla Zane waited in a kitchen. Despite their best efforts to remain calm and poised, the two senior citizens were on the verge of breaking down. They had no idea what was going on, and they could only assume the worst.

Just before their son's arrival in Phoenix the night before, a well-dressed man had knocked on Gordon and Carla's door. He said he was looking for Sean Kemp, who supposedly resided at that address. The Zanes were attempting to help the stranger when a loud pounding came from their back door. With the Zanes momentarily distracted, the well-dressed man had forced his way into the house, shoving the unsuspecting couple to the ground. Recovering from the chaos, Gordon and Carla were startled by the sight of a black pistol aiming down at them.

Gordon and Carla were gagged, bound with duct tape, and forced to witness the slaughter of their beloved pet as they waited for Tanner's arrival. Unable to warn their son of the impending danger, the parents anxiously watched his fate unfold when he arrived at their home. Two mysterious assailants had quickly subdued Tanner and dragged him out into the garage. That was the last time they had seen him.

The nighttime drive had been unpleasant and unnerving. Confined in the back of a stuffy moving van, Gordon and Carla had absolutely no idea where they were going. Ten agonizing hours later, they were escorted from the moving van and into a modestly furnished mountain home. They now sat quietly at a small table, eating a makeshift breakfast of peanut butter sandwiches, as the assumed leader of their captors paced in front of them.

"Listen up," the leader began. He was balding and overweight but he carried himself with purpose, like he was no stranger to working outside the law. "You're being held as collateral while your son does some work for us. When he's finished, you'll be released and dropped off somewhere in the Arizona desert. By the time you find your way home and call the police, we'll be a distant memory."

Gordon found the courage to speak. "Where's our son?"

"Not here," the leader said, offering no other explanation.

"Is he all right?" Carla asked, trepidation in her voice.

"I assume so, but I'm not taking care of him now, am I?"

"Is he in some kind of trouble?" Carla followed up.

"Look, I'm not running the show. My job is to keep you locked up until the boss tells me it's time to let you go. Got that?"

"What do we call you?" Gordon asked.

"You can call me Karl," the leader responded. "Those two fellas over there are helping me out." He gestured toward a pair of street thugs sitting on the couch in the living room. All three men looked like hardened criminals, and they were armed with guns.

Gordon gazed around the room. "Where are we?"

"That's not important, but this is, so listen up," Karl said. "You'll do what we tell you. If you try to escape, we'll kill you, just like we killed your stupid dog. Got that?"

Completely out of their element and with no other options for survival, Gordon and Carla Zane reluctantly nodded their heads in agreement.

———•———

Tall escorted Tanner out of the bathroom and into the main area of the cabin. After studying his surroundings for a moment, Tanner realized there would be no roughing it here. The main floor had a large kitchen at one end and a spacious family room with a two-story vaulted ceiling at the other. A stairway wrapped around its edge and went upstairs to four bedrooms, each with a door overlooking the main floor below. The professionally furnished interior had a rustic western feel that seemed to clash with the large flat-screen TV in the family room. Looking toward the modern kitchen, Tanner noticed two other kidnappers in addition to the blond-haired driver of the Suburban. All three men looked serious with their SIG Sauer P220 handguns tucked into their waistbands.

"Let me introduce everyone since we're going to be working together," Tall began. "That's Charles, standing by the fridge. You already met him earlier this morning," he said, pointing toward the blond man with glasses. "Sitting on the left is Michael, and next to him is Magic. I'm Patrick, the second-in-command here."

Michael was the shortest of the group, with a military-style haircut and dark eyes that stared penetratingly at Tanner. Michael appeared to be a man of few words. Magic's wrinkled T-shirt and faded blue jeans highlighted his youthful and nonthreatening appearance. Magic seemed to be about Tanner's age, while the other men appeared to be in their late forties or early fifties. Tanner figured he could probably hold his own against Magic, but with their athletic and well-conditioned appearance, Tanner knew he wouldn't last very long in a fight against the others.

Tanner heard the fridge open and turned just in time to see Charles tossing him a Mountain Dew. Reaching out, Tanner clumsily grabbed the aluminum can before it hit the ground.

"We can be hospitable if you work with us. I'm sure you'll agree that drinking a cold Mountain Dew is a lot better way to spend the day than peeing your pants and getting punched in the gut." Charles said.

Tanner nodded slightly in agreement and then opened the can, taking a long, cold drink. His tongue tingled as the yellow liquid raced down to his empty stomach.

"Get Tanner some breakfast," Patrick said. "I'm going to check in with the boss and then hit the shower." Patrick went upstairs to his room, leaving Tanner in the care of the capable men in the kitchen.

"Well, you don't have to stand there all day," Charles said, pointing to a chair at the table. "We know this ain't the sabbatical you wanted, but it won't be a prison unless you make it that way."

Charles hoped that Tanner felt the positive vibe he was sending out. During the first couple of hours of captivity, Charles knew that Tanner would try to identify with a captor and find some common ground. He was playing a compassionate and supportive role, hoping that Tanner would unconsciously start trusting him. That trust would be a crucial psychological component in getting Tanner to cooperate.

"What do you want to eat?" Charles casually asked as Tanner took a seat by himself at the large table. Tanner was famished. He hadn't eaten anything since lunch the day before. Still holding the can of Mountain Dew, Tanner quickly finished it off and asked if he could have another with a bowl of Cheerios. As Charles opened the door to the fridge, Tanner noticed several twelve-packs of soda chilling inside. The kidnappers even knew his favorite drink. Tanner was frightened but impressed.

"Cheerios ain't going to cut it, boy," Charles said, handing Tanner another soda. "I'm making pancakes and eggs. You haven't eaten anything in a while. You must be hungry."

Tanner was startled by the man's friendly and casual demeanor. It was an obvious contrast to Patrick's military-like intimidation. He silently watched Charles cook breakfast, Tanner's brain was going full-throttle. All his synapses were firing, trying to get a grip on what was happening. *Relax, concentrate, and observe,* Tanner told himself. *If they were going to kill you, they would have done it already. You're valuable to them. Don't lose your value. Buy time, and figure a way out of this mess.*

Magic spoke up, bringing Tanner out of his thoughts. "My name's Magic. I'm the newest guy on the team. We're going to be working closely together. I'll be your shadow on the computer stuff. Everything you do on the hacking front, I'll watch and make sure you're doing it right. Know what I mean?"

"You guys got the wrong person for this," Tanner spoke up, finding a little bit of confidence. "I don't hack anymore. I'm clean now," he said.

"Yeah, but I figure that hacking is like riding a bike. Once you learn, you never forget," Magic countered. "Besides, if you want to leave, you'll do the job."

"Breakfast is done," Charles said, interrupting the exchange. Coming over to the table, Charles put three pancakes, two eggs, and a couple of strips of bacon on a plate in front of Tanner.

Tanner realized it wasn't much use to argue his reformed ways right then, so he ate quietly while the others chatted. He'd learned long ago that listening was an educational experience. Tanner could learn a lot about people and their backgrounds by listening and observing.

"The Dodgers choked in the ninth inning last night," Michael told the others.

"They can't wrap it up when it matters. The playoffs start soon.

They gotta get focused or they won't get the wild card from Colorado," Charles said.

"None of that matters. Baseball is just filler until football gets going, and my Raiders are going to be for real this year," Magic said. The other two men laughed.

Tanner listened to Michael, Charles, and Magic talk sports. Although Tanner was a big sports fan, he wasn't interested in bantering right now. Instead, he paid attention to his kidnappers' speech and dialect to see if he could figure out where they were from. Unfortunately, they sounded like average Americans. Tanner's captors could have easily been three guys talking sports around the water cooler at his work.

"Tanner, what's your team?" Charles asked.

"I'm not much for baseball. NBA is my thing," Tanner replied cautiously. His response caused all three men to chuckle.

"Then you must appreciate our names, if you're into basketball and all," Magic said with a smirk.

Their names. How could I have missed it? Tanner scolded himself as he mentally rehearsed his captors' names—Michael, Charles, Magic, and Patrick. He immediately recognized the significance of the names from the NBA. All they needed was a Larry and they'd have the starting five from the 1992 Dream Team.

"Yeah, the 1992 Olympics," Tanner said. "I didn't catch it the first time."

Everyone finished their breakfasts about the time Patrick came back downstairs, looking refreshed and more alert. Patrick had shaved his beard, leaving a goatee. Walking over to the kitchen counter, Patrick grabbed a cup of coffee and a banana for breakfast. Tanner could sense the jovial mood in the room yield to Patrick's serious demeanor.

"Tanner, you can see that we're calling the shots around here. Don't be an idiot. Foolish actions will be reciprocated with physical pain," Patrick said flatly, sipping his coffee.

Patrick turned and nodded to Magic, who walked out into the garage. He came back a moment later holding what looked like a large black wristwatch. Taking the device from Magic, Patrick showed it to Tanner.

"Ever seen one of these?" Patrick asked rhetorically. "It's an ankle monitor. It's used for tracking people under house arrest, but this one is more sophisticated than what's used on common criminals," he said, handing it back to Magic. Stepping over to Tanner, Magic reached down and securely snapped the device onto Tanner's right ankle. "It has a GPS transmitter, so we can track your location anywhere in the world within a couple of feet. Inside the cuff is a small, tamper-resistant electrode. If you try to remove or destroy it, an alert will immediately notify us. You'll have this on your ankle the entire time you're here, as will your parents at their safe house."

Tanner was relieved to hear mention of his parents. "Where are my parents? Are they okay?" he asked.

"They're safe. We're holding them as collateral to make sure you do your work," Patrick said. "But don't lose your focus worrying about them. Keep your mind here, on present matters. That's the best thing you can do for them right now."

Patrick's cell phone suddenly rang, echoing loudly in the large house. He motioned for Tanner, Charles, and the others to go outside, so he could take the call in privacy. Stepping out onto the front porch between his escorts, Tanner shielded his eyes from the bright morning sun. "Where are we?"

"In the mountains," Magic responded sarcastically.

Charles spoke next, redirecting the focus away from Magic's failed attempt at humor. "As you can see, there's nobody around. You could walk for hours in any direction and only manage to get lost," he said as he led the group around the cabin toward a small barn at the back of the lot. "That's our utility shed," he said, pointing to a smaller building that complemented the exterior of the larger cabin. "Inside we have a generator that is fed by an underground fuel tank. Next to the barn, you can see a propane tank that heats the furnace and water heater. Two satellite dishes on the house provide our communications. We are completely self-sufficient here. No need to go to town for anything," Charles announced triumphantly.

"We're also completely secure here," Michael said. "We have motion sensors hidden at ten, fifty, one hundred, and one thousand meters around the house. The road in has several cameras that relay video back to our command center. It's all state-of-the-art stuff. We can tell if a squirrel farts a mile out. We also have a significant arsenal in the barn that could hold off a small army. Nobody is coming to your rescue."

Tanner wasn't sure why he was getting the lecture, but in bragging about their fortress, his captors were also inadvertently disclosing other bits of information. These guys were professionals and were definitely backed by someone with extensive funding to execute such an elaborate operation. *Interesting.*

Finished with the ad hoc tour, the kidnappers escorted Tanner back inside to Patrick.

"I assume you noticed all the security precautions we have. You won't get away," Patrick said. "But, still, I can't realistically believe that you won't try to escape. So I've thought of another fail-safe."

Reaching into a cabinet drawer, Patrick pulled out a large pair of pliers. Suddenly the other kidnappers reached for Tanner. He fruitlessly tried to shake off his attackers, but it was no use. Patrick forcefully grabbed Tanner's right leg, securing it the same way a blacksmith holds a horse's leg when shoeing the hoof. Removing Tanner's shoe and sock, Patrick gripped Tanner's big toe in the vise of the pliers.

"This will hurt," he said as he forcefully jerked on Tanner's big toe. Tanner's scream blasted out of the house and into the open meadow. Unfortunately, nobody was around to hear it.

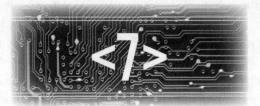

SEPTEMBER 4, LOS ALAMOS, NEW MEXICO

An hour north of Tanner's location, on Highway 4, Dr. Jodi McDonald was working feverishly at Los Alamos Labs. Her team was almost done with the initial testing sequence on the quantum computer. Once she had the preliminary numbers, she would write up a report and give it to the lab directors. Then it would be time to prepare for the upcoming quantum computing conference in Europe.

She knew her team's groundbreaking work on quantum computing would create another technology gold rush, just like the personal computer did in the early 1980s. Start-ups would dot the globe as entrepreneurs scrambled to get in on the first wave of this new technology. Many scientists theorized the awesome power of quantum computers would increase the ability to do complex calculations ten-thousandfold. Rendering DNA molecules, charting the expansion of a supernova, or resolving complex mathematical problems would take seconds instead of months. However, Jodi knew that not all of their research would go public. The pinnacle of their effort, the nitrogen vacancy diamond, would remain a tightly classified secret. The prototype diamond was the key to the phenomenal power of quantum computing.

It was also a technological treasure that powerful people would kill for.

Tanner's incarceration at the mountain retreat was ironically close to his Albuquerque home. If he'd had more time to explore his surroundings, he might have even recognized some of the familiar landmarks of the Jemez Mountains. The volcanic mountain range in northern New Mexico divided the region in two, with New Mexico State Highway 4, the main artery coming into the area, passing just five miles due west of Tanner's secret location.

The hidden lodge where Tanner was kept had been constructed three years earlier by the CEO of a health-care company in Albuquerque. Originally built as a summer retreat, the isolated building was located on three hundred acres of private land in the Santa Fe National Forest. At an elevation of 6,800 feet, and an hour's drive to either Albuquerque or Los Alamos, the cabin was the ideal location to run the kidnapper's operation. Inside, Tanner sat on the couch with a large ice pack on his foot, attempting to soothe the pain shooting up from his broken toe.

"Sorry about that. It's nothing personal, just business," Charles said empathetically as he gestured toward Tanner's toe. "I got some pain meds if you want."

Tanner leaned back and elevated his foot on the edge of the sofa, trying to limit the swelling in his toe. Looking over at Patrick, Tanner felt both anger and frustration at what had happened. Tanner was usually a person to act, but in this situation he was completely helpless. He knew fighting back would be pointless, but that didn't stop him from having the overwhelming urge to get up and take a swing at Patrick.

"Just give me a couple of Tylenol," Tanner said weakly. Even though he really could use an opioid-based pain pill, he didn't want another medication-induced trance. He'd had enough of that from the night before.

Coming back into the room, Charles gave Tanner an unopened bottle of Tylenol. "Thanks," said Tanner.

"No problem. I did some time as a medic. Let me know if there's anything else you need. Keep your foot elevated, and ice it on and off every twenty minutes."

Tanner nodded at Charles's instructions, curious that he had used the word *medic*. Most people would have said *paramedic* or *doctor* if they had formal medical training. Tanner knew *medic* was an army term, and that meant Charles had some ties to the military.

"Just be glad it was your toe," continued Charles. "Toes fix easy and don't need to be in a cast. It will take about four weeks for you to get back to normal, but in the meantime, you'll be able to limp around with this." He picked up Tanner's shoe. Taking the switchblade from his back pocket, Charles cut off the top end of the shoe, creating a makeshift walking boot.

With Tanner confined to the couch, Charles, Michael, and Magic eagerly went to work on their tasks. Despite what Hollywood portrayed in the movies, surveillance duty was tedious, monotonous, and boring. However, the shadow work they had done wasn't all for naught—it was indeed a critical part of the overall objective. For the past two months, Patrick and the others had observed and dissected Tanner's life. They knew intimate details, like his preferred toothpaste and favorite drink. They knew how much he spent on food and entertainment. Most important, they knew that Tanner didn't date or have family close by in Albuquerque. Their scheme had been planned to coincide exactly with Tanner's sabbatical. Everyone in Tanner's life was expecting him to be gone, and that meant nobody would miss him.

For two hours the kidnappers unpacked and set up computer equipment in the garage. Tanner recognized the names of hi-tech companies on the boxes—HP, Cisco, and EMC. The kidnappers were setting up a small data center in the garage, complete with an AC unit to keep the area cool. All afternoon they racked servers, switches, and SAN equipment.

"Hey, what do you think of our gear?" Magic asked enthusiastically. "We got all the best stuff for you. Quad-core blade servers loaded with 64 gigs of RAM, 1 gigabit LAN switches, and an IP SAN. This place will be screaming."

Tanner was impressed despite himself. The computer equipment was the cream of the crop and expensive. These guys were well funded.

"I also got any operating system or software you want. Let me know what you need and I'll install it," Magic offered.

"How do I know what I need? I don't even know what you're trying to accomplish," Tanner said.

"The boss gets here the day after tomorrow. He'll explain everything. In the meantime, we're supposed to get the computer equipment staged and ready to go," said Magic.

"So you've got a lot of horsepower on the server side, but how do you get Internet up here?" Tanner asked doubtfully.

"Good question. You're already thinking, I like that," Magic said. "Remember the two satellite dishes out there on the roof? One is a receiver for watching TV." He motioned toward the 55-inch LCD TV in the family room. "The larger satellite dish is for Internet broadband. We got a little device on our end that encrypts the data before we transmit it, so there's no chance of anyone eavesdropping on us."

Tanner decided it was a good time to do a little probing. "It sounds like you know your way around computers."

"Yeah, I've done some computer work here and there. I'm definitely the most technical guy of the bunch," Magic said.

"Why don't you just do the hacking job?"

Magic set down the computer monitor he had just unpacked. Making sure the other two kidnappers were in the garage, he lowered his voice. "You know, that was the original plan. But then I saw how big a job this was and how little time I had to do it. That's when the boss told us to get an expert in here," Magic said.

"How did you know to find me—or know that I could do the job?" Tanner said.

Magic was just about to say something, and then he caught himself. "Hey, I know what you're trying to do, but I'm not saying anything more. You'll just have to wait until the boss gets here to get your answers."

With that, Magic picked up his monitor and headed out to join the others in the garage.

SEPTEMBER 5, MOUNTAIN SAFE HOUSE, NEW MEXICO

Tanner woke up Monday morning with an aching pain in his foot. Looking down at his big toe, he saw that it had swelled into a black-and-blue mass. Reaching for some Tylenol, Tanner swallowed a couple of pills with a swig from a warm can of Mountain Dew from the previous day.

Tanner had spent the night on the couch in the great room. At first it wasn't comfortable, but Michael eventually pulled out the hide a bed, giving Tanner more space. With three pillows stacked up to elevate his foot, Tanner eventually dozed off after midnight.

Throughout the night, Tanner had at least two people guarding him. The men seemed to rotate in eight-hour shifts, with one guard sitting near Tanner while the other was off in the kitchen. That way, Tanner figured, if he did try to make a move and surprise one of his captors, the other one would have ample time to react and take Tanner down.

Tanner woke up briefly at 4:00 a.m. to use the bathroom. Magic and Michael were both awake, one playing solitaire at the kitchen table and the other reading a spy novel in the recliner next to Tanner. About 7:00 a.m., Michael and Magic were relieved of their watch. Now the friendly Charles and the sadistic Patrick were on duty.

"Hey, if you're hungry, I'll get you something to eat," Charles said. He was sitting at the table doing a crossword puzzle. Patrick sat in the recliner across from Tanner, just staring him down. *That dude is creepy. Where does he think I'm going with a broken toe?* Tanner thought as he turned his gaze from Patrick to Charles.

"I'll just have some Cheerios for now," said Tanner.

"Suit yourself, but I'm making me some omelets," Charles responded.

Patrick offered to help Tanner to the bathroom, which surprised Tanner because he didn't think Patrick had a nice bone in his body. When he got back from the bathroom, Tanner noticed that Charles had folded away the hide-a-bed and propped up some pillows for Tanner's foot.

"Here's another ice pack to start your day. Keep icing your toe for the first twenty-four hours. There's not much else you can do but protect it from getting hurt again," Charles said.

While Tanner waited for his breakfast, Patrick outlined the plans for the day. "Michael and Magic are getting some sleep upstairs, so let them be. We'll wake them around noon, and then I want you and Magic to get the data center ready. Our boss gets here tomorrow. He'll expect to see results."

Tanner nodded and then countered with a question. "How do I know my parents are safe? You have to let me see that they are okay."

"What difference does that make?" Patrick responded curtly. "If they're dead or alive, it doesn't change the fact that you're stuck here working for us."

"Yeah, that's true. But peace of mind can go a long way in helping me focus on my work, and extending an offer of trust can't hurt either."

"Trust is for suckers," Patrick said, sneering. "But we'll see what the boss says. Maybe you'll get lucky."

Soon it was lunchtime, and all four captors were awake. Charles made an easy meal of soup and sandwiches for everybody. Tanner would rather have had a burger from McDonald's, but he was grateful for something to eat.

"Okay, Tanner, we've got to rock 'n' roll," Magic said as Tanner finished his lunch. "See that large desk over by the fireplace? That's going to be your workstation. You've got four monitors there, each connected to a computer with a high speed network link to the servers in the garage."

Tanner pushed back a bit. "Look, when I was in the hacking game, I wasn't just some script kiddie poking around on the Internet," he said.

"So I'm guessing that you want me to do some serious black hat work; something that's very risky and very illegal."

After a brief pause, Patrick responded with a slight smile. "Yeah, you're a smart guy. That's why you're here. Let's hope you know how to keep your mind focused and not let it wander off where it can get you into trouble," he threatened. "Your only goals for today are, one, get the computer gear working, and two, prevent any other broken bones." The final comment drew a small chuckle from the other kidnappers.

"But don't break any fingers! He'll need those for typing," Magic chimed in.

Tanner gazed down at his ugly toe. It looked like a dog had chewed on it. He decided to try one last time to convince his captors he was the wrong guy for the task. "The last time I did any hacking was years ago. Everything has changed since then. It's a whole different game now," he said.

"What do you mean?" Charles asked.

"When I was hacking, I had to speak and breathe computers. I took years to figure out how to do it right. Now most of the information that I had to learn firsthand is out on the Internet. There's canned hacking tools and guides all over the place. You don't need my help. I bet Magic could do whatever you needed."

Patrick laughed. "I think you overestimate Magic's skills." Tanner glanced at Magic in time to see a frown cross his face.

"But it doesn't make sense. Why go through all the trouble of kidnapping me when my skills are so outdated? Why take such a risk?"

Patrick turned toward Tanner. His icy stare ended the conversation. "I think it's time for you to stop asking questions and shut up."

In a small, childish act of defiance, Tanner turned away from the others and crossed his arms. Leaning back into the couch, he reminisced about when he was at the top of his hacking game. The small business he had set up back in college had fizzled out when Jeff Kessler quit school early to pursue other financial opportunities in California. The following year, Tanner graduated with a bachelor's degree in both computer science and mathematics. He passed on several legitimate job offers and decided instead to pursue hacking full time.

Tanner remembered one Sunday morning in particular when he was manipulating the City of Albuquerque's database—a great time to hack because IT staffing was scarce. He was deleting a client's arrest warrant when he came across some seemingly innocent information. The city's zoning commission had been working with a private developer who wanted to build a new mall on the northwest side of town. Reading through the minutes of the zoning meeting, Tanner learned that the developer planned to purchase a hundred acres of farmland for a two-story mall once the zoning change was completed. Tanner could see that the owner of the farmland was guaranteed to make a fortune. Cross-referencing the parcel of land in the Bernalillo County database, Tanner quickly approached the farm owner about a purchase. She was an elderly widow who had sold off all her dairy cows and equipment to avoid fore-closure. Using the money he accrued from his college hacking business for a down payment, Tanner offered to pay the widow a meager amount for her land. The seventy-four-year-old woman, who was anxious to move back to Texas and live with her daughter, readily accepted the offer. The purchase was completed, and Tanner held the land for just five months before the city council officially approved the zoning change. The mall developer approached Tanner and offered him $200,000 more for the land than he paid for it.

The handsome profit from the real estate deal helped Tanner see that he had been going about the hacking business all wrong. He was hacking to make others rich. Tanner decided it was time for a change. He started using his hacking skills to make himself wealthy. With his illegal access on the city and county networks, Tanner researched and speculated on future real estate deals in the area. Acting quickly to buy the land before developers could acquire it, Tanner soon accumulated over $400,000 in his bank account.

That was about the same time when the Internet really took off. Cor-porations quickly realized the Internet could generate huge sales reve-nue, and they all rushed to become dot-com aware. However, Tanner was one step ahead of the game. He had already purchased dozens of dot-com domain names that were unique to specific businesses. When a corporation found out that Tanner already owned the rights to their spe-cific domain, he would agree to sell the name back to the business for a sizeable payment. Using this cyber-squatting technique, Tanner quickly doubled his money.

For Tanner, the Internet was a magnificent dream. It was the Wild West of information technology, and just as the outlaws of the past century roamed across the Old West without restraint, Tanner roamed freely through cyberspace. Quietly and anonymously, Tanner became a super-hacker on the Internet. For years he manipulated and controlled thousands of computer nodes across the world as he continued to accumulate wealth. It seemed there was no limit to Tanner's hacking fortune—until a traumatic family event shocked Tanner so much that it made him question everything he had done.

September 6, Mountain Safe House, New Mexico

Tuesday morning came after a better night's rest for Tanner. His toe wasn't hurting nearly as much, and the Tylenol seemed to keep the pain at bay. But Tanner now understood why a broken toe prevented his escape. Running required a toe-to-heel motion, something that was impossible to do in his injured condition. Gentle and slow walking, however, was possible when he shifted his weight to his heel instead.

The safe house actually had two different computer workstation arrangements. One was the primary hacking center where Tanner would do his work. The other workstation was isolated in the far corner of its kitchen and was turned around so Tanner couldn't see what was on the two monitors. He guessed that the computer system was for viewing all the surveillance cameras and motion detectors around the cabin. Charles was currently sitting there, probably monitoring the live feeds from the wireless security cameras while eating his breakfast.

Just before 9:00 a.m., the satellite phone next to Charles started chirping. Because of their remote location at the safe house, ordinary cell phone service was unavailable. To communicate with the outside world, the kidnappers used satphones. Charles grabbed the ringing satphone and answered with an anonymous "Yes?" Listening for a second, he responded, "Roger that. See you in fifteen minutes."

"That was the boss checking in. His ETA is fifteen minutes," Charles relayed to the rest of the team.

Tanner again caught Charles's use of military lingo. He was definitely ex-military.

A few minutes passed, and a loud beeping sound from the control center alerted the group to the oncoming visitor. Although the car was still a half-mile out, the motion-activated security cameras relayed a picture of an SUV as it worked its way up the dirt road. Though they were expecting their boss, the kidnappers still didn't take any chances. Grabbing two SIG Sauer SIG556 patrol rifles from the garage, Patrick and Michael walked out onto the porch. Charles stayed inside and continued monitoring the video feeds while Magic kept an eye on their hostage. Before long, Tanner heard the familiar sound of an engine off in the distance. Straining to look out the front window, Tanner saw his forest-green Toyota 4Runner coming to a stop.

A man cautiously emerged from the truck, making sure not to startle the guards with the large machine guns on the porch. Satisfied the situation was normal, Patrick and Michael relaxed and walked out to greet their leader. The group of men turned and walked up the gravel path toward the porch. Inside on the couch, Tanner anxiously watched the front door as Michael and Patrick entered, followed by their boss. Taking his first good look at the leader of the kidnappers, Tanner suddenly felt the air rush out of his chest. Speechless, he stared in shock as Dr. Larry Killpack waved and said hello.

Tanner was dumbfounded. The sight of his next-door neighbor caused his mind to race in a thousand directions simultaneously. Feeling nauseated as massive amounts of adrenaline poured into his bloodstream, Tanner lurched forward and threw up all over the coffee table in front of him.

"I knew you'd be surprised, but that's not the reception I was expecting," Dr. Killpack said, stepping back to avoid the mess. "Tanner, you look white as a ghost. You better lie down and relax. Michael, Magic, get some towels and clean up this mess."

Tanner reclined back on the couch, attempting to catch his breath, while Michael and Magic did the unpleasant duty of cleaning up. After a few minutes, the coffee table was wiped clean, and Tanner had recomposed himself. With his brain running at the speed of light, Tanner connected all the dots. His next-door neighbor must have been the focal point for the entire operation. Larry was close enough to Tanner to track his every move, and with the tools and technology he had seen, Tanner wouldn't be surprised if they had bugged his entire house.

Tanner didn't know it, but that was precisely what had happened. Posing as satellite TV installers, Patrick and Michael broke into Tanner's home two months ago. They tapped Tanner's phone line and hid miniaturized surveillance equipment throughout his house. The hi-tech devices recorded all the audio and video in the rooms below, including capturing Tanner's computer username and password. Everything Tanner had said or done over the past two months was recorded and analyzed by his eavesdropping neighbor.

"Tanner, do you want a drink or anything? I imagine you're feeling overwhelmed," Larry said, sitting in the chair across from Tanner.

Tanner sighed. "I should have known it."

"Actually, there's no possible way you could have known. What normal, law-abiding person would ever assume that their neighbor would be a criminal? It's just too preposterous," Larry sympathized. "Tanner, we need you so we can be successful. As such, you must understand how you fit in the overall picture. Just about two months ago, we infiltrated your life. We monitored every aspect of your existence and know more about you than even your parents, who, by the way, are safe and secure in another location," Larry said.

The mention of his parents made Tanner sit forward. "How do I know that? Will I be able to talk to them?" he asked anxiously.

"Yes, in due time," Larry said. Tanner yearned to punch Larry in the face. He glanced at Patrick, who was standing guard with an automatic rifle resting across his chest.

Larry saw Tanner's eyes flick over to Patrick, and he smiled.

"I know what you're thinking, kid. Before you do anything rash, remember that you are unarmed and outnumbered five to one. After all you've endured, wouldn't you like to know what this is all about?" Larry asked. "Magic, get Mr. Zane a drink while we chat. I have a fascinating secret to share."

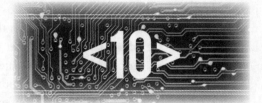

September 6, Mountain Safe House, New Mexico

Tanner tried to maintain a poker face. He was simultaneously experiencing two conflicting emotions—rage and curiosity—but the former would have to remain checked. Patrick and Michael were both watching Tanner closely for the first sign of aggression.

"I've spent the past couple of days reviewing our progress with our employer, and I have received approval to move on to the next phase of our operation," Larry began. "At this point, secrecy and spy stuff don't really benefit us anymore. So let's be perfectly honest with each other." Larry leaned toward Tanner. "Are you familiar with Los Alamos National Labs?"

Tanner nodded his head in response. Most people who lived in New Mexico were aware of the Lab and the scientific work that was done there.

Larry continued. "The Lab conducts a wide variety of research beyond nuclear weapons. One particular area of interest to us is supercomputing. You see, Tanner, there's a battle going on between nations, and it's not a war of violence, but a struggle to control information. Quantum computing is the newest weapon in this digital battle, and only those nations who have quantum computers will be superpowers."

Tanner listened intently, noting two phrases that caught him off-guard: *supercomputing* and *superpowers*.

"For the past several years, a team of scientists at Los Alamos has worked on a new generation of supercomputers. Based on the principles of quantum physics, they've created a quantum computer that is faster than all the computers on the planet combined," Larry stated.

Tanner had heard about the theory of quantum computers when he was in school. Some of his professors had talked about new research into the technology, but the discussion was always theoretical, like it was something that wouldn't be feasible for decades.

Larry's voice brought Tanner back to the moment. "At the core of this exceptional quantum computer is a man-made diamond—the most valuable diamond in the world. Stealing it from a top-secret facility is impossible, so we need to hack into the network and get the classified plans on how the diamond was made. That's why you are here," Larry said. "The diamond is the key to quantum computing, and quantum computing is the atomic bomb in global information warfare." Larry paused, letting Tanner process what he had been told.

"I can tell you're rethinking your assumptions. You see, Tanner, I'm a doctor, but not in the medical field as you've thought. I have a PhD in psychology, and I know your psyche. I bet you're wondering why someone from the United States government would hack into their own national laboratory."

That was exactly what Tanner was thinking. He had assumed these guys worked for some secret branch of the CIA or NSA, but clearly that wasn't the case. These guys had skills and money. They were definitely backed by a government—just not that of the United States of America.

Tanner spoke after a moment, breaking the silence. "So you want me to hack into the network at Los Alamos and steal the plans for a super-secret diamond," he said.

"Precisely," said Larry. "You're the perfect candidate for the job. You have tremendous hacking skills, but you're also anonymous. And being single with few family ties means no one will miss you while you work for us over the next two months."

"Why me?" Tanner asked, probing for more information. "Surely you have the ability to do this job on your own. Look at the money and resources you've invested in this place." Tanner gestured at the elaborate cabin. "Plus, you were able to track me down out of complete obscurity, which was probably more difficult than just social engineering some worker at the Lab. Why not just steal the diamond yourself?"

"We're more like spies, not hackers," Larry countered. "Besides, you were specifically recommended for this job by an old friend."

That brought Tanner to a halt. Someone knew enough about his hacking past to recommend him for this role? He was confident that he had effectively buried any evidence of his previous hacking life when he'd converted to Mormonism, yet someone close to him knew about his illegal activities. Who had betrayed him?

"Okay, let's say that I am the best person to steal your information," Tanner said, trying to stifle his renewed fear. "It's still an impossible task. The world changed after September 11th. Information security has become a top priority. It would take me months just to get past the perimeter security and firewalls. I'd also have to spend hours doing surveillance of the facility. Points of contact would have to be made, including a bunch of other on-site work, which I assume you won't let me do. It's impossible," he concluded.

Larry laughed. "Tanner, I think you underestimate your abilities. You of all people should know that with enough time and resources, any computer network can be compromised. We will get you the help and equipment you need. Besides, I know you've never been one to turn down a challenge, and I don't believe your ego will let you do it now."

"My ego has nothing to do with it," Tanner countered. "You're crazy if you think that I'm going break into a national lab and hand over such a valuable piece of information to you. This isn't like I'm going after someone's Social Security number. We're talking treason here."

Larry chuckled. "Treason? Who said anything about treason?"

"Look, you guys don't have the technical brains to make use of a quantum computer. So I can only assume you're going to give the information about this diamond to someone else," Tanner said.

"This hasn't anything to do with treason or 'us versus them.' We're just businessmen with unique skills. Our employer is paying us to get this information. What he wants to do with it afterwards doesn't concern us," Larry said.

"What if I just refuse to do it out of principle?"

"Are you saying you're morally opposed to this?" Larry asked. "It's not like we're asking you to kill someone. You're just getting some information, that's all."

Tanner decided to lay it all out. "Yeah, I am totally against it. I swore off hacking years ago when I became religious. Doing this job goes against every principle I've embraced. Not only is it illegal, it's wrong."

"And that's why we have your parents. We knew you'd need some strong motivation." Looking Tanner right in the eye, Larry delivered his ultimatum. "You need to decide right now what is more important— your parents or your morals. It's just that simple."

Tanner paused. An awful feeling swelled inside of him. He was at a stalemate. The kidnappers had already demonstrated their resolve by breaking Tanner's toe and killing the family's pet. Tanner knew they wouldn't hesitate to kill again. On the other hand, he realized that if he did the job, he would be breaking some of the promises he made to God when he was baptized. He felt like he was being forced to choose between his family and his faith. With no clear right option, Tanner yielded to the basic instinct of survival. He had to do the hacking job. He just hoped when the Day of Judgment came for him, God would understand.

Tanner took a defeated breath. "Okay, I'll do it," he said. "But first I have to talk to my parents."

Larry picked up the satphone and punched in some numbers. Larry waited a second and then said, "This is Larry. Put Tanner's parents on the phone." Larry then handed the phone to Tanner with a word of caution. "I'm putting it on speakerphone so we can hear your conversation. If you begin to say something we don't like, we'll cut the call, and that will be your last communication with your parents."

Tanner took the phone. "Mom, Dad, it's me, Tanner. Can you hear me?"

"Yes, we can hear you," was his father's anxious reply. "Tanner, what have you gotten yourself into to? Are you involved in drugs?"

Larry quickly leaned forward and answered, "Mr. and Mrs. Zane, your son is not involved in drugs, nor has he broken the law. He is being held captive, much like yourselves. Tanner has a job to do for us. When he is finished, you'll all be released. In the meantime, don't do anything stupid that would compromise your son's safety."

"Tanner, are you okay? We're worried about you." Tanner's mother voiced exactly what every concerned mother would say.

"I'm okay," Tanner lied, looking down at his broken toe. "Just do what they say. It will be fine. Are you all right?"

"We're terrified, but surviving," his dad replied.

Larry quickly pulled the phone away from Tanner. "That's all for now. Please follow your son's advice and do exactly what we say. Good-bye," he said, and disconnected the call.

SEPTEMBER 7, MOUNTAIN SAFE HOUSE, NEW MEXICO

The following morning, Tanner's work schedule was explained to him. He would work eighteen hours a day, seven days a week until he had the classified quantum diamond information. Now, just before 8:00 a.m., Tanner had finished his breakfast of eggs Benedict (which he didn't like) and was now setting up his computer workstation. Two large whiteboards had been placed at each end of the room for note taking, and the furniture had been moved to the side, providing an open work area.

"I've got it set up the way you wanted," Magic said as he connected the last cable. He was helping Tanner put the finishing touches on the computer equipment while the other kidnappers finished their breakfast.

"I guess it's time to break my promise," Tanner said.

Magic looked up from behind the desk. "What's that?"

Tanner let out a sigh. "I promised my grandmother that I'd never do this again."

"What are you talking about?" Magic asked. He walked around the desk and took a seat next to Tanner.

Tanner looked distressed, like he was about to confess to a priest. "When I was in the hacking game years ago, I made a serious fortune. We're talking seven figures."

46

Magic let out a slow whistle. "That's a million bucks."

"It was more than that," Tanner said. He gazed at the far wall, like he was searching his memory for a time he wanted to forget.

"Man, I'd die to have that kind of cash," Magic said.

"It wasn't as cool as you'd think. It was anticlimactic when I made my first million," Tanner said.

"What are you talking about?" Magic seemed puzzled that someone wouldn't be ecstatic to have a million dollars.

"That's what most people don't get. Money doesn't really change anything. I was still the same person with a lot of the same problems," Tanner said.

"Yeah, but then you had money," Magic said.

Tanner turned toward Magic. "It was all a façade. I thought I was living the life, doing my own thing, not taking orders from anyone . . ." Tanner's voice trailed off.

Magic saw the anguish on Tanner's face. Something about the past still haunted him. "Then what happened?"

"Then," Tanner said, pausing, "my grandmother got ripped off. She got caught up in a phishing scam. The email looked legitimate, like it had come from her bank, but instead it came from a group of hackers in Europe. They stole her identity and cleaned out her life savings. She lost everything in an instant."

"That's why you quit," Magic said.

Tanner nodded his head. "I realized I wasn't any better than those hackers who scammed my grandma. My first big score came after I conned an old woman into selling me her farmland for practically nothing. I had basically done the same thing to her that the hackers had done to my grandma. I felt so guilty that I gave up hacking."

"What did you do with all that money?" Magic asked.

"My grandma was fighting cancer at the time, and she had tons of medical bills. I secretly funded her entire treatment and even paid off her mortgage. The cancer got her a few months later, but at least she got to spend her last night in her own home," Tanner whispered. "At her funeral I silently promised her that I would do everything I could to clean up my act. So I gave the rest of my dirty money to charity and started looking for God."

"Just like that?" Magic asked.

"More or less," Tanner confirmed. "Now you guys are forcing me back into the game, but I'm not sure I have the stomach for it this time around."

Magic slapped Tanner on the knee. "Well, you better find some way to do it, because it's show time."

Larry, Patrick, and the others were seated against the walls of the large family room. Tanner sat in an office chair at the front, preparing to address his makeshift class of thugs. His first and most pressing task was to take charge. "Okay, I don't like this situation. But, as you are aware, I have no choice. My ticket to freedom is stealing these classified documents," Tanner said. "To be successful, I have to call the shots on the hacking front. I'm the one who has the technical background and the skills. If you want that information, I'll have to be the leader."

Larry snickered. "Very well. However, Magic will watch and double-check everything you do. He'll be your shadow for the next two months. You'll only work when he is available. If Magic has to stop to take a break, you'll wait on the couch until he's done. Any communication to the outside world like phone calls, emails, chat rooms, or blogs will have to be approved by me. We have nine other toes to break if you desire," he said, motioning toward Tanner's feet.

Tanner acknowledged Larry's response yet still felt odd as he spoke to the group. On one hand, he was a prisoner, held captive against his will. On the other, he was lecturing his kidnappers like a university professor.

"Most of the hacking stuff we'll be doing will come from my memory. To protect myself, I never documented anything, but I've been out of the hacking game for years and I'll be rusty. We have limited time, so I'll be assigning all of you tasks." They had agreed the night before that Tanner could have all five men at his disposal, especially since he wasn't able to leave the compound.

Tanner started with his first lesson. "I want to establish a basic understanding of computer hacking. Everyone needs to know this so we're on the same page, working together. Despite what you may have seen in the movies, hacking isn't some guy sitting at a computer terminal, trying to guess someone's password. Hacking is more of a process, a methodology, to exploit computer vulnerabilities. Lesson number one: why force our way through the front door of a computer network when we can just get someone on the inside to give us the information?"

"What are you talking about?" Patrick asked.

"Our target is Los Alamos National Labs. There's no way we're getting on the secure facility, into the restricted building, and accessing the classified network to steal this information. We're going to need someone's help on the inside."

"No one is going to help us steal that information. That's crazy," Patrick said.

"They will because we're going to trick them into getting us access to the internal computer network," Tanner said. "It's called social engineering, and it's one of the most effective yet overlooked tools of the hacking trade."

"What's social engineering?" asked Charles.

"It's basically manipulating people into giving out their confidential information. Some of the best hackers in history—like Bannon, Foster, and especially Mitnick—were experts at this. They did more damage with a telephone and a friendly hello than with a thousand computer systems."

"Kind of like con men, right?" Charles said.

"Exactly," Tanner said, remembering when he conned his way into the chemistry professor's office back at college. Back then, Tanner had learned the hacking value of being friendly. Tanner continued, "It won't be easy, but there's an upside. Years ago, it took me lots of time and discipline to compromise a person's account information. I spent huge amounts of time looking for important documents in the trash, stealing letters from mailboxes, and working the local bars to meet people and gain their trust. But now, with social networking sites like Facebook and

Twitter, getting personal information is significantly easier. They might as well just call them 'social engineering' sites instead of social networking," Tanner joked.

Tanner couldn't believe the stuff people put out on the Internet. Personal information like birthdays, phone numbers, and street addresses that used to take him months to discover were now freely and intentionally published on the web. Tanner remembered reading an article last year in the Albuquerque newspaper about the dangers of Internet predators. A police officer from the Internet Crimes Task Force had spoken at a high school assembly. For a demonstration, he invited two of the most popular teenagers to come up on stage with him. Using only publicly available data he got from social networking sites, the officer started reciting the students' personal information, beginning with their full name, date of birth, home address, and extra-curricular activities. He knew when they were at sports practice or at home. He knew the names of their closest friends and their associated addresses. He knew where the students liked to hang out on Friday night. He even knew the students' personal cell numbers. According to the article, silence fell over the assembly as the officer's point was powerfully delivered: people put way too much personal information out on the Internet.

In this way, Tanner was different than most of his peers. He didn't like putting any personal information out on the net because he knew that once it was out in cyberspace it could never be erased. Tanner was a consumer of web information, not a producer. Except for a couple of email addresses and the occasional online purchase, Tanner Zane was an unknown guy in cyberspace.

Tanner paused as he brought his mind back to his current situation with his kidnappers. "Here's how it's going to work. We're going to start with a broad search. We're going to scour the Internet and examine all the popular social networking sites and blogs of anyone who mentions Los Alamos. Chances are the vast majority of the people who live in Los Alamos work at the National Labs. We'll target those people first and analyze their information to see whom we can exploit," he said as the group nodded in understanding.

Tanner continued. "We need to find an unsuspecting victim, someone with access to the classified network in the lab, but who's a little too trusting and naïve. From my experience, I've found the best place to start is with a secretary or an administrative assistant. Those people usually have full access to their superiors' computers and associated information, but they don't understand the sensitive nature of it."

He turned his chair around and brought up a web browser on a large projection screen for everyone to see. "We're going to start our search by going to the authoritative site for the lab." He typed in the URL of the lab's official site. He quickly found the link to the lab's online phone book. "Isn't it nice of them to list all the employees who work at the lab for us?" Tanner said with a sarcastic laugh. Suddenly, his fingers started flying across the keyboard. He wrote a script, or small program, to download all the HTTP code from the public-facing Internet site. The script crawled the home pages, extracting the names of any individuals it found. The results were amazing. In just a few minutes, he had the names of nearly five hundred scientists, engineers, and department heads. He printed off five copies of the results.

"Okay, here's our initial list of targets," Tanner said as he distributed the information to the Starting Five, what he called his captors in reference to the starting members of the Dream Team. "Each of you get on your laptops and start searching all the popular social networking sites and blogs to see what you can find out about these people. One of these folks is going to help us get that diamond."

The day quickly passed, and midnight soon rolled around. With no weekends to recuperate, Larry knew that he couldn't push Tanner nonstop. If he did, it wouldn't be long before Tanner started experiencing the Law of Diminishing Returns. They decided to end the day's work at midnight. Locking out Tanner's access to all the computers, Magic started a data backup and went to bed. The team had had a successful day, compiling a nice list of forty or so people who lived in the Los Alamos area and worked at the National Labs.

Tanner made some final notes on a whiteboard before going to bed. Larry and Charles had already gone to sleep, leaving Patrick and Michael to guard Tanner. Sometime in the early morning hours, Tanner knew Patrick and Michael would change shifts with the others and a new day would begin. Exhausted from the tedious work, Tanner went to bed. He took a moment for his personal prayer routine before crashing on the couch, wondering which of his past acquaintances had told the Starting Five about his secret hacking identity.

September 8, Mountain Safe House, New Mexico

Tanner woke up to the smell of breakfast emanating from the kitchen. The clock on the wall displayed 7:18, and Tanner could see that Charles was cooking at the stove. Outside, the sun had just peeked over a distant mountaintop, casting a yellow glow on the polished wood floor of the house. Tanner hadn't ventured outside except for his initial tour several days ago. Every now and then, he would take a prolonged look out one of the bay windows and try to make sense of his surroundings.

Tanner hobbled over to the bathroom for a shower. Larry tagged along just to make sure Tanner didn't do anything mischievous. The swelling in Tanner's toe had gone down somewhat, revealing an unusual black-and-purple pattern. Fortunately, the over-the-counter medicine was keeping the pain in check, but Tanner still couldn't walk without a major limp. In his injured state, Tanner probably didn't even need the ankle monitor.

Letting the hot water soak his head, Tanner had a hard time chasing sleep from his mind. For several hours in the middle of the night he had lain awake trying to figure out who had revealed his hacking identity to Larry and the others. Tanner thought about the people he had met over the years. The only person who knew Tanner could do any computer hacking was his old friend Jeff Kessler. But Tanner hadn't spoken to Jeff since college, and back then Tanner was a novice hacker, certainly not anybody who had the astute hacking skills needed to break into a top-secret government lab.

With Patrick and Michael sleeping upstairs, the others were ready to get to work. They had divided the list of people into two groups. One list consisted of scientists who worked at the lab. It was easy to identify those people because their titles usually included *Dr., PhD*, or something similar. The other list was comprised of the worker bees: people who looked like they might fit the profile of secretary or administrative assistant. Most of these individuals lacked the academic credentials found in the group of scientists. Tanner knew his list wasn't perfect, but social engineering involved a lot of stereotyping, something that Tanner didn't especially like to do.

"Tanner, are you ready for another day's work?" Larry asked as he sipped his hot coffee.

"Yes, but it's not going to be exciting. It will be a lot like yesterday," Tanner said. "We have to narrow down our lists to a dozen or so really good candidates. Once we have solid targets, we can begin infiltrating their lives."

With Tanner seated at his computer workstation and Magic by his side, the group picked up where they had left off the night before. They continued searching for names and addresses on the Internet and cross-referencing them to the list of employees they had gotten from the lab's website. Tanner was amazed but not completely surprised, at all the private information they found in their initial search.

"Look at this," Tanner said. "This person has his entire genealogy listed on his personal web page. It's a complete list of names, birth dates, and everything."

"Yeah, so?" Charles asked.

"So a lot of programs ask for a mother's maiden name to reset a password or something like that. Now we have that valuable piece of information. We can use it later on if we need to impersonate him."

"I just found a Facebook post with someone showing a copy of their new driver's license," Magic said. "She's complaining about how her hair looks in the photo, but she has all the other information on her license right here." He laughed.

Tanner shook his head in disbelief. "Some people just don't get it. They complain about the government and privacy concerns, and they go out and post a picture of their driver's license on the Internet. You know how easy it would be to make a fake ID with that? We could steal her identity in a second."

It seemed that the Internet had fostered a massive wave of narcissism across the world. People were blogging and tweeting about every little detail in their lives, as if anyone else really cared. But Tanner knew that was one of the draws of cyberspace. A person could have a completely fictitious identity, like a twelve-year-old boy pretending to be a sexy college girl in a chat room. Or with sites like Twitter coming online daily, an individual could let all their friends know when they were at work or on vacation. *Good information to know if we needed to break into a house*, Tanner thought.

Every bit of data Tanner and the Starting Five collected was stored in a database for faster searching and indexing. Computers were wonderful things, especially useful for analyzing and finding similarities. Sometimes, Tanner and the group would start down the trail of a potentially good name only to have it go cold when they encountered a restricted web page or a false email address. Despite the occasional setback, they continued to work and refine their list of targets.

Soon it was time for lunch, and Michael and Patrick joined the other members of the Starting Five at the dining room table. As usual, Tanner ate alone on the couch; Patrick felt it would be safer if Tanner wasn't close by to hear any confidential information discussed during meal times. The Starting Five were quietly talking about something when Tanner chimed in. "We're going to have to visit Los Alamos at some point," he said to no one in particular. "Once we choose our targets, I'll have to follow them around for a couple of days and see what I can learn from their behaviors."

"Impossible," Larry replied. "You are not allowed to leave the cabin. One of these guys can do the legwork for you," he said, waving his hand toward the other men.

"That's not good enough. I need to be on-site to be effective."

"It ain't going to happen, buddy," Charles said. "We got a video camera that we can use to get some footage for you, but like the boss man said, you're staying here."

"Look, do you want that quantum diamond information or not? When I used to hack, I would spend hours doing surveillance of my target, just like I'm sure you did with me. I need to see what's out there that I can exploit," Tanner countered, almost yelling.

"Forget about it. You'll just have to let one of us do the work for you," Larry said abruptly, ending the conversation.

Tanner didn't like being told no, so feigning disappointment wasn't hard, but inside he couldn't have been happier about the response. Not once in the entire conversation did Larry say it was too far to Los Alamos or that it would take too long for his men to get there. With that insight, Tanner concluded that the mountain hideout was reasonably close to Los Alamos, or close enough that distance wasn't a consideration in getting there.

September 11, Mountain Safe House, New Mexico

The next two days passed in the same manner, and Tanner continued to behave as Larry and the others demanded. Tanner knew that if he could buy enough time, more and more clues would appear to help him discover his whereabouts. At meal times, Tanner took several minutes to discreetly survey the cabin. He noticed that the stainless steel appliances in the kitchen looked new and that the edge of the carpet on the stairs hadn't been worn down yet. Clues like these led Tanner to believe the cabin was relatively new, probably built within the last couple of years.

Tanner also watched how the Starting Five interacted. He paid close attention to everyday routines like eating, writing, and talking. Innate actions like these, learned in childhood, were extremely difficult to bluff over long periods of time. Tanner also noticed his captors' lack of oral hygiene, something that might seem trivial to other people. But Tanner knew that most of the world didn't have access to quality dental care like the citizens of the United States. He might have dismissed this as a coincidence if just one of his kidnappers had poor dental work, but seeing the stained and crooked teeth on all of them was revealing. These guys were foreigners. The only exception was Magic, who seemed to be from a younger generation and was more Americanized than the other men.

The Starting Five had just finished their breakfast and were now gathered in the large living room with Tanner. Now that they had narrowed down the list of potential social engineering targets to a dozen people, Tanner decided it was time to move in a different direction.

"I think we have a solid list of people, so we're ready to move on to the next part. This should be easy for you. Let's choose our top five prospects and infiltrate their lives. I need to know everything about them. Where they live, how many kids they have, and where they shop. One of these targets will provide us with something useful that we can exploit. We already have a lot of their personal information from the Internet, but nothing is better than on-site intelligence. So who's going to Los Alamos to do the legwork?" Tanner asked.

Larry decided that he, Patrick, and Michael would spend the next week doing surveillance in Los Alamos. They would track each of the identified targets and gather as much information as they could about the area. In the meantime, Tanner, Magic, and Charles would begin working on the technical aspects of computer hacking.

Larry, Patrick, and Michael wasted no time packing their gear and left for Los Alamos just before noon. With the others gone, Charles was now the senior man at the cabin, and he didn't wait long to implement his style of leadership.

"Tanner, come on over and have some lunch with us. You don't need to eat alone, at least not while I'm in charge. I never liked that stupid rule anyway." Tanner could sense the remaining two captors starting to relax, and he secretly hoped the environment wouldn't be as oppressive with Patrick gone for the week.

Tanner, Charles, and Magic worked feverishly all day, and soon it was time to call it quits. However, there were only two guards left to watch Tanner at night, and they too would have to get some sleep. Tanner wondered how they would address that problem. He didn't have to wait long to find out. Charles grabbed a pair of handcuffs from the garage. Securing Tanner's left ankle to the steel frame on the fold-out bed, Charles threw a sleeping bag and a mat on the opposite end of living room floor for himself.

●———●

From a budget motel room in Los Alamos the following morning, Larry, Patrick, and Michael planned their work. Their objective for the week was reduction and selection. They needed to narrow down the list of potential targets to a select few. Once they had their top choices, they would begin the infiltration phase.

While the Starting Five had little in the way of IT skills, they were all experts at military tactics and physical security. They'd received additional training as spies after they completed a tour of duty in their army. Released from their governmental duties because of political division and unrest, Larry and the others had moved to America years ago, offering their unique services to any client with a large enough checkbook. Upon successful completion of this particular job, they would each get a million dollars from their anonymous employer.

Finishing their complimentary continental breakfast, they grabbed the surveillance gear and headed out to the black Suburban. Patrick took the driver's seat while Larry navigated from the passenger's side, capturing video with the digital camcorder. Michael had his laptop on the backseat, using a cellular air card to maintain a link to the computer systems back at the safe house. Referencing the list of potential suspects, Michael called out the first name and directed Patrick to their target's home.

———————

Back at the cabin, Tanner, Charles, and Magic focused on creating a computer routine to sift through the data sent back from the field team in Los Alamos. They hoped to cross-reference any significant information and match it to their list of targets.

"Guys, I'm going to need a couple of things from my car," Tanner said, starting his programming routine on the computer. "I always listen to music while I code, and my MP3 player is out in my 4Runner. Will you get it for me?" Tanner asked before making his second request. "I'll also need my bass guitar, please."

Charles laughed. "Bass guitar? What are you going to do with that, serenade us?" he asked.

"Only if you want to listen," Tanner countered. "I like to play it when I brainstorm. Focusing on musical notes relaxes my mind and helps me solve complex programming problems. Nothing opens up my mind like some classic Police," Tanner said.

"Just don't play it all night," Magic replied.

"Don't worry," said Tanner. "I left my amp at home, but if this computer has a quality sound card, I can plug into it and use the PC speakers instead."

Magic grabbed Tanner's car keys and headed outside. He soon came back with the MP3 player and a black guitar case.

"I think I got it all," Magic said. "But first I need to check this stuff out. I got to make sure you don't have any trick gadgets in here. I don't want to get shot with a poisoned dart from your guitar," he said half jokingly.

Magic looked over the MP3 player and guitar and was satisfied that everything was benign. The MP3 player was the standard kind found at any electronics store. The bass guitar also looked okay, but Magic wasn't quite sure what he should be looking for if something was out of the ordinary. The only serious threat from the instrument would be if Tanner swung it like a club. Searching the inside of the guitar case, Magic pulled out an unusual cable. "What's this?" he asked.

"That's a customized adapter for my bass guitar. It takes the standard guitar lead and converts it to USB. With the right software, I can digitally record any notes I play right to the computer. It's a pretty cool setup. I'll show you later tonight," Tanner said, setting the guitar case on the ground next to him.

"So when are we going to get past this fact-finding stuff and do some real hacking?" asked Charles.

"We are hacking. We're just not doing any of it on a computer yet," Tanner responded. "But this reconnaissance stage is the most important part. End users are always the biggest threat to computer security, but made-for-TV dramas often skip over this fact because it's not very glamorous. But trust me, if we put in quality time and do this right, the next steps will fall into place."

"Okay, but this is boring me to death. I can't stay awake," Magic replied.

Tanner hobbled over to the fridge and grabbed two Mountain Dews. "That's what this stuff is for. Mr. Dew has gotten me through many a sleepy night while programming." He kept one and tossed the other to Magic. With a laugh, Magic caught the can in mid-flight.

"Let me give you a scenario," Tanner said as he sat back down in his office chair. "We could try to hack through the perimeter firewall on the lab's computer network, but it would never work. Don't forget, this is the same place where they keep all sorts of secrets about nuclear weapons, and other countries would kill for that kind of information," Tanner said. "But if we can isolate two or three people who are in a vulnerable position from financial or social problems, we can blackmail them to escort us through the back door. Once we get inside the lab's perimeter defenses, then we'll start some serious computer hacking."

As Tanner spoke, a new thought came to his mind. *The quantum computer diamond is a big prize and all, but why isn't the Starting Five stealing more valuable information, like nuclear secrets from LANL?* Tanner knew the answer as soon as he thought of the question. *These guys don't want nuclear weapons because they must be from someplace that already has nuclear technology.* Pursuing this line of thought, Tanner swiftly made a mental list of countries with known nuclear capabilities—United States, England, France, Russia, China, Israel, Pakistan, India, North Korea, and possibly Iran. Tanner dropped England and France off the list. They seemed unlikely to steal quantum-computing information, especially from an ally. India and Iran didn't seem to fit the bill given their political climate. Israel might be a possibility because Tanner knew they spied on everyone, including their allies. But two countries stood out above the rest—North Korea and China. North Korea didn't seem like it had the economic base for a quantum computer. Tanner knew North Korea's current standard of living resembled Stalin's reign of the Soviet Union during the 1950s, and since North Korea couldn't even feed its own people, a next-generation supercomputer seemed trivial to such a backward country. Crossing North Korea off his mental list, Tanner was left with Russia and China. As he thought about it, China made more and more sense. China was an emerging superpower. They had a huge labor pool but little intellectual capital. In fact, Tanner remembered reading on the web that China got most of its technology through corporate espionage—and a quantum computer would be on the cutting edge of technology.

● —————— ●

Up at Los Alamos National Labs, in Building 72, Jodi McDonald grinned enthusiastically. Everything was coming together nicely. All the testing and validation with the quantum computer was done. She now had the green light from her superiors to present the non-classified parts of their research at the International Conference on Quantum Information and Computation. The conference this year was in Switzerland, and Jodi was thrilled to be going back. She hadn't been to Europe in several years, and she looked forward to the all-expenses-paid trip. Unfortunately, the department's budget couldn't afford to send everyone to Europe, so Jodi had the unpleasant task of selecting just two individuals to take with her. She hated this part of being a manager, and she sometimes wished that she could do research exclusively. Picking up her desk phone, she dialed her administrative assistant's extension.

"Hey, Becky, this is Jodi. Are you free around two? I need your help to arrange travel plans for some folks on the team." Rebecca Lewis was a wonderful administrative assistant, and everyone in the Applied Quantum Computing department, or AQC, liked working with her. Becky had a sixth sense for predicting what her boss needed before she even asked. It was an awesome trait that compensated for a brilliant but scatterbrained boss, like Jodi.

———•———

For dinner it was grilled chicken, potatoes, and steamed broccoli. Tanner couldn't complain about the menu; Charles was a good cook, and Tanner never went to bed hungry. Of course, he missed his occasional Big Mac from McDonald's. Maybe he could convince Larry to bring one back from Los Alamos. Tanner decided to stick with water for dinner. He had reached his quota of soda for one day. Despite the cases of soda stored in the pantry, Tanner noticed there wasn't any beer or wine in the cabin. Tanner didn't drink anymore because he gave up alcohol when he joined the LDS Church. It was one of the hardest things he'd had to do for his religion, but it surprised him that his captors didn't have a beer once in a while. Maybe the Starting Five didn't want alcohol around because it could cause serious problems, especially for guards who were supposed to be watching someone twenty-four hours a day.

"We've made some good progress," Tanner said at dinner. "We just might make our deadline next month."

"Well, you've got us going in the right direction. Keep it up and Patrick might not break any more of your toes," Charles said, chuckling.

"What's his deal? I mean, I'm doing the work. He doesn't have to keep threatening me," Tanner said.

"It's just his style, but he's mellowed out a lot. You should have seen him ten years ago. He probably would have broken a couple of your ribs. Those things are a lot worse than a broken toe," Charles countered.

"Sounds like you guys have been together for a while," Tanner probed.

"Magic's the newest addition to our group, but the rest of us go way back. Larry has always been the boss. I guess he earned that with his degree. We work well together—"

"That's enough talking for now," Magic said with irritation in his voice. Turning toward Tanner, he deliberately changed the subject. "Tanner, are you going to play that bass tonight?"

"Sure, if you'll let me. I was serious about what I said. Playing the bass relaxes me. When I get jammed up with a tough computer problem, I like to play a few songs to clear my mind."

"Yeah, you're good," Charles responded without thinking. "I don't have musical ability like you."

Tanner was gleaning all sorts of interesting tidbits tonight. First, Charles talked about how most of the Starting Five had been working together for a long time, and now he acknowledged that Tanner was a good musician, which meant they had definitely been eavesdropping on his house. These guys were good, but they couldn't fake their background forever. As they became more comfortable with Tanner, they instinctively let their guard down. It was human nature to do so, and in that way, Tanner had already begun using his social engineering tactics on them.

———•———

The working day ended just after 11:00 p.m. Charles decided to give Tanner a break and let him demo his bass guitar and how it interfaced with the computer. Tanner hadn't played for almost two weeks, and he was excited to pluck some tunes. Taking his Fender Bass guitar from its case, Tanner connected the adapter cable to the USB port on the computer. Then, putting the headstock of the guitar up against his chin, he gently plucked the E, A, D, and G strings one at a time. Satisfied that it was sufficiently tuned, he spoke to Magic. "Hey, I'll need access to a website to show you how this works."

"What website?" Magic responded skeptically.

"It's a website that has a freeware sequencer that I can download. I need it so I can play the music through the computer speakers," Tanner said, keying the URL in the browser only to have the web page automatically blocked by the proxy rules Magic had created.

"Let me check it out first," Magic stated. Putting in his password to bypass the proxy filter, Magic examined the site. "The site looks okay, but I can't let you download the freeware program. It might have a virus."

"That's fine. There's an online version I can use. All I have to do is create a username and download the MIDI driver," Tanner responded.

"I'll create an account for you, but I'll keep the password. That way I control when you log on, and I can make sure you don't try to communicate with anyone on the Internet," Magic responded as he set up a bogus account and email address.

"Okay, I've logged in. Now what?" asked Magic.

"Click on the link to download the driver." As Magic did that, the guitar made a connection to the computer, showing up as a new device. Ready to play, Tanner plucked a few notes on his bass. As he did, the notes where digitally transposed onto the website, showing which note was played.

"It's a neat application," Tanner said. "I can play a song and it will compose the music in a MIDI format for others to see. This is how I taught myself to play the guitar, but I did take piano lessons when I was little, so I already had some basic music theory."

"Can you find other music that people have uploaded and play it?" Charles asked.

"You bet. That's the fun part. People compose their own songs, post it on the website, and let others try it. Check out this one." Tanner clicked the mouse on the music repository and scrolled down the alphabetized list to find a song. The website loaded the score, and Tanner began plucking an upbeat bass line, filling the cabin with a smooth reggae beat.

"I don't ever buy sheet music. I just log into this website and play songs that people have composed," Tanner said, manipulating his bass guitar in a relaxed, uniformed movement. For the next forty-five minutes, Tanner played bass lines from all sorts of songs, entertaining his guards and freeing his mind from its physical prison for a moment.

SEPTEMBER 15, OUTSIDE LAS VEGAS, NEW MEXICO

Gordon and Carla Zane woke up that morning excited for the day's activity.

"Are you ready for your adventure?" asked Karl, the boss of the group.

"Yes. Thank you for allowing us to go," responded Carla in her usual polite manner.

"We're not animals, Mrs. Zane. In fact, we are under strict orders not to harm you unless you try to escape," Karl responded.

"Will we get to talk to our son again?" asked Gordon.

"That's not my decision. Larry will determine when your son has earned the right to call you."

After breakfast Gordon and Carla got ready to go outside. Compared to Phoenix, the temperature here was a cold fifty degrees. They grabbed their sweatshirts and stood ready at the back door.

"Here's the deal," Karl spoke as he brought out a pair of handcuffs. "It will be easier to guard you if you are handcuffed together. I'll lead the way with the two of you following behind. My buddies will bring up the rear, armed, of course."

Walking toward the back side of the mountain property, Karl spoke to them as they started up a gradual dirt trail. "This is an easy path that goes for about a mile into the forest. Can you handle it?" Tanner's parents each answered yes, and Karl continued. "If you behave and obey the rules, we might be able to make this walk a daily occurrence." Grateful at the prospect of getting out each day, the Zanes willingly agreed.

———•———

Larry, Patrick, and Michael's week-long surveillance campaign was almost over. Just a few more days and they would regroup with the others back at the Jemez Mountain safe house. Larry was eager for that because nobody had slept much during their busy week. The previous night had been especially brutal—they spent the early morning hours quietly shuffling through their targets' trash cans, looking for any important personal information. It surprised Larry how few people used a shredder to destroy sensitive documents like credit card statements or phone bills. They hit the jackpot at one house in particular, grabbing all sorts of papers with names and addresses—even a credit card application with a Social Security number on it. Unfortunately, they didn't have enough time to sort through all their findings, so they stuffed everything in trash bags to be scrutinized back at the cabin.

After returning to the cheap motel for a couple hours of sleep, Larry and his team soon found themselves back at work. Their first order of business was a quick bite to eat at the local coffee shop. "We need to check out the security at the Lab today," Larry said, sipping his coffee at an isolated table in the café. "But we have to be discreet. I suggest we do remote surveillance with a 'stupid tourist' maneuver."

"We should probably have one person in the car for that. It might look suspicious with all of us. Also, our black Suburban with tinted windows won't make the security patrol feel at ease. I suggest we rent another car to approach the gate," Patrick said.

"Good thinking," Larry replied. "Let's finish up here and head down to the rental car place." Los Alamos had a small airport with a smaller rental car fleet, but it would work for their purpose.

A short time later, Larry watched Michael head toward the entrance of LANL in a white Ford Escape. Michael's voice came through Larry's secure satphone. "I'm on my way up to the main gate. Are you ready?"

"Roger that," Larry responded. After dropping Michael off to rent the car, Larry and Patrick had taken up a reconnaissance position at the Los Alamos Medical Center. The hospital was over a narrow canyon immediately across from the main entrance to the Lab. "We see you now," Larry said as he spotted Michael in the Ford Escape crossing over the Omega Bridge.

———•———

Michael hung his camera across his neck and threw a road map on the passenger seat next to him. He liked playing the stupid tourist role, and he was excited to see what the Lab had for physical security. It was after 9:00 a.m., and the morning rush of workers into the facility had thinned out. Michael slowed down and hesitated as he neared the security checkpoint. He wanted to convey a sense of indecision to the security patrol to see how they would react when something didn't seem right. His behavior had the desired effect. The security guard had already noticed Michael's erratic movement and was motioning for him to slow down. Stopping at the checkpoint, Michael professionally scanned the area with his peripheral vision. He noticed the tall chain-link fence that encompassed the entire facility. A few yards behind the checkpoint was an olive-green Hummer with a 50-caliber machine gun mounted on its top. Finally, Michael quickly surveyed the guard as he approached the car. He was in fatigues and a black shirt, and on his hip was a 9mm pistol.

"Can I see your ID, please?" the officer said. Even though he was most likely a rent-a-cop from a security company, this man was all business and could definitely handle any trouble that might come his way. Michael also noticed how the guard instinctively placed his hand on his firearm as he spoke, ready for a quick draw if needed.

"Uh, what ID? Like my driver's license?" Michael said with a dumb expression. Glancing behind the guard, he saw another sentry in the gatehouse. Leaning on the wall next to him was a machine gun. The second guard watched Michael with hawklike eyes for the first sign of trouble.

"Sir, this is a restricted area. You need proper ID to enter. You'll have to turn around," the guard said, tensing slightly.

"Hey, I'm just looking for the bombs. Do you know where they are?" Michael responded with feigned ignorance. Quickly, the guard took a step back and un-holstered his weapon. The sentry in the guardhouse picked up his machine gun and approached the car.

"Whoa! Hey, wait . . . slow down," Michael said. "I'm from out of town and I'm just looking for the museum that shows how they made the atomic bomb for World War II. A friend of mine in Albuquerque said to come up here and check it out. I don't mean to cause any trouble."

"I suggest you be careful what you say around here, sir," the guard replied. Then, relaxing a bit, he put his gun back in his holster. "You're probably looking for the Bradbury Science Museum, but it's not here on the Lab campus. The museum is over on Central Ave and Oppenheimer Drive." The guard then gave instructions to Michael on how to get to the museum. Carefully turning his car around, Michael waved good-bye to the security officer, who looked relieved to see the stupid tourist leave.

Michael drove off, heading back across the Omega Bridge, but instead of going over toward the museum, he rendezvoused with Larry and Patrick in the parking lot of the medical center. "Well, that was enlightening," Michael said as he got out of the rental car.

"Yeah, we saw the security guard tense up in our binoculars. You must have said something that caught him off guard," Patrick observed.

"I asked him where the bombs were," Michael said with a laugh.

"That will get their attention for sure," Larry replied. "I'm surprised they didn't arrest you."

Michael continued. "The gate is well guarded by two sentries with pistols and machine guns. Even if we could get past the main gate, it looks like every building is isolated by another fence with more razor wire. I bet there's additional security access controls for those buildings."

"Tanner was right. We're going to need help from someone on the inside to do this job," Patrick responded.

•———•

Tanner ate his lunch hastily, hoping to get a little extra time on his bass guitar before starting work again. For the past couple of days, he'd had a nagging thought in the back of his mind, and he hoped some music would help him focus on an answer.

While Charles and Magic ate their lunch of spaghetti and meatballs, Tanner plugged his bass guitar and headphones into the computer. The headphones weren't the best at reproducing the low tones of a bass guitar, but they allowed him to play quietly without disturbing the others. Tanner decided some smooth jazz was just what he needed. Moving his fingers up and down the frets, Tanner slowly played a quiet jazz bass line, allowing his mind to wander.

For nearly three weeks, Tanner had been at work, preparing to hack into one of the most secret and secure national laboratories in the world. Los Alamos National Labs was the birthplace of modern nuclear technology and the keeper of nuclear secrets. Again, his mind went back to the question from the other day. *These guys are taking a huge risk and spending a lot of time to penetrate LANL. Why are they so interested in quantum computers?*

Tanner ruled out money as an option. If it was money they were after, they would steal nuclear secrets and sell it to al-Qaeda for a boatload of cash. Instead they wanted the classified plans to a prototype quantum computer. *So why does a group of criminals want the plans for a quantum computer? Are they going to sell the information to cyber-terrorists?* The word "terrorists" resounded in Tanner's mind as he thumbed the D string and stopped, staring blankly at the wooden floor. A wave of intelligence flooded over Tanner. His gut knotted up as if he had just been sucker punched by Patrick again. The reality of why the Starting Five wanted a quantum computer became clear, and Tanner's quiet fear turned into panic.

SHAOXING, ZHEJIANG PROVINCE, CHINA

The bright autumn sun highlighted the emerald hills that landscaped the entire city. *The air pollution isn't nearly as bad here as it is in Beijing,* Yang Dao gratefully acknowledged as he looked out the office window on the fourth floor. Even though he was still getting used to the new facility, Yang Dao was pleasantly surprised with the arrangements. Just six months ago, he relocated his entire cyber-warfare operation from Beijing to Shaoxing in the Zhejiang province. The members of the First Technical Reconnaissance Bureau now occupied a massive concrete building overlooking the valley below.

Major General Yang Dao was indebted to China for his career in the army. At age sixty-two, he had worked his entire life in the military and was now a powerful man in the communications and espionage branch of the People's Liberation Army. But Yang Dao hadn't spent his entire life in China. Early on, his superiors had recognized Yang Dao's academic abilities and made sure that he was properly educated. Getting his basic schooling in China, Yang Dao later moved to England to study economics, of all things. *Quite a contradiction for a man living in a state-run nation,* thought the major general, and he smiled. Since he was educated in Europe, outside the indoctrination of the Chinese government, Yang Dao was able to understand reality. He wasn't blinded by the communist rhetoric that flowed from Beijing. The major general fully understood that lasting change for his country couldn't be based on the fallacies of Chairman Mao. It had to be based on the principles of economics.

Yang Dao remembered the mistakes made by the former Soviet Union almost twenty-five years ago. The Soviet Union collapsed, not against the military might of the United States, but against the economic machine of America. The major general saw many of the same parallels between the former Soviet Union and his own country. Unless China continued to embrace capitalism, his country would eventually wither away, taking its place behind the other communist countries that failed to compete in the global economy.

Fortunately, the leaders in Beijing had recognized over the past decade that corporate espionage was an extremely reliable method to compete in a free market. The Chinese weren't shy about flaunting the trade secrets and patents they had stolen from all around the world. Yang Dao had been to Shenzhen many times, and he had seen the knockoff merchandise and electronic counterfeits pilfered from America and manufactured at one hundredth the price. Despite his nation's recent economic renaissance, Yang Dao knew that China was a manufacturing giant, not an intellectual superpower. China had to steal technology to survive.

And we will continue to do so, the major general concluded with resolve. It had been two years since the inception of his brainchild project. The idea came from one of his deeply planted spies in the United States, who learned of a prototype quantum computer that was powerful enough to steal digital secrets right off the Internet. Unfortunately, repeated attempts by his own cyber-warfare specialists in the First Technical Reconnaissance Bureau had failed to obtain the classified plans from Los Alamos. That was why Yang Dao decided to hire someone in America to help him out. With luck, the man in California would succeed in obtaining the plans for this magnificent device. Then Yang Dao would construct his own quantum computer and begin a massive espionage campaign that would solidify his country's rise to superpower status.

———•———

Shor's algorithm, Tanner thought as he recalled what he had learned in his computer cryptology class back in college. Created by a brilliant mathematician named Peter Shor, the algorithm provided a way to solve supercomplex mathematical equations. Tanner now understood why someone would want their own quantum computer. With a quantum computer, a group of cyber-terrorists could use Shor's algorithm to crack the core encryption and security protocols of the Internet.

Ever since the Internet had become a household phenomenon, organizations and businesses had realized the need for secure communication. The Internet was filled with private data like Social Security numbers and bank accounts, all guarded and secured by a concept called PKI, or public key infrastructure. Tanner recalled how his college professor explained public key infrastructure to the class using a medieval metaphor. In ancient times, a courier of the king would deliver a secret message to his troops, sealed in wax, with the king's official seal. When the commanding general received the letter, he could determine two important things. One, the letter was an official message from the king because it bore his seal. And two, the letter hadn't been tampered with because the wax seal was not broken. For added security, the king and the general could also agree on a form of encryption or a method of transposing the plain text message in a way that would appear as gibberish to everyone but the two of them. Julius Caesar had done something similar to communicate with his troops by shifting each letter in the message three characters down in the alphabet.

Tanner had learned that the same encryption concepts were used in modern times, but instead of using envelopes and wax seals, modern electronic communication used certificates and keys. Each computer on the internet had a randomly generated code, or key, to ensure its privacy. The key was created using a tremendously complex mathematical equation—so complex that it would take a room full of supercomputers a million years to solve the equation and crack the key. By the time the code was cracked, the timeliness of the original message would have passed, making the information useless. Speed was paramount in cracking a key, and by implementing Shor's Algorithm on a quantum computer, an encrypted key could be compromised in seconds instead of centuries. The impact would be unfathomable. Secure communications would be compromised. Government secrets would be brought to light. Information in any corporate database would be stolen. Massive identity theft would occur across the world. Personal information would become part of the public domain.

The phone rang in Yang Dao's office, startling him from his thoughts.

"Hello," the major general answered. He didn't need to say anything else because he was highly confident that this was the man he had hired.

"Hello, Major General," the man on the other side of the phone responded. His code name was "Reagan," a jab at the former president who hailed from the same state as the phone call. "I just got an update from my team in New Mexico, and the project is moving along nicely. I'm a little concerned that no hacking attempts have taken place, but my team leader said they're still in the information gathering stage," Reagan reported.

The espionage operation was set up in two separate organizations to isolate and protect identities. Reagan was the ringleader. Yang Dao had hired him to steal the classified information from Los Alamos. Realizing that the risky endeavor was too much for just him to handle, Reagan subcontracted the kidnapping and hacking work out to Larry and the others in New Mexico. Yang Dao and the team in New Mexico knew very little information about the each other's existence. Reagan had meticulously organized his operation this way, allowing him to coordinate everything from the safety of his California location.

"Should I be concerned at your lack of progress?" Major General Yang Dao queried. He was taking a big risk to trust Reagan completely.

"I've got a good plan in place. I'm confident that we'll get you the information before the deadline," Reagan concluded.

"Very well," responded Yang Dao. "I anticipate your status update next week."

SEPTEMBER 19, MOUNTAIN SAFE HOUSE, NEW MEXICO

Larry and the others arrived back early in the morning after a week and a half of surveillance in Los Alamos. They brought hours of video footage, pages of surveillance notes, and sacks full of trash to analyze. Somewhere in this mountain of data, Tanner was confident they would find their unsuspecting accomplices. However, with Larry back in charge, the relaxed and sometimes jovial mood of Charles and Magic disappeared. They were all business again. As before, Tanner ate his breakfast alone, and it wasn't long before Larry noticed the bass guitar sitting in the corner of the room.

"Why is that in here?" Larry asked, pointing to Tanner's black-and-white Fender Bass.

"We brought it in along with his MP3 player, so he could have some music," Magic responded.

Larry's faced turned stern. "I didn't authorize that," he said

"We checked everything out, and it's legit. Tanner usually plays it after lunch and before bed to relax. As you know, he likes his music, and he seems more productive with it," Charles said on Tanner's behalf.

"But why is it connected to the computer?" Larry continued.

"He doesn't have his amplifier with him, so he plugs it into the computer and pipes the sound through the speakers. We opened access to one

74

specific website so he can read music on it," Charles replied, not trying to hide anything from his boss.

"Show it to me," Larry said. Magic brought up the website on the computer for Larry to see. They spent a good twenty minutes thoroughly going through all the links on the website. Tanner finished his breakfast of bacon and waffles silently, watching them do their work. He knew it would be counterproductive to get involved in the discussion.

"I guess it's okay," Larry said. "And if it helps Tanner focus, he can play thirty minutes at noon and before bed." Larry turned toward Charles and Magic; he was more firm. "All that stuff was supposed to be cleared through me. No more web access or accounts without my authorization. Is that understood?" Charles and Magic both agreed, looking sheepishly at the floor. "Tanner, finish up your breakfast, and let's get started. We've got a ton of things to look at," Larry commanded.

The entire day was devoted to sifting through the data. The group divided into three teams. Patrick and Magic were busy going through the trash, sorting out the documents that contained personal information from the worthless scraps of paper. There were eight different piles, one for each of the preliminary targets they had selected. Working next to them, Michael and Charles scanned through the surveillance notes, looking for any correlation with the information that was found from dumpster diving. Tanner and Larry were in the third group. Skimming through eighteen hours of video, they watched for any clues or information that would help them in their selection. The three teams busily worked through the morning and into the afternoon, stopping momentarily for a quick lunch. Only the occasional question or comment broke the silence as everyone focused on their assignments.

At 10:45 p.m., Larry addressed the group. "We've hit it hard for one day. I think we've all got a massive headache from hunching over papers and notes. I know my eyes are about to fall out from watching video clips all day. Let's stop and pick it up tomorrow." Nobody argued. Leaving the documents and notes on the floor or taped up on the wall, the Starting Five moved to the kitchen for a quick snack.

"Can I play my guitar for a bit?" Tanner asked.

"Sure. You deserve it after today. I'm beginning to appreciate your approach to choosing our targets. Magic, go ahead and log Tanner in to that music website," Larry said.

Tanner's eyes were on fire. Dry and raw from staring at a computer screen all day, he didn't want to spend any more time reading music on a monitor. Instead, he opted to just sit on the couch and close his eyes. Effortlessly, he quietly played a melodic bass line as Larry and the others quietly chatted.

"Hey, do you know any Rush?" Larry asked.

"A little bit. Why?"

"They're my favorite group. Their *2112* album is a classic," Larry said.

"Maybe I'll play some tomorrow, but right now I need something more relaxing," Tanner responded, trying to let the stress dissipate from his mind.

September 20, Mountain Safe House, New Mexico

Sunday was a special day in the safe house. It was the start of pro football season, and Larry turned the TV to the NFL network and quietly left it on in the background so everyone could sneak a glance at the scores.

"Okay, let's get down to it," Larry said as the Jets played the Broncos in an early season game. "I've got to report to my boss on our progress, and I want to let him know who our final three targets are—gold, silver, and bronze."

Patrick spoke to the group. "We have some data on all eight of our candidates. The details range from sparse to extremely rich for a couple of people. We sorted the information by individual and selected our top three choices."

"Tell us what you've got and why," Tanner chimed in.

"Our bronze medal," Patrick said, playing on the Olympic theme, "goes to Curtis Huntsaker. He's a single male, age twenty-five. We followed him going to and from work, but we aren't sure what he does at the Lab. In his spare time he likes to smoke pot. We caught him in a couple of drug transactions. We paid his seller five hundred dollars for the information we got about Curtis. We could blackmail him on the drug angle," Patrick offered.

"That might backfire on us," Larry said. "Drug addicts' actions are often unpredictable. In fact, the only thing we can count on from Curtis is his desire to get high. What else have you got?" Larry asked.

Michael started talking next. "That's why we put Curtis Huntsaker as our third option. We have two other choices that have significantly more potential. Our silver finalist is a man by the name of Ken Calloway. Ken is forty-four and has been married to Karen for twenty years. He has three kids, all teenage girls, but we don't know their ages yet. He's probably a scientist or engineer at the Lab, as his license plate 'PHD4ME' proudly states, but we aren't sure what technical area he works in. He drives a BMW and spends a lot of money, as we found out from several unshredded credit card statements in the trash. But here's the kicker: it looks like the mom and daughters are spending him into the poor house. From what we can tell, he's maxed out seven or more credit cards, carrying a total balance of well over eighty thousand dollars of debt. We aren't sure if his family knows the financial mess he's in, but debt is a great gateway for extortion."

Tanner took note of Ken's financial problems, recalling that money troubles were the number-one reason for people committing espionage. That's why it was practically impossible to get a security clearance after declaring bankruptcy.

"And who's our gold medal winner?" Tanner asked.

"That belongs to Ms. Rebecca Lewis," Patrick said. "She's a single female, thirty-five years old, and never married. We tailed her for a couple of days and discovered she likes to spend her evenings in Santa Fe at the local bars. She has a resume posted on a national career website. She listed her current position as an administrative assistant in the AQC group at Los Alamos. AQC stands for Applied Quantum Computing, the same department where the quantum computer research is taking place. Clearly, that's a huge score. Rebecca hangs out in clubs with a lot of other single people, which would make her an easy point of contact."

"Where did you find all that information?" Larry asked.

"She put most of it on Facebook and Twitter. She documents almost every part of her life on the Internet. Welcome to the age of social networking," Magic said.

"Tanner, what do you think about our targets?" Larry asked.

"I'm highly optimistic about the top two targets in particular, Ken Calloway and Rebecca Lewis, but the drug user might be risky. Also, it will stretch us too thin to go after three targets. I suggest we focus our efforts on the two best choices and play both of them simultaneously," Tanner said. Looking around at the nods of agreement from the others, he changed the subject. "Now that that's decided, what's the physical security like at the Lab? Could we get in if needed?"

"Negative," Patrick responded. "We scouted the entire facility. There's a ten-foot chain-link fence that surrounds the entire perimeter. There are only two main entrances, one on the north side by Los Alamos and one on the south by White Rock. There are armed guards at the entrances. Inside, the more secure buildings are behind another fence with an additional checkpoint."

"That's what I figured. The only way we can hack their network is with the help of someone on the inside," Tanner stated resolutely.

That night, after wrapping up for the evening, Tanner again played his bass guitar. But this time, the music was bumpy and offbeat.

"What are you playing? That doesn't sound like anything to me," Charles said.

Tanner didn't take his eyes off the digitized sheet music on the computer screen. "I'm trying to learn a new song. Sorry, it's not very melodic."

Accepting that they didn't understand that he had to practice new music sometimes, Tanner put on his earphones and continued to play for the next half hour.

• — •

The following morning, Larry called California using his secure satphone. California was an hour behind New Mexico, but since it was Monday morning, Larry figured that Reagan would be up and going by now. Walking outside to make sure no one overheard his conversation, Larry dialed the number.

"Hello," Reagan answered the phone on the fourth ring.

"This is Larry."

"I hope you have some good news," Reagan stated with some irritation. "I'm getting a little concerned at your lack of progress."

Larry took the jab in stride. He knew from experience that every operation had hiccups along the way. Larry was confident that he would deliver the classified plans to Reagan on time.

"We've narrowed down our targets to two people. Tanner thinks they're a good selection." Larry went on to explain what they knew about Ken Calloway and Rebecca Lewis.

"How come you haven't started hacking into the lab yet?" Reagan asked. "It's almost been a month."

"You're the one that insisted we use Tanner for this job. You said he was the best," Larry quickly countered.

"He is the best and definitely the man for the job. But if you need to, squeeze him to move the project forward. I want to hear that you've hacked into the network when you call next week."

"Tanner isn't slacking, but it's taken a while for us to collect the information on the people we're going to exploit. Tanner says successful hacking begins with identify theft," Larry said.

"Speaking of Tanner, don't let him communicate with anyone. He's very resourceful," Reagan warned.

"I've done this stuff before!" Larry said, upset that Reagan would question his abilities.

"Very well. I expect to hear good news next week, though," Reagan countered.

"I'll call you later," Larry said. He didn't like to be told how to do his job, but Reagan was the man writing the paychecks, so he held his peace and went inside to talk to Tanner.

"I just spoke to my boss," Larry began, addressing the group. "He thinks we're falling behind schedule. Tanner, you better find a way to move faster, or I'll see if Patrick can find other ways of motivating you."

Tanner looked down at his broken toe before responding. "I'm moving along the best I can, but we're losing time because I have to train everyone on computer hacking. I told you it would go a lot faster if I could be on site at Los Alamos and see things for myself instead of having to rely on you."

"Don't waste your energy getting mad at me," Larry said, rolling his eyes. "Use it to figure out another way to pick up the pace. We need to be into the Lab's network by next week."

"Next week? That's completely unrealistic," Tanner replied.

"Why? We've selected our targets and already collected enough information to exploit them. I say we start the face-to-face interaction."

"That could be risky," Charles countered, trying to defuse the situation. "If we rush in too quickly, we risk frightening off our targets."

"I don't care. I'm trumping everyone. Tomorrow we begin the face-to-face contact with Ken Calloway and Rebecca Lewis!" Larry commanded.

The team spent the rest of the day finalizing their plans on how to contact their targets. After a fierce debate, they agreed on two approaches. Charles would focus on Rebecca Lewis, using a dating website and a potential romance as entrance points into her life. He was the sweet talker in the group and the most likely to gain Rebecca's trust. Larry and Patrick would take a direct approach with Ken Calloway, leveraging his financial crisis to convince him to commit espionage. Tanner would immediately start working on a computer program that would exploit the computer network at Los Alamos. With only four days to do his work, Tanner figured he'd have to start pulling some all-nighters.

Tired and stressed out, Tanner was grateful when 11:30 p.m. arrived. He definitely needed to play his bass to relax. Tanner took out his guitar, hooked it up to the computer, and had Magic log him in to the website. Looking at the newly posted music, Tanner searched for a user who might have posted a song in the past day.

Monday signified the beginning of the workweek for most people, but Tanner and the crew at the cabin had been working nonstop. Tanner was fully back into the hacking lifestyle, committing crimes he promised he'd never do again. He hated himself for exploiting innocent victims, yet a small part of him couldn't deny the intoxicating rush that came from doing something illegal again.

"I've created an account for Charles on several of the dating websites that Rebecca Lewis uses," Tanner told Larry. "I've also doctored up his profile to match what Rebecca looks for in a man. Hopefully she'll respond with interest in a first date."

"Good work," Larry replied before turning to Charles. "How are you going to handle the arrangements?" Larry asked.

"It would be best if I spent the next week in Santa Fe, close to the places that Rebecca likes to visit. I'm going to try and find a furnished apartment to rent. My angle is that I just moved into the area to work at the Lab. I'm a divorced forty-five-year-old with a couple of teenagers who live with my ex-wife. After I gain Rebecca's trust, it's up to Tanner to get me that CD thingy," replied Charles.

"It's called a rootkit," Tanner said.

"What's the rootkit again?" Michael asked.

"It's a collection of programs designed to take control over a computer.

The basic idea is that Rebecca Lewis will run this CD on her computer at work, and it will activate the rootkit," Tanner explained.

"But why would she run the CD if she knows it has a rootkit on it?" Patrick asked.

Tanner let out a sigh. "She won't know it has a rootkit. She'll think that she's running a regular CD with pictures or music on it, but in the background this rootkit will execute," he said.

"Okay," Charles agreed. "I get close enough to her so she feels comfortable running this CD with a rootkit on it."

"That's right. You do the romancing, and I'll do the hacking," Tanner said flatly. "Let's also hope she isn't current on her security training. I'm sure there are all sorts of policies at the Lab against bringing media in and running it on the internal network. That's why you'll have to turn on the charm. Blind her with love so she'll do what you want."

"Well, the love doctor is in the house," Charles said with a macho laugh.

"Charles, plan for seven to ten days in Santa Fe. Pack up your gear and take a laptop to keep in touch. We'll want a daily report," Larry said.

"Don't force your relationship on Rebecca, but you don't have a lot of time to waste either, so you'll have to find a delicate balance between the two," Tanner warned.

"Got ya," Charles said, heading off to pack his gear. He seemed to think romancing "this Becky gal" was going to be the best part of the job.

Satisfied that Charles was ready to go, Tanner turned to Larry and Patrick. "I imagine you're more skilled at extortion than I am, so I don't think you'll need any pointers from me," Tanner said. "What's your plan for dealing with Ken Calloway?"

"It's pretty straightforward," Larry replied. "We're going to approach him and see if he's interested in a business deal that would help fix his money problems. We know he's in a big mess, so hopefully he'll play along."

"Are you going to stay in Los Alamos?" Tanner asked.

"We'll stay there for the first day or two and see how it goes. Once we have our initial agreement in place, we'll be ready for your hacking routine," Larry stated.

"Okay, I'll pound out the CD with the rootkit and try to have one ready for Ken by the end of the week," Tanner promised. Larry and

Patrick went to pack their gear. Before long, Charles was off to Santa Fe in Tanner's 4Runner. Following closely behind, Larry and Patrick headed out in the black Suburban for Los Alamos. Watching the last SUV leave, Tanner spoke to Michael and Magic. "We won't have any time to party while those guys are gone. It's going to be a busy week for all of us."

Up to this point, Tanner's main focus had been on the social engineering aspect of hacking, but now he was moving into the technical nuts and bolts. He just hoped he could still remember how to construct a good rootkit.

"So is this rootkit just going to try and guess a person's password?" Michael asked as he sat down next to Tanner.

"No, it's more much more elaborate than that," Tanner said. "I once read in a security magazine that passwords like '123456', 'iloveyou', and 'monkey' used to be so common that hackers did guess them out of dumb luck. But most organizations now require a password to be at least eight characters long and not be a word found in a dictionary. That's over 200 trillion different combinations if you use all letters and numbers on a keyboard. Trying to guess a password with that complexity is impossible. Instead I'm going to focus on security exploits and vulnerability scanners."

"What are those," Michael asked.

Tanner went on to explain the hacking concept to Michael and Magic. "Every computer program or software routine out there has some weakness somewhere. That's just the inherent nature of computers."

Michael looked perplexed. "Don't the companies that write these programs try to fix the holes?"

"Of course," Tanner said. "They're always fixing problems, but computers are so complex that it's impossible to secure everything. New vulnerabilities are being discovered all the time."

"But how do you know which exploits or vulnerabilities to use?" Magic asked.

"Back in the day it took years for a hacker to find security holes, but now, with the Internet, it's a lot easier. We'll search some hacking websites to see what specific vulnerabilities are out there. Then I'll write a bunch of computer routines to check for those vulnerabilities and put those in my rootkit," Tanner explained.

"People actually put that information out there on the Internet?" Michael asked.

"You bet. Hackers all over the world are constantly looking for new ways to get access into a computer system or network. When they find one, they put their discoveries out on the Internet to share with other hackers. Other hackers then write programs to find these known bugs or weaknesses in an application or operating system. These programs have a very high rate of success since most people don't proactively patch their computers."

Magic nodded his head. He was catching on to how basic this process was. "You're going to create one of these rootkits to give to Ken or Rebecca to run on their computer. It's going to find some kind of security hole on their computer, and then give us access to the entire Lab's network."

"That's the idea," Tanner said, smiling.

———————

"There he is." Larry looked up as Patrick spoke. Both men were sitting in the black Suburban at the edge of the parking lot. Looking through his binoculars, Larry identified Ken Calloway as he walked into the only grocery store in Los Alamos. Their target was overweight, balding, and deeply in debt.

"How will you approach him?" Larry asked. Patrick was the person with the most spy-craft training in the group, and he was the one who would make the initial contact with Ken Calloway.

"We need a public location where I can have a casual conversation without triggering any suspicion, like a park or restaurant," Patrick said.

"Let's follow him and see where he goes after this. Maybe he'll grab a bite to eat," Larry speculated. About ten minutes later, Ken came out of the grocery store, carrying something. Focusing his field glasses, Larry tried to see what was in Ken's hand.

"It looks like one of those small paper sacks they give you with a prescription," Larry said as Ken crumpled up a piece of paper and threw it in the trash can just outside the store.

"Let him go for now," Larry said. "I want to see what he threw away." Larry hopped out of the SUV with a newspaper tucked under his arm and casually walked up to the same trash can. Throwing the newspaper away, Larry faked frustration as if he'd thrown away more than he wanted. Reaching into the trash can, he withdrew the sports section and the crumpled up paper that Ken had just tossed in a few seconds earlier.

Then going into the store, Larry bought a bag of chips to complete the masquerade before returning to the SUV. Opening up the crumpled paper, Larry could see it was an information sheet for the prescription drugs Alprazolam and Zolpidem. Smiling, Larry said, "It looks like Ken's stressed out and having trouble sleeping. Maybe his money problems are a lot more serious than we thought."

———•———•———

Apparently, Charles's trip to Santa Fe had taken longer than expected. Coming down Highway 502, he'd had to wait thirty minutes while the police cleared a car accident on the bridge that crossed over the Rio Grande. But eventually he'd gotten to Santa Fe and found the rental office to an apartment complex specializing in long-term stays. After visiting with the landlord, Charles had paid cash for a month's rent on a furnished one-bedroom apartment.

Later that night, Tanner read the two field teams' reports at the main cabin.

"It sounds like Charles is ready to go on a date tomorrow. Well, it's not really a date, but he's agreed to meet Becky for lunch at a sandwich shop up by the Lab," Tanner said to the group as he read through Charles's report.

"That's a good first step, but knowing Charles, he'll want a base hit on the first date," Michael said jokingly.

"What about Larry and Patrick?" Magic asked.

"They struck out. They didn't get a chance to approach Ken, but they did manage to get his cell phone number off a prescription receipt. They're going to send him an anonymous text message. I think that's a good icebreaker," Tanner said as he responded to Larry's email.

Tanner was glad evening had come. He'd spent all day at the computer, even eating his meals there, as he drafted the steps of his rootkit. Tomorrow would be a serious research day, as he would try to find a dozen security exploits to implement. Calling it quits, Tanner picked up his bass guitar. "Magic, would you mind hooking me up on the web page so I can play my bass?" Tanner asked.

"Sure thing," Magic responded. He logged into the music website for Tanner, who warmed up by playing "Walking on the Moon," a score he had memorized long ago. After a couple of minutes playing the rhythmic melody, Tanner changed to unevenly plucking the strings.

"It sounds like he is practicing again. I wish he would just stick to the music he already knows," Michael said to Magic. Tanner heard Michael's comment and took it as a hint to put on his earphones.

●————●

Charles was having fun. He stayed up until midnight, chatting with Becky online. They seemed to have really hit it off. For some reason people seemed to have less restraint when mingling in cyberspace, and Becky was no exception. She let loose a fountain of information for the two hours they chatted. Charles told her that he was new in the area and working at the Lab as a chemical engineer. She responded by verifying that she worked as an administrative assistant at the Lab. Charles continued probing her with seemingly trivial questions, just as Tanner had instructed the previous day. Becky was all too willing to talk. The Internet provided a false sense of security, and Becky rambled on for hours, revealing many aspects of her work and life. When Charles finally said good night, he had composed almost four pages of notes, but with it being so late, he decided he would sleep first and then send his notes off to Tanner in the morning.

It was the last day of September. Tanner had been in captivity for almost an entire month. He hadn't spoken to his parents in weeks, but Larry and the other kidnappers assured him that his parents were alive and well. Charles had spent the past week in Santa Fe, preparing for his first date with Becky Lewis. Larry and Patrick had been busying tracking Ken Calloway. With everyone focusing on their assigned tasks, Tanner and the two remaining kidnappers got to work. "What's on the schedule for today?" Magic asked.

The day had begun the same way as the others for the past month. To break up the monotony, Tanner had been growing a goatee for the past week. His toe was feeling better, but he still moved with a slight limp, hoping to show his captors that he didn't need another broken toe.

"We're going to surf the web for more security exploits and vulnerabilities," Tanner said.

"How many of those do we need? We've already found almost a dozen," Magic said.

"We've got to have at least twice that amount. The computers at the lab won't be susceptible to most of the vulnerabilities we find, so I need to put at least two dozen in my rootkit to make sure one of them is successful," Tanner said.

Tanner was surprised by how much information was available on the Internet about hacking. When he was in his prime, hackers' tools and secrets were confidential and passed on by word of mouth only, but now there were literally thousands of websites devoted to hacking a computer system. Some of those websites even provided step-by-step hacking instructions. Other enterprising hackers were taking a business approach, selling prepacked hacking programs that only required a user to click on a button to exploit a computer.

"Why can't we just use the security holes we've already found?" Michael asked.

"Those big vulnerabilities are too well known. We've only got one shot at this, and I'm betting the computer guys at the lab have already patched the system for those exploits. We need to find some newer vulnerabilities that aren't well known yet. That will give us the best chance of success," Tanner explained.

Michael shook his head in frustration. "This computer stuff is way over my head. I should have taken Charles's gig. He's the one having all the fun."

———•———

Back in Los Alamos, Charles was getting ready for his lunch date. He left Santa Fe early to check out the place where he would meet Becky. Dressed in Dockers and a blue dress shirt, he appeared both handsome and professional. He knew first impressions were critical in situations like this, and he wanted to follow up his week of online courting in a positive way. Arriving fifteen minutes before noon, Charles took a corner table at the sandwich café and ordered an iced tea.

Becky had been so excited about her date that she hardly slept last night. After saying good-bye to Charles, she lay in bed, wondering what he would be like in person. Becky's dating life had been listless. Even the bars and dance clubs seemed to be filled with egocentric men or indecisive boys who still hadn't moved out of their parents' basements. Becky hoped that Charles wouldn't fall into either category. As she parked her car next to the restaurant, Becky took a moment to check her makeup and hair one last time, making sure it was perfect.

Charles recognized Becky as she came in the door. Wearing a red blouse and casual black skirt, she presented herself in a professional and beautiful, manner. She looked a little older than the picture on her online profile, and her long hair was a shade darker. Waving to get her attention, Charles motioned for her to come over to the table. He greeted her with a friendly handshake and smile. "I wasn't sure if you were going to make it. We were up pretty late last night," Charles said with a casual laugh.

"We *were* up late. I only got a few hours' sleep before I had to get up for work. It's about an hour commute from there to the Lab, but I prefer living in Santa Fe," Becky said with playful smile. Charles tried to be even more impressive in person than on the Internet. He portrayed a quiet confidence in addition to his mature looks.

"I'm glad you came for lunch. I'm so new in the area that I hardly know anyone," Charles said.

"Thank you for inviting me. I really like this café. They have the best roast beef sandwiches around," Becky said. After ordering their meals, Charles picked up the conversation from where it had ended the night before.

————•————

On the other side of town, Patrick waited for Ken Calloway at the Bradbury Science Museum. Last night Patrick sent Ken an anonymous text message requesting a meeting at the museum. The text message stated that Patrick knew about Ken's financial situation and that Patrick had a business deal to help him get out of debt. Of course, Ken texted back, wanting to know what it was all about, but Patrick responded by saying he needed to meet face-to-face to discuss the details.

"He's not going to show," Larry said, talking to Patrick on a small two-way radio. Larry was waiting outside in the Suburban, anxiously anticipating Ken's arrival.

"Give him another couple of minutes. We've got to be patient and take our time to fish him out," Patrick said, moving to the next exhibit. It was a scaled replica of the Fat Man atomic bomb that was dropped on Nagasaki, Japan.

"I've been sitting out here for almost an hour, and I haven't seen anyone come or go that remotely looks like our target," Larry countered.

"I'll send him another text message," Patrick said. Grabbing his sat-phone, Patrick started a text message only to be stopped by Larry's voice talking excitedly over the radio.

"Wait, here he comes. I just saw the BMW pull up. He's parking now."

"Okay, keep an eye on him and make sure he's not bringing any friends along," Patrick said.

Ken Calloway had been fighting an internal battle of conscience for more than twelve hours. Ever since he got the text message last night, his mind had gone back and forth on what to do. Ken had worked at the Lab for decades, and he knew from his annual security training that situations like this were always a possibility. Especially during the Cold War, Ken had been trained on the different approaches the KGB might use to try to steal classified information. But the Cold War was over, and Ken wasn't really a scientist. He was a civil engineer in the Construction Management department, and he didn't have access to any of the classified secrets at the national lab. However, with his debt piling up, he was becoming increasingly desperate, even to the point of considering espionage to pay off his bills. *Talking to a guy about a business deal isn't really espionage, is it?* Ken rationalized as he entered the building.

Ken walked around the museum, looking for a man in a yellow dress shirt holding a coffee cup. Ken's heart was beating rapidly. Again, he cursed himself for being overweight because just walking around the museum was a workout. Turning the corner, Ken saw Patrick standing against a large display.

"Patrick?" Ken called out quietly, almost to the point of Patrick not being able to hear him. Patrick had been watching the reflection on the glass that covered the map he was looking at, and he had seen his target approach from the far side of the museum. Patrick turned around and extended a friendly handshake.

"Relax, I don't bite," Patrick said with a smile and a laugh, trying to put Ken at ease. He was obviously scared.

"I almost didn't come. I had second, third, and even fourth thoughts," Ken said nervously.

"Hey, I'm not going to force you to do anything you don't want to do. You can head back to work right now if you choose. I can always find someone else to be my business partner."

The suggestion had the desired effect. Fearful of losing the chance to make some quick money, Ken responded that he was willing to talk.

Patrick guided Ken slowly through the museum, acting like they were chatting about the exhibits. "Ken, I'm a business man who needs information. I'm looking for someone who would be willing to do a small and simple task in exchange for one hundred thousand dollars," Patrick said, dangling the carrot. "I know you're having big financial troubles at home, so I thought I'd offer to help you first."

"How do you know about my problems?" Ken asked weakly, realizing it didn't matter. Obviously, Patrick had connections because he knew Ken's phone number, where he lived, and how much debt he had accrued.

"I'm a resourceful businessman, but let's focus on you, Ken. Your high-maintenance wife and kids are sending you to the poor house. From what I can tell, it's only a matter of months before you lose your home."

Embarrassed at Patrick's intimate knowledge of his dire financial situation, Ken looked down at the carpet before responding. "I keep trying to make ends meet, but I'm falling behind so fast."

"It's time for you to step up and take control. Stop letting your wife and kids manipulate you. It's time to put your foot down," Patrick said, both mocking and motivating Ken at the same time.

"I know, but I'm in such a deep hole I can't get out."

"That's why you're meeting with me today, right? You're looking for a way out of this mess," Patrick guessed. "I can help."

"I'm a patriot, not a traitor. Even if wanted, I couldn't get you information on nuclear weapons. I don't have classified access."

"Hey, I'm a true-blue American too. I wouldn't ask you to betray our country's nuclear technology," Patrick said, establishing a relationship of trust.

"What? I thought for sure that's what you wanted," Ken said.

"There's a lot of other cool stuff at the Lab besides nukes. I'm interested in computers, superfast computers, only found here at the Lab."

"What kind of supercomputers?" Ken asked. He was relieved that he didn't have to steal nuclear secrets. Patrick went on to give Ken a brief explanation of the quantum computing research going on at the Lab. Patrick purposely told Ken the truth, knowing that the truth, sprinkled with lies, was a lot more effective.

"The best part is that you don't really have to do anything. I just need you to put a CD in a computer and hit enter. That's it," Patrick explained.

"What's on the CD? A computer virus?" Ken asked.

"No, Ken. Viruses destroy data. I want to get a copy of it. This CD will run a little program that will go out on the network and email me some information. You don't have to steal anything. Just thirty seconds of work for one hundred thousand dollars. That's a pretty good deal if you ask me."

Ken was gaining more interest in Patrick's project. Surely copying some information wasn't all that bad. "Okay, what's the catch?" Ken asked.

"What do you mean?"

"There's always a catch," Ken replied.

"I just laid it all out for you, Ken. No hidden agendas. I'm a capitalist, not a criminal."

Ken paused for a moment, looking at a diagram on how nuclear weapons worked. When he left for this secret meeting, Ken thought for sure that Patrick would ask him to steal nuclear secrets. That's what the security office at the lab always said the enemy wanted. But Patrick was an American, not the KGB. He just wanted the quantum computer technology first so he could profit from that, and there's nothing wrong with making some money. *How much harm could a computer do?* It didn't take long for Ken to commit to the proposal. "Okay. What do you want me to do?"

Patrick smiled. He never doubted that Ken would agree to do the job. If Ken weren't interested, he wouldn't have met with Patrick in the first place. "That's a smart choice. We both win. You'll get out of debt, and I'll get the quantum computer."

Patrick spent a few more minutes, discussing how to proceed. In a couple of days, Ken would return to the museum where he would find a package taped under the second sink in the men's bathroom. Inside would be the CD with the instructions on what to do.

"How will I get my money?" Ken asked.

"After we see that you successfully ran the CD, we'll send you additional instructions on how to get your money. But for now, here's a down payment," Patrick said, stuffing a roll of hundred-dollar bills into Ken's pocket. Patrick then turned and started walking away. "Check your cell phone for further details," he said before going out the front door.

Once outside, Patrick didn't go straight back to the Suburban. Instead he walked in the opposite direction, giving Larry a chance to spot a tail, but no one ever came. The only person Larry noticed was Ken as he came through the front doors of the museum a few moments later. Satisfied that Ken was acting alone, Larry waited for him to leave before picking up Patrick.

"Is he in?" Larry asked as Patrick climbed in the front seat.

"Absolutely," Patrick responded with a grin.

—————•—————

Across town, Charles's lunch with Becky was going very well—so well, in fact, that Charles didn't even worry about whether she would accept a second date. He already knew it was going to happen.

"Thank you so much for lunch. I really had a great time," Becky said.

"You're very welcome. It was a lot of fun meeting you. I would like to do it again sometime," Charles emphasized. "Are you free later this week?"

"Yes, I am," Becky said with a slight giggle. She would have gone out tonight if Charles had asked.

"Let me give you my cell number," Charles said. He texted his cell number to Becky in exchange for hers. "I better get going. I have a meeting with HR to start my security clearance paperwork."

Becky turned her head to the side, obviously expecting a quick kiss on the cheek, but instead Charles extended his hand. Giving Becky a firm handshake, he thanked her again for the date and said good-bye. *Always leave them wanting more*, Charles thought as he passed through the door and into the parking lot.

—————•—————

Driving back to work, Becky was smiling so much that her face hurt. Charles was everything she had hoped for, and even though her head told her to slow down, her heart was saying otherwise.

"How was lunch?" Jodi McDonald asked as she passed Becky in the hall back at work. Becky had told her earlier in the day about her anticipated lunch date.

"He was fabulous. I won't say he's Mr. Right, but he's definitely a finalist," Becky said, smiling even more.

"That's a pretty big assumption after just one date," Jodi said.

"We just hit it off. It's like he's known me for a long time. We're going out again later this week."

"He sounds like a great guy," Jodi said with a slight pause. Even though Jodi wasn't much older than Becky, she had known Becky for a long time and felt like an older sister to her. "Maybe I should meet him sometime just to give you my impression."

"That's a great idea. We'll all have lunch together. Then you can see how wonderful Charles is," Becky said as she floated off down the hall.

Tanner decided he was ready to start the rootkit. He wished he'd had more time to explore his options, but with just three days to create a successful hacking routine, he was running out of time. Narrowing down his list, Tanner chose several lesser-known security exploits that would have the highest probability of success.

"Okay, here's what I'm going to do," Tanner announced to Magic and Michael. "There are a lot of technical details here, so I'll just give you a quick overview." Michael and Magic were listening on the couch while Tanner stood by one of the large whiteboards, drawing out his plans. "The first thing I want to do is sniff the Lab's computer network. This will help me map out which servers are available to exploit. It's similar to how a thief would scout out a neighborhood, looking for the easy targets. Then I'll execute a scan to find out which ports the servers are listening to. Ports are openings through which computers communicate. The port scan is like a thief checking for unlocked windows or doors. The next step is to identify which communication protocols are enabled. If the system administrator at the lab is doing his job, most of these common services will be turned off. But we might get lucky and find a service that isn't locked down or that's vulnerable to a buffer overflow. I'm also going to probe to see if the application accounts still have their default passwords. It's amazing how often people forget to change those. Finally, I'll check for application vulnerabilities like SQL injections, which can allow direct access into a database."

Finished listing all his steps on the whiteboard, Tanner turned back toward Michael and Magic. Both men had blank looks on their faces. Tanner laughed. "Guys, that was the quick and non-technical overview, but I guess it was still too much," he said. It was going to be a long night.

October 1, Outside Las Vegas, New Mexico

Carla Zane sat next to her husband, drinking fresh orange juice at the kitchen table. Both of them watched the sunrise over a mountain ridge covered with Piñon pines. In the kitchen, Karl and one of his men were fixing a breakfast of scrambled eggs and English muffins. The other sentry had gone to sleep after taking the night shift guarding the couple. The Zanes were both trying to remain positive despite their situation. The fall mornings were beautiful, yes, but right now they should be traveling along the Oregon coast with their son, not locked up in a remote mountain home somewhere.

"Will we be able to talk to our son today?" Carla asked her captors.

"You've asked me that same question every day since you got here," Karl replied.

"But can't you call and ask?" Carla pleaded.

"We're not supposed to do that. We're to remain isolated and only call in an emergency."

"But it's been so long, and we're worried sick about him. We've done everything you've asked of us. I think that should entitle us to a phone call," Carla begged. She began to cry.

Karl knew she was right. Both Mr. and Mrs. Zane had been extremely easy prisoners. Neither of them had caused any problem, so maybe just one quick phone call wouldn't hurt.

"I'll see what I can do," he said. "Maybe I'll try checking in later today."

———•———

Larry and Patrick checked out their cheap motel early and headed back to the cabin. Convinced that Ken Calloway would cooperate, there wasn't much else the two could do without Tanner's rootkit.

"We're on our way back," Larry said to Michael on the secure satphone as he and Patrick headed down Highway 4 in the black Suburban. "Tell Tanner that we've got to have his program ready to go by this weekend."

"He stayed up all night working on it," Michael told him.

"Okay, I want a full update when I arrive," Larry said, and the line went dead.

Michael had also stayed up all night watching Tanner work. With his ankle monitor still in place and the other ankle handcuffed to the desk, Michael figured Tanner wouldn't go too far.

"That was Larry. He's on his way back and wants a full update when he gets here," Michael said.

"Okay," Tanner said curtly. Still working at the keyboard, he was in the zone, as he liked to call it. Occasionally, he would get into this pure programming mind-set, and he wouldn't stop for fear of messing up his groove. Tanner had made great progress working all night, but he knew he couldn't go on like this for three days. He'd have to stop for a few hours of sleep this afternoon.

Michael brought over a bowl of cold cereal for Tanner.

"It's not much, but here's an easy breakfast. You can't live on soda alone," Michael said.

"Thanks." Tanner took a quick spoonful of cereal.

An hour later, the black Suburban pulled up and parked in front of the cabin, and Larry and Patrick got out and walked through the front door.

"Good morning," Larry said tersely as he went into the kitchen and poured himself a cup of coffee. After taking a sip, he headed over to Michael and Tanner. "Where's Magic?" Larry asked.

"He should be up in a moment. He went to bed last night about 2:00 a.m. We weren't sure when you'd be back, so we decided to split up the guard duties," Michael said. "But don't worry, Tanner's ankle has been cuffed to the computer desk all night, and we disabled the Internet connection so he couldn't communicate with anyone on the outside."

"Okay, let's sync up," Larry said, deciding it wasn't worth getting into an argument as to why only one person was guarding Tanner. They were all under pressure to get this project done, and with that sense of urgency, they were going to have to make exceptions.

Tanner finished his programming statement and turned to the group. His bloodshot eyes verified that he hadn't slept in a while. "I'm almost one-third done, and I think I can have it finished by Friday."

"Good," Larry said, and then he briefly explained how Patrick made contact with Ken the previous day. "Take a break this afternoon and get some sleep," Larry ordered. Then, turning to Michael, he asked for an update on Charles.

●————————●

In Santa Fe, Charles started his day with a morning run. The capital city of New Mexico was over seven thousand feet above sea level, and the cool morning air had a slight chill. Running down the side of the road, Charles geared up for a big day. Tonight would be an official date with dinner and a movie. Charles was excited, but he still thought of this as a job. He didn't even consider the possibility that Becky was already falling for him.

●————————●

A satphone in the cabin started ringing just after lunch. Grabbing his phone from his pocket, Larry answered, recognizing Karl's phone number on the caller ID.

"This is Karl. We have a problem. Mrs. Zane is begging to speak with her son. Every day she asks me, and it's getting unbearable."

Larry sighed. He knew that eventually he'd have to let Tanner talk with his parents. It had been almost four weeks since they'd briefly spoken to each other. Larry decided that right now might not be a bad time. A surprise phone call would mean Tanner wouldn't have any time to organize his thoughts and try to communicate a secret message to his parents. "Okay, I'll put him on." Larry walked over to Tanner and handed him the phone. "It's your parents. Make your conversation quick and simple," he ordered, turning on the speakerphone.

"Mom, is that you?" Tanner asked, rubbing his bleary eyes.

"Yes, it's me. How are you?" she asked.

"I'm all right, Mom. How are you? Is Dad okay?"

"Yes, we're both fine. We've been locked up in this house the entire time except for an afternoon walk in the woods," Carla said.

"That's more than I've been able to do. I've been sitting at a computer the entire time," Tanner responded, knowing he had gained a couple of pounds from his inactivity.

"What are you doing? Why do they want you?" It was his father's voice now on the phone. Larry jumped in before Tanner had a chance to answer.

"Sorry, Gordon, but Tanner won't be answering that question. You can hear that he is alive and fine. I hope that satisfies your curiosity," he said. He took the phone back and finished the call, talking alone with Karl.

Tanner was thrilled with the unexpected call with his parents. He assumed they were okay, but still he worried. Ironically, he was more concerned about his parents' well-being than his own situation. He wished he could have talked more, but he was so tired he was about to pass out. Taking a long stretch, Tanner decided that it was a good time to take a nap. "Wake me up in three hours," Tanner said to nobody in particular. Then he fell fast asleep on the couch.

●————●

Sitting at her desk, Becky Lewis alternated between working and monitoring her cell phone. Even though she had it set to both ring and vibrate, she still checked it often to see if Charles had called or sent a text message. It had been just twenty-four hours since their lunch date, and despite Jodi's advice to take it slowly, Becky wanted to see Charles again.

"Checking your phone won't make him call any sooner," Jodi said as she dropped off some documents to be faxed.

"I know, but I'm worried that I might miss a message," Becky said.

"Take it easy," Jodi cautioned. "He's not going anywhere. As a matter of fact, you're probably his only acquaintance right now."

Becky smiled. "I'll introduce you to him, and then you can see how wonderful he is."

"Okay, but in the meantime, can you send these off to payroll for me?" Jodi asked. "I keep forgetting their fax number."

"You should store it in your smartphone. You keep everything *else* in there," Becky said in a half-joking manner.

"I already have my entire life programmed in there. Heaven forbid I should ever lose that thing. I'd be completely lost without it." Jodi took it out and checked it. "I've got to run to a meeting. I'll chat with you later about Mr. Right." She turned and headed off to a conference room.

Jodi had barely turned the corner when Becky's cell phone started chirping. Checking the caller ID, Becky saw the name "Charles" appear on the screen. Quickly composing herself, she answered the phone. "Hello."

"Hi, Becky. This is Charles. I hope I didn't get you at a bad time."

"No, it's fine. I just finished up something, so I can talk for a minute."

"Hey, I'm wondering if you'd be free for dinner tonight. I'm usually pretty strict about having my first date be dinner and a movie."

"Well, what about yesterday? Was that a date?" Becky playfully asked.

"I really enjoyed having lunch with you, but I feel like I need to spend more than fifteen dollars for it to be considered an official date. I'd like to take you out for a nice dinner. I heard about a good restaurant in Santa Fe that I'd like to try."

"I'd love to go," Becky replied, trying to curb her enthusiasm.

"What if I picked you up about six o'clock? That way we can have dinner before hitting a movie," Charles said.

"Sounds great," Becky responded, quickly telling Charles where he could pick her up. Usually, she didn't give out her home address so soon, but Charles was different. She could tell that he was a good guy.

October 1, Mountain Safe House, New Mexico

Tanner felt someone shaking his arm, rousing him out of a deep sleep.

"It's almost dinnertime. I figured you'd want something to eat before getting back to work," Magic said.

"Thanks," Tanner replied, sitting up and rubbing the sleep from his eyes. Even though he'd had only a little time to rest, Tanner was confident he'd be able to work late into the night. Looking over at the kitchen, he spied Michael making some kind of meatloaf surprise. Aware of Michael's previous cooking experiments, Tanner decided he would skip dinner tonight.

"We just heard back from Charles. He has another date," Patrick said from the command center in the corner of the room.

Tanner sat back down at the computer, Magic watching over his shoulder. Tanner had determined that Magic was just a script kiddie. He knew enough about computers to be dangerous, but that was it. With Magic's rudimentary computer knowledge, Tanner thought about trying to code a secret message in his rootkit program, but he wasn't sure what that would accomplish. First of all, Tanner didn't know whom he should contact. Second, the police wouldn't believe an anonymous email message from a rootkit, and without being able to respond and maintain an effective conversation, his plea for help would be disregarded.

"Tanner, are you going to have that done by Friday?" Larry asked, bringing Tanner back to the present.

"I hope so. I'm going to see if I can find any canned scripts posted on a black hat website. That way I won't have to code everything from scratch."

Patrick walked over, joining the conversation. "You keep saying 'black hat.' What does that mean?"

"It refers to a hacker's motive. If someone is hacking in a malicious way to destroy data or make a profit, they are called 'black hat' hackers. If someone is hacking for an ethical purpose or to find security vulnerability, they are referred to as 'white hat' hackers. I was definitely a black hat in my day."

"So why did you quit?" Patrick asked.

At the risk of sounding theatrical, Tanner took the opportunity to explain his conversion to the Mormon Church. "Back in the day, I was an elite hacker. I thought I was living the high life, but I always felt hollow inside. Then one day my grandmother got cleaned out by some identity thieves. She lost everything. I realized I wasn't any better than those guys who stole all her money. I felt so guilty for what I had done that I quit hacking and reformed my ways. I even found God and joined a church along the way," Tanner explained.

"Yeah, but now you're hacking again, going against everything you changed for," Larry pointed out.

"I know, and it's killing me inside," Tanner acknowledged. "But I guess that's how life is, right? Everything's not black or white. We gotta make the best decision we can and hope that God forgives us if we're wrong."

"That's why I never believed in God," Patrick said. "Religion keeps people so soft they don't act in their own best interest."

"I used to think that way," Tanner countered, feeling more confident now. "But don't you wonder if there's something more to life than just kidnapping innocent people?"

Patrick went livid. "You keep talking like that and you'll get a bullet in your Christian head!" he shouted.

"Easy, Patrick," Larry said. "Tanner's religious beliefs are irrelevant. And if he doesn't get those classified plans, I'll let you take the first shot at him."

Charles pulled up to Becky's apartment just before 6:00 p.m. Parking Tanner's 4Runner in a handicapped space, he went inside the complex and climbed the stairs to apartment number 238. Knocking on the green door, Charles hid his shock when Becky answered. Dressed in a low-cut blouse, jeans, and nightclub-style heels, she definitely wasn't mimicking her business attire from the day before. For a moment Charles felt overdressed in his tan Dockers and light green polo shirt.

"It's good to see you again," Becky said, leaning forward and giving Charles a quick kiss on the check.

"You look great," Charles responded in a gentlemanly fashion. "Are you ready for dinner?"

"Yes," Becky responded enthusiastically.

"Then we're off," Charles said. He escorted Becky down the stairs to the waiting 4Runner. He opened the door and gently helped her into the passenger seat.

As they drove to dinner, Charles wondered how fast Becky was willing to take their relationship. Her behavior presented a bit of a dilemma. Charles needed to have an emotional relationship with Becky, not just a physical one. He needed Becky to trust him enough that she wouldn't hesitate to run the rootkit on her computer at work.

Charles had made reservations at a new Southwestern-themed restaurant. Pulling into the parking lot, he was glad he did. The place was packed.

"I hope we can get in. It looks crowded," Becky said, studying the mass of people at the entrance.

"It's a good thing I made reservations," Charles replied, confident they wouldn't have to wait in a line. Showing again that he was a gentleman, Charles helped Becky out of the SUV and escorted her through the crowd to the hostess. "I have a reservation for Charles Smith," he told the hostess, who showed them to a booth in the corner of the restaurant. After they ordered, Charles asked Becky about her day.

"It was good. Sorry if I sounded a little flustered when you called me. I had just gotten done talking with my boss," Becky said as their drinks arrived.

"Was he grilling you?"

"Actually, he's a she, and she's a little overprotective at times," Becky said. She took a sip of her drink.

"Why's that?" Charles probed.

"Well, it's not a big deal, but I've worked with her for years, and she feels like she has to screen all my dates. I really like her and she's a great boss, but sometimes it feels like she's my older sister."

"Does she think we're moving too fast?" Charles innocently asked, already guessing the answer. The way Charles listened and how he seemed so interested in her trivial work situation impressed Becky.

"Yeah, she said that in a way."

"Well, I don't bite. I promise you that. I've already been married once, so I'm not looking to rush into anything," Charles said with a calm demeanor. He was playing the situation perfectly.

"That's what I told her, but she doesn't seem to believe me. I told her she would have to meet you and see for herself that I'm right," Becky said.

"That's a great idea. I'd be happy to ask your boss for permission to date you," Charles said in a sarcastic tone, causing both of them to laugh. Charles and Becky enjoyed a fabulous dinner at the restaurant. They talked like old friends, telling each other of their dreams, goals, and even some of their fears. Charles spoke of his failed marriage and how he had learned a lot about himself during the bitter divorce. When he mentioned his kids who were now living with their mother, he faked some emotion and let a few tears well up in his eyes. Charles was a master con artist, and he pushed all the buttons necessary to manipulate Becky. If Larry and the others had been around, even they would have been awed with Charles's fake sincerity.

When the check came, Charles paid the ninety-dollar tab in cash, again impressing Becky. She had already calculated the dinner expense in her mind, and she was waiting to see if Charles would flinch at paying such a large bill.

"Shall we go?" Charles asked, getting up from the table.

Becky giggled. "Yes, let's do something fun."

"So tell me more about what you do at the Lab," Charles probed as he escorted Becky out of the restaurant toward the car.

"Oh, it's not very exciting," Becky began. "I'm basically an administrative assistant for the AQC group."

"What's the AQC group?"

"It's the Applied Quantum Computing group. The scientists in the department develop new computers that run super fast, but a lot of that techie stuff is way over my head. I basically just manage the office and take care of personnel matters like travel and payroll. It's not all that exciting, but it pays the rent," Becky continued as she climbed into the SUV.

"I think that would be an awesome group to work with. If I hadn't specialized in chemical engineering, I might have gone into computers. I bet you guys do some cutting-edge stuff," Charles said.

"I probably shouldn't be telling you this," Becky began. She gave him a look that suggested she was trying to impress Charles. "But the group made a huge breakthrough over the summer. I'm not sure exactly what it was, but all the scientists stayed up late one night celebrating and talking about reinventing the computer."

"Wow! There must be some really cool technology being developed there. I wish I could see it," Charles said with a slight disappointment in his voice.

"Well, after you get your Q Clearance, I might be able to pull a few strings and get you a tour. Especially if I continue giving my boss glowing reports of our dates." Becky laughed.

"That might be hard to do. It sounds like she doesn't like me," Charles said. He causally drove the 4Runner toward the movie theater.

"Oh, don't worry about her. Jodi is skeptical about anything new. It's the scientist in her."

"I bet it's hard working for a boss who's a rocket scientist," Charles probed, hoping to get more information on the project leader. "I know I'd have a hard time working for someone who was so smart."

"She is supersmart, but she's very scatterbrained. She has to program all the details of her life into her phone so she won't forget anything. She even has her passwords stored in there. I keep telling her to delete them. If the security department found out, they'd freak."

"Or worse, she'd lose her phone and forget who she was," Charles joked, causing Becky to break into hysterical laughter. It was a good thing she had her seat belt on or she might have laughed herself right out of her seat. Charles wondered if Becky realized the consequence of her loose talk. He might not even need Tanner's rootkit thingy. Jodi McDonald's phone might have all the information they needed.

The romantic comedy wasn't Charles's first choice, but the movie wasn't for him. From what he could tell, Becky really enjoyed it. He even managed to put his arm around her during the film. She warmly received his gesture, snuggling up next to him for the last hour. For a brief moment Charles had a slight attack of conscience, realizing that Becky was completely oblivious to his true motive. *Too bad we didn't meet under different circumstances*, Charles thought as the movie ended. Becky was a nice girl, and Charles might have seriously considered dating her if she wasn't the primary target for helping Tanner hack into the lab.

"Did you like the movie?" Charles asked as they walked out of the theater into the dark night.

"Yes, I loved it, and the dinner was fabulous. I haven't had this much fun in a long time," Becky said. "Of course, I haven't met anyone as fun as you either."

Charles wasn't completely clueless. He saw how much Becky was coming on to him. All night long her nonverbal communication screamed interest, but Charles had other plans. He wasn't interested in romance right then—he wanted a quantum diamond. Charles laughed to himself as he thought about the irony of his situation. Usually it was the girl who wanted the diamond.

October 2, Mountain Safe House, New Mexico

The secret cabin, high in the Jemez Mountains, was abuzz with excitement the following morning. Charles's report from the night before was nothing short of spectacular. Successful hacking usually required a lucky break, and now the team had one. The revelation that the project leader—the main scientist nonetheless—had the access codes to the classified quantum computer project stored on her cell phone was unbelievable. Tanner marveled at how dumb some people were, even those with PhDs.

"How does this information from Charles change our plan of attack?" Larry asked Tanner. The team had just finished breakfast and was preparing for another day of work.

"It's definitely a game changer. It's going to make things much easier, but we still need to run the rootkit to map out the computer network and determine which server has the classified documents about the quantum diamond. The rest could be really easy after we lift her account and passwords from her smartphone."

"Can't we just steal the phone and crack it?" Michael asked.

"That's not likely to work. Once she realizes she's lost her cell phone, she'll change all her account information. We need to get the information off her phone in such a way that she doesn't know we stole it," Tanner said.

"How do we do that?" Magic said. It was the million-dollar question.

"I'll have to do some research on that. I've heard that cell phones can be hacked, but I've never done it. For now, we'll still proceed as planned," Tanner decided.

———•———•———

Ken Calloway finished his fourth cup of coffee. He knew that much caffeine wasn't helping calm his nerves, but he hadn't slept a wink last night. Today was going to be an awful day. Yesterday his wife's Cadillac Escalade had been repossessed just outside their home. It took less than one minute for the repo man to hook up the SUV and haul it away. Fortunately, his kids weren't home at the time to hear the hour-long fight that had erupted between him and his wife.

Ken figured the Cadillac would be repossessed any day now. He hadn't made a payment on it in four months. His wife was completely unaware of the family's financial troubles, and the horror of seeing her SUV towed away was both frustrating and humiliating. Despite his reassurance that it was all a mistake, Mrs. Calloway stormed off to her bedroom, locking the door behind her. Ken took refuge on the sofa, downplaying the situation to his daughters when they came home for the night. Amid his financial meltdown, Ken had decided he would steal anything Patrick wanted. Running his hand through his thinning brown hair, Ken wished Patrick would contact him. He needed that money, and needed it soon.

"Ken, are you okay? You look worn out," Bill Lopez, a coworker, said, looking over his computer monitor at him the next morning.

"I'm all right. I just had a hard night last night. My back has been bothering me, and I didn't sleep very well," Ken lied.

Bill and Ken both worked in the construction management department at the Lab. Neither one of them was a scientist; they were civil engineers who designed the construction projects around the Lab.

"We have that meeting in fifteen minutes on the new plutonium facility in TA-55. Do you want to go, or should I?" Bill asked.

"Why don't you go? I've got some stuff I need to finish up here."

"Okay, but you'll have to go next time," Bill said. He grabbed his stuff and headed out the door. The technical areas at the Lab were spread out over a huge campus, and the engineers had to plan ahead when traveling to meetings. Sometimes it took a fifteen-minute commute to get to the outlying buildings.

Now that Ken was alone, he decided he would risk making a phone call to Patrick. Grabbing his jacket, he headed out to his car. Once inside, he retrieved the mysterious phone number from his cell phone history and hit send.

———•———

Patrick's satphone started chirping, announcing the incoming call to everyone in the cabin. Looking at the phone's display, Patrick was surprised to see the number. He immediately recognized the caller. "It's Ken," he announced to the team. "I told him that I would get back to him by Friday."

"Hello?" Patrick said into the phone.

"Is Patrick there? I need to talk to Patrick," said the frantic voice on the other end.

"This is Patrick. I thought we agreed not to talk until Friday."

"I know, I know, but I'm really in a jam, and I need your help," Ken said. He went on to explain how his wife's SUV was repossessed the night before and about the ugly fight that came afterward. "I need the money. I need it now. When can we move forward?" he asked anxiously.

"Patience, Ken, you'll get your money. I'm almost ready. I want you to go back to the museum on Friday during lunch and do what I told you. Do you remember your instructions?"

"Yes, I remember."

"Good. All the information will be included in the package. I'll have people watching to make sure you do it right. The program on the CD will send out an email, letting me know that you executed it correctly. If you try to disable the program, there will be an anti-tampering mechanism which will destroy the CD and your chances of getting your money," Patrick said bluntly.

"Okay, okay. I won't do anything stupid," Ken responded.

"Good. I know you'll follow my instructions," Patrick said and hung up the phone.

"Do you think it's a trap?" Larry asked.

"I doubt it. He sounded like he was in a tight jam. We know from the credit information we found in his trash that he had several notices for late payments on the SUV," Patrick said.

Larry walked over to Tanner at the computer. "Tanner, we'll need to have that rootkit done by Friday morning."

Slowly nodding, Tanner didn't respond. Instead he just kept plugging away at the keyboard.

———•———•———

That afternoon, Charles sent Becky another text message. Usually Charles was more laissez-faire in his dating methods, but with the crunch to get the rootkit running, he didn't have the luxury of time. His goal wasn't just another date with Becky, but a date with Becky and her boss—because her boss's cell phone was the target now.

I had a great time last night. When can we get together again? Charles said in his text message.

———•———•———

Up at Los Alamos, Becky's cell phone chirped, signaling an incoming text message. Coincidently, she had been talking with Jodi about the upcoming seminar on quantum computing when her phone interrupted the conversation.

"Don't tell me. It's Mr. Right," Jodi said with obvious sarcasm.

"Yes, it is," Becky responded with a smile. She had been waiting all day for a message from Charles. Grabbing her cell phone, she quickly responded to the text while Jodi shook her head in disbelief.

I'm busy tonight, but I'm free tomorrow, Becky wrote back.

Dang, I've got an appointment tomorrow with the realtor. Can we get together on Friday night? Charles asked.

Love to. Give me a call tomorrow, Becky wrote, much to Jodi's disappointment.

"Becky, you've got to slow down with this guy. It's hardly been a week and you're going on, what, your third date?"

"Fourth, if you count our all-night chat session, but who's keeping track?" Becky answered with a giggle.

"So when do I get to meet this guy?" Jodi asked.

"Let me see how it goes this weekend. Maybe he can meet us for lunch next week, and I can show you how wonderful *Charles* really is," Becky said, putting emphasis on his name as if he was from royal lineage.

———•———•———

Tanner rubbed his eyes and stood up for a stretch. He had been at the computer for almost eighteen hours, and every part of his body was sore. The clock on the wall showed 2:38 a.m. He desperately wanted to get some sleep, but he had to keep pushing forward. Larry demanded the rootkit to be done on Friday morning so Patrick could take it up to Los Alamos. That left Tanner less than thirty hours to finish, assuming he didn't sleep until it was done. However, he wasn't as young as he used to be, and pulling all-nighters wasn't as easy as it had been ten years ago. Hobbling over to the kitchen, he opened the fridge, looking for a cold Mountain Dew.

"Getting another drink?" Larry asked. Larry and Magic were guarding Tanner while the other men slept.

"Yeah, I can't stay awake," Tanner responded.

"How's it coming?" Larry inquired.

"Right now I'm testing the routine and fixing bugs in the execution script. After that, I only have the anti-tampering and completion routines to add before I'm done."

"How are those going to work?" Magic asked.

Taking a long drink of his soda, Tanner leaned on the granite counter before responding. "The tampering script is a routine that will check to make sure none of the software code has been altered. Using a checksum algorithm, it will detect any changes in the date, size, or attributes of the rootkit and overwrite the data before anyone can dissect it." Grabbing a handful of Doritos from an open bag, Tanner continued. "The success script is not as complicated. Once the program completes, it will shoot out a quick email to Ken with a fake bank account. He'll never get any money," Tanner said.

"It sounds like you're almost done," Larry noted.

"Yeah. I wish I had more time to test it all out," Tanner said. "If I wasn't under such a tight deadline, I'd try to create some designer malware. That's the future of hacking."

"What's designer malware?" Magic asked.

"Most computer malware, like viruses or worms, indiscriminately target the entire spectrum of computers. They infect any host and try to spread as far as possible," Tanner began. "Mass destruction is their goal. But in the future, hackers will focus more on designer malware. Those hacking routines won't spread out and mass-infect systems on the net. Instead, those hacking programs will attack specific computers that are tied to unique functions like ATM machines or nuclear

reactors. Designer malware will be super focused and super dangerous," he said as he hobbled back to his computer, gearing up for more
hours of coding.

Tanner struggled through the rest of the night, working on the
rootkit. In a strange way, he was excited to see the fruit of his labors.
Despite having sworn off hacking years ago, part of Tanner still loved
the thrill that came with exploiting IT security—it ignited the rebel-
lious side of his ego. Tanner had never before made a rootkit of this
magnitude, and the uncertainty of how it would all work was exhilarat-
ing to him.

At about 7:00 a.m., Patrick and Michael came down to relieve Larry
and Magic of their guard duties. Tanner also took the opportunity for a
quick nap. Two hours later, he was up and at the computer workstation.
With his MP3 player so loud that Patrick and Michael could probably hear the music through the headphones across the room, Tanner
downed two more Mountain Dews while his fingers flew across the
keyboard.

"The guy is an animal," Michael said, watching Tanner work. He was
preparing lunch in the kitchen.

"Too bad he's not going to live to see the brilliance of his work,"
Patrick said. It had been known from the beginning of the project that
Tanner and his parents would be killed. Larry and Patrick had already
planned the unfortunate car accident that would claim the life of Tanner
Zane and his parents.

"I wonder if he knows that he has less than two weeks to live," Michael
said to no one in particular.

———•———

Tanner worked feverishly all afternoon. When it was time for dinner,
he opted instead to stay at the keyboard and continue programming.
Staying up all night always caused Tanner to lose his appetite because his
stomach seemed confused as to whether it should be digesting or resting.
Finally, about 9:00 p.m., he stood up and yelled out "Done!" so loud that
everyone in the cabin heard him.

"You're finished?" Larry asked as he walked over to the computer
workstation from the kitchen. "I thought you had another day to go."

"I still need to run my final testing, but I'm done with all the coding,"
Tanner said with an exhausted smile.

"It better be ready for me to deliver tomorrow," Patrick said gruffly, trying to defuse Tanner's celebration.

"What about the one for Becky? When will that one be done?" Larry asked.

"As soon as I'm finished cleaning up this rootkit, I'll start on the second. It shouldn't take quite as long because I'll be able to cannibalize a lot of the programming routines from the first rootkit," Tanner said.

"How is Charles going to convince Becky to run the CD?" Magic asked.

"I put the rootkit in a hidden folder on the CD. The rest of the CD is full of those pictures of kids that I had you download yesterday. Charles is going to give the CD to Becky and tell her it's a slide show of his kids. When she runs the CD, it will also execute the rootkit in the background."

"What pictures?" Larry asked.

"Oh, they're just some random pictures that I found on Facebook. Someone uploaded her family album, and I copied the photos," Tanner said. "Now, since I've been working all day, I'd like to unwind by playing some music. Magic, if you'll log me into the website, I'll see if I can find the sheet music for Rush."

Magic started up the web application while Tanner took out his bass guitar. Searching the online music database, Tanner found the score for "Tom Sawyer" and started playing the rhythmic bass notes. Larry listened for a couple of minutes before grabbing his secure satphone and heading out on the porch into the cool night air. Hitting the speed dial for a number with a California area code, Larry was excited to deliver the good news.

"Hello," Reagan said, answering the phone on the second ring.

"The rootkit is finished. All that's left is the final testing, but it will be ready to go tomorrow as promised," Larry said.

"Excellent. That's good news. How long before you get some data back from the lab?"

"Tanner figures it will take a couple of hours to scan and collect all the information about the computer network. We hope to establish a back door by the beginning of next week. Then we can launch deliberate attacks against the computer system that stores the data about the quantum computer."

"That sounds reasonable," Reagan said.

"There's something else," Larry said. "It's highly likely that the team leader over the quantum computing project has her passwords stored on her smartphone. Tanner is looking into the possibility of lifting that information without her knowledge."

"Why not steal her phone?" Reagan asked, just as Larry suspected he would. Reagan was ignorant about technical stuff. He might even have his own passwords stored on his smartphone.

"If we steal her phone, she'll immediately change her passwords because she'll know the information has been compromised. So we need to steal the passwords in such a way that she doesn't know they're gone," Larry explained.

"I want that quantum diamond information by the end of the month. That gives you just under two weeks to get it," Reagan demanded.

"I don't think that will be a problem. I feel better about our goal now that the rootkit is done," Larry stated.

"Once we have our information, what's your plan for dealing with Tanner and his parents?" Reagan asked, changing the subject.

"We're thinking of staging a deadly car crash. Make it look like a tragic accident on a remote New Mexican highway. The car and bodies will be burned beyond recognition by the time the cops find them," Larry said.

"You know the importance of tying up loose ends. Call me back Monday with a report. Good luck," Reagan said.

* ———— *

Inside his car, Reagan checked his watch. It was just after 8:00 p.m. local time, which meant it was 10:00 a.m. the following morning in China. Taking another secure satphone out of his locked glove compartment, Reagan dialed the number from memory.

"Hello," a man answered in broken English.

"Hello, General. I have an update. My team leader reports good progress. He plans on executing the network scan at the Lab sometime tomorrow. This is an important first step in locating the classified plans for the quantum computer."

"When do you expect to have the information?" Major General Yang Dao asked.

"I expect to have the information in hand within the next week or two. Upon successful completion of the project, all nonessential personnel will be terminated. I assure you that every possible lead will be cut off," Reagan stated confidently.

"Thank you for your update. I expect to hear further good news next week," the major general said before hanging up his phone.

Tanner wanted to sleep in the following morning, but he forced himself to get up and head for the shower instead, hoping the warm water would help him wake up. In the bathroom, Tanner paused to look at himself in the mirror. His goatee had fully grown in, and he was surprised at how different he looked. Interestingly, his facial hair came in lighter than his normal brown hair, which had grown too long without a haircut over the past month.

After getting dressed, Tanner hobbled out to the kitchen for some breakfast. Patrick and Magic were awake, replacing Larry and Michael for the daytime shift. Tanner grabbed a soda and a bowl of cereal before heading toward the computer workstation.

"How long do you think you'll need to finish up the rootkit?" Patrick asked as he made a fresh batch of pancakes for the morning crew.

"It's just after seven, and I suspect it will take two to three hours to finish. It should be ready for your trip up to Los Alamos at noon."

"That's cutting it close, but I'll let Ken know that we're scheduled to meet during his lunch break," Patrick said.

Tanner picked up his MP3 player and selected one of his favorite groups to listen to. With the upbeat music blaring through his earphones, Tanner was ready to go. For the first hour, Tanner's code repeatedly failed with various programming errors like missing semicolons and incomplete select statements. Once Tanner fixed all the coding errors, the rootkit effectively completed but delivered unpredictable results. Tanner reviewed his work and fixed the logic errors that were producing the inconsistencies. Finally, with twenty minutes to go before his noontime deadline, the rootkit completed successfully.

"Hey, I just got an email," Magic said, sitting over at the monitoring console. The rootkit forwarded an anonymous email to another generic email account, which then routed it back to the security console at the cabin.

"What does it say?" Tanner asked.

"It says 'Success.' That's it," Magic responded.

"There should be an attachment. Did you get it?"

"Oh yep, there it is," Magic replied. Opening up the attachment, Magic saw a list that contained information about the local computer network in the cabin, including server names, IP addresses, and firewalls. It even had detailed information on the two network printers they used in the cabin. "Tanner, you're amazing," Magic said.

"Yes—yes, I am," Tanner said, smiling broadly.

• —————— •

About eighty miles away in Santa Fe, Charles was also starting his day. Tonight would be a big step in his ongoing relationship with Becky. Somehow he needed to arrange a meeting with Becky's supervisor without creating any suspicion or jealousy. Charles had to move forward despite his uncertainty because Larry had called last night, emphasizing the importance of getting access to Dr. McDonald's smartphone. At least Charles didn't have the near-impossible task of trying to hack a cell phone. That was Tanner's issue to deal with.

• —————— •

Ken Calloway thought this day would never come. His wife had kicked him out of the house last night, still furious that her car was repossessed. Taking refuge in one of the few hotels in Los Alamos, Ken considered his bleak situation. His daughters had stopped by to visit at the hotel, but despite his best efforts to calm their fears, they'd left with tears in their eyes. Seeing his daughters distressed hurt Ken more than anything his wife had said. He was determined to fix the situation and regain his kids' respect.

Unfortunately, like so many of his fellow Americans in debt, Ken thought the path to financial freedom was increasing his income, not controlling his spending. The fastest way for Ken to make more money was working for Patrick on the side even if it involved doing something illegal. Letting his emotions control his destiny, Ken responded to Patrick's text message saying that he was ready to pick up the package during his lunch break.

Back at the cabin in the Jemez Mountains, Tanner's celebration was short lived. With the first rootkit done, he now had to focus on hacking Jodi McDonald's smartphone, something he'd never attempted and didn't have a clue how to start.

Tanner looked across the room. Patrick was getting ready for his trip to Los Alamos. With latex gloves on his hands, he sealed the package containing the rootkit and instructions in a tan mailing envelop. "Okay, let's go," he called out to Larry, who had just gotten up after only a couple hours of sleep.

"We'll call you once we confirm Ken has taken the package," Larry said. Both men walked out the door with their SIG Sauer P220 handguns tucked behind their backs.

Turning toward Magic and Michael, Tanner spoke. "I need both of you to help me. Get on the web and google anything you can about hacking smartphones. I'm sure somebody has successfully done it already, and that will be a good starting point for me. I need to understand the basic process of how to do it."

Larry had planned to get to the Bradbury Science Museum early. He wanted to recon the area and make sure they weren't walking into a trap. Fortunately, Ken had never met Larry, so as an added security measure, Larry would be the one to place the package.

Driving around the block several times, both Larry and Patrick relaxed as they parked the black Suburban in the museum parking lot.

"Tape the package under the second sink in the bathroom," Patrick said as Larry got out of the SUV.

Larry walked up to the museum entrance and made a casual sweep of the area, looking for anything out of the ordinary. Everything appeared to be normal, so he went into the main lobby to check out the exhibits. Larry didn't want to rush directly to the bathroom. It would be too obvious. Instead, he headed over to the exhibits that showed the history of the Lab and the Pajarito Plateau. After spending fifteen minutes looking around, Larry casually headed toward the men's restroom and into the first stall. Closing the door, he took out a roll of tape and the small envelope that he'd tucked under his shirt. He put a couple of strips of tape on the outside of the package and got ready to make his move. Listening to make sure nobody else had entered the restroom, Larry quickly walked out of the stall and taped the package on the underside of the second sink in one quick motion. He finished the illusion by washing his hands before exiting the restroom and moving toward the parking lot.

"Easy as that," Larry said, getting into the front passenger's seat of the SUV. Patrick pulled the Suburban away from the building and parked down the street.

·————·

Ken arrived just after noon. Getting out of his car, he went into the building and headed straight for the restroom. He figured there was no point in being nonchalant about his reason for being there. With no one in the restroom, he bent down and looked under the counter by the second sink. There it was—a tan mailing package taped to the underside of the porcelain sink bowl. Ken pulled the package off the sink, took out the unmarked CD and instructions, and threw the envelope in the trash. In less than two minutes he was walking back out to his car in the parking lot.

·————·

"He doesn't waste any time, does he?" Larry observed, looking through binoculars from the SUV.

"That's the funny thing about traitors. Once someone decides to commit espionage, it's forward full throttle. I guess people figure there's no point in trying to hide it," Patrick responded.

"Let's wait another ten minutes, and then I'll go back in and check to make sure he took the CD," Larry said. They watched the BMW pull out of the parking lot and drive away on Trinity Boulevard.

At the same time that Ken was taking his first steps toward espionage, Charles decided it was a good time to call Becky.

"Hello, Charles," Becky answered with a pleasant voice.

"Hi. Did I get you at a bad time?"

"No, I'm on my lunch break. I was hoping you'd call me."

"Are we still on for tonight?" Charles asked.

"Most definitely, but how about I choose the activity?" Becky asked. Charles was momentarily taken back. His mind quickly sorted through all the different possibilities of what she could be planning.

"That's a little bit out of my comfort zone, but why not?" Charles said.

"Great. How about you come over to my place at six?"

"I'll be there," Charles confirmed.

Ken needed to get lunch before heading back to work. Taking a quick detour at the drive-thru of a local fast food restaurant, he ate in the car as he approached the security checkpoint. Even though there was no possible way that anyone knew what he was about to do, Ken still felt anxious as he pulled up to the armed uniformed sentry. Showing his Lab ID to the guard, Ken tried to act at ease.

"Anything wrong, sir?" the security officer asked.

Ken felt small beads of sweat forming on his forehead.

"No, I'm okay. I just had to run to get lunch and hurry back for a meeting. I guess I need to get in better shape," Ken lied.

"Have a good afternoon," the guard said, handing the ID badge back to Ken.

A few minutes later, Ken arrived at his building. Parking his car, he took out the instructions from the pocket of his jacket. Reading over the information once more, he made a mental note of the steps: 1) insert CD into a computer, 2) click on the run button that pops up, 3) when the CD ejects, remove it and cook it in a microwave for two seconds to destroy the data.

The instructions seemed straightforward to Ken. Deciding that he didn't need to keep any incriminating evidence around, he crumpled up the note and stuffed it in the bottom of the paper sack with the trash from his lunch. Ken threw everything away in a black trash can just outside the entrance to his building. Going straight to his desk, Ken loaded the CD into his own computer and executed the rootkit.

As soon as Ken clicked on the "run" button that popped up on the monitor, the rootkit came to life. The initial step copied the hacking routines from the CD to a hidden location on the internal hard drive. This action took less than a minute, after which the CD was ejected, but the real work was just beginning. First, the rootkit initiated a full network scan. Using the NMAP protocol, the program queried all the available IP addresses and ports on the network, listening for any response from an unsuspecting computer. With this information, the rootkit started building a map of the network topology and underlying operating systems. This was the most time-consuming step; it had the potential to run for hours on a vast network. But Tanner's routine didn't wait for the network scan to finish before executing additional steps. Once a server was identified, the rootkit targeted that specific computer and began probing for security vulnerabilities to exploit.

The rootkit stealthily went about its task the entire afternoon and into the early evening. Just after 5:00 p.m., the shift changed at the network operations center, or NOC. Located on the other side of the LANL complex, the NOC was responsible for monitoring and securing the vast computer network at the Lab. One specialized tool the NOC had in its arsenal was a computer system called an intrusion detection system, or IDS, which analyzed the network traffic at the lab. When Ken started the rootkit, the IDS hardly noticed the increase in connection request attempts across the network. However, as the rootkit continued to expand out and execute over the IT infrastructure, more and more connection requests occurred. After several hours, the rootkit hit critical mass and triggered an alert on the IDS. The alert caught the attention of the operations agent, who had just started his evening shift.

"Jim, do you know if the network group has any penetration testing scheduled for this evening?" the first level agent asked his superior.

"Nothing is on the work list. What have you got?" Jim Fredrickson, the supervisor, asked as he walked over to the agent's computer monitor.

"The IDS is detecting a lot of network activity in Building 64. That's in the Construction Management Office. At first I thought it might just be the nightly backups kicking off, but the activity log shows a ton of connection requests. It's hard to tell for sure, but it kind of looks like a port scan."

"Isolate the source IP address and cross-reference it to the computer owner, but don't shut down the network port yet," Jim Fredrickson said. "I want to see where this is going."

• — •

Back at the safe house, Tanner and Magic huddled around the computer workstation with an anticipation that made it seem like Christmas Eve. Messages from an anonymous email server in Europe had started trickling in about ten minutes ago. Tanner designed the rootkit to route the information it generated through several anonymous hosts before forwarding it to a generic email account used by the Starting Five. It was a simple but effective process to obscure the email's final destination.

"Is there anything interesting yet?" Larry asked, taking a bite of his turkey-and-cheese sandwich. He and Patrick had gotten back from Los Alamos several hours ago.

"It's just starting to come in. I knew it would take a while to collect any data from the initial port scan," Tanner explained.

"Whoa, look at this!" Magic shouted. He opened an email attachment containing the IP addresses that the rootkit had already discovered on the network. "There are hundreds of IP addresses here, and each one corresponds to an individual computer!"

"See this," Tanner said, pointing to the list on the computer monitor. "It looks like the IP addresses are broken down by subnet and hostname. I bet the network team designed it that way to quickly identify all computers at the Lab. That's good news for us because we can easily determine which computers belong to Dr. McDonald and her team," Tanner said.

"How long will this keep running?" Michael asked.

"It depends on how big the network is. It could go for a while," Tanner said. They settled in to wait.

• — •

The situation wasn't improving, and Jim Fredrickson decided he had seen enough. The connection requests on the network were increasing, and additional alerts were coming from the IDS.

"Did you isolate the network traffic to a specific computer?" the supervisor asked the operations agent.

122

"Yes. It belongs to Ken Calloway in the CM Division. I tried calling his desk, but seeing that it's almost six, I'm guessing he's gone for the day."

"Okay, shut down the ethernet port for that computer and get it off the network. I'm going to escalate this to the incident manager," Jim replied.

———•———

"What happened?" Magic asked. The incoming emails seemed to have stopped.

"I don't know," Tanner countered. "Click on the attachment in the last email we got. I programmed the rootkit to send out an error log if it didn't complete normally," he explained. Reading through the log file, Tanner slammed his hand against the desk in frustration. "It looks like the computer system that was running the rootkit got disconnected from the network."

"What does that mean?" Patrick asked.

"It most likely means that we got caught. The IT security group probably got a whiff of our rootkit and pulled the plug on the computer before it could complete," Tanner said.

"How could they do that?" Magic asked.

Tanner took a second to calm down before explaining. "Most serious IT organizations have specialized equipment that monitors the computer network for anomalies. If the equipment detects anything out of the ordinary, it triggers an alert or automatically disconnects the offending computer system from the network. I took this into account when I created the rootkit, but I've been out of the hacking game for almost a decade. There's probably newer technology now that can detect even subtle hacking attempts."

"So it was a failure?" asked Larry.

"It's too soon to tell. Let me look through the data we collected and see what information we have to work with."

October 3, Santa Fe, New Mexico

Friday night's date with Becky felt like it had a lot more riding on it than the previous ones. Charles's usual easy-going and carefree attitude was replaced with anxiety. He wasn't sure what to expect tonight as he pulled into the apartment complex where Becky lived. Composing himself, Charles knocked on Becky's door.

Becky answered the door in a tight-fitting pink sweater and jeans. Her brown hair was pulled back, not in a ponytail, but in an updo style that attractively highlighted her oval face. Charles heard some smooth jazz playing in the background, and looking over at the candles glowing on the table, he saw this was going to be an intimate evening.

"You look great," Charles said to Becky. She reached around Charles's waist and pulled him in for a kiss.

"I'm so glad that you came," Becky said. Looking into her twitter-pated eyes, Charles could tell she was in love. For a moment he wished this relationship was the real thing, but he quickly discounted his personal feelings, knowing that this romance wasn't meant to last.

"What are you cooking?" Charles asked.

"Chicken parmesan. It's a recipe that my grandmother gave me. She was a second-generation Italian and could make the most wonderful food," Becky said as she finished putting the food on the table. "Now, if you'll pour the drinks, I think we can begin."

———•———

Back at the cabin hideout, Tanner's thoughts had turned somewhat optimistic. The rootkit had collected a large amount of useful data even though it didn't complete.

"Okay, it's not as bad as I first thought," Tanner said, addressing the group. "We got a ton of information and even some details about different system vulnerabilities. More importantly, it looks like we've identified which computer systems belong to the Applied Quantum Computing group. That's the good news, but there's something else I discovered that presents a bigger problem," Tanner added.

"What's that?" asked Larry.

"Even if the program had completed successfully, we wouldn't have gotten to the classified information. From what I can tell, it looks like the rootkit ran on an open network," Tanner said. He proceeded to explain the concept of network isolation. "It's common practice to have two separate and distinct computer networks wherever classified data is maintained. One network is for unclassified information like email and web surfing, while the other one is restricted and isolated internally. To steal the information about the quantum computer, we'll have to be physically connected to the classified network."

"How can we possibly do that?" Patrick asked in a doubtful voice.

"We can't, but Becky can. I'll tweak the second rootkit so it will download the files about the quantum computer to a hidden location on the CD. She'll give the CD back to Charles unaware that it contains the classified information."

"But we don't know Becky's account information or her password. How are we going to be able to access those files?" Larry asked.

"We don't need Becky's credentials. We can download the files using Jodi McDonald's account information once we steal it off her smartphone," Magic said, following Tanner's plan.

"Yep—hacking Jodi's cell phone is now the critical part of the operation," Tanner said.

———•———

The NOC at Los Alamos National Labs was a hive of activity. It had been almost two hours since the supervisor notified the IT security group of the network scan. Now, five experts from different organizations were huddled in a conference room, debating about what to do next.

"It looks like the unauthorized network scan started about 1:20 p.m., but we didn't see it show up on our IDS until after five," the network engineer, Jean Addison, explained. "Most likely the scan didn't trigger the alert threshold until then."

"Why wasn't the threshold set lower so we could get notified sooner?" asked the operations agent.

"It's a balancing act to determine where to set the threshold. If we set it too low, we'll get spammed by false alerts, but if it's set too high, we'll miss the indicators of a legitimate attack," Jean responded.

"I think the real question is why Mr. Calloway ran this network scan in the first place," said Kyle Samson, the incident manager in charge of coordinating the investigation.

"Allegedly ran the network scan. We're not sure it was actually him. Someone might have just used his computer," chimed in Brigit Hepworth from the legal group. Brigit was a dinosaur at the Lab; her tenure exceeding everyone else's in the conference room. She'd drafted the original Lab policy stating that all security incident teams must include a member of the legal department to make sure nobody tainted the investigation.

"We have all the facts right here in the logs. The time the network scan started, how long it ran, and which computer systems it queried. It definitely came from Ken Calloway's computer," countered Jean, perturbed by how lawyers always manage to muddle the facts.

"But what about the emails? We know the program sent off several dozen emails," the operations agent said.

"We're still working on that," jumped in an engineer from the messaging team. "But it doesn't look good. We counted thirty-six emails sent off-site. The destination was an anonymous email relay system that masked the final email address. The relay server is in Europe, and it will take a lot of legal work for us to get a copy of their system logs."

"So what's the damage?" asked Kyle, steering the group back to its focus.

"Moderate but not severe, I'd say," said Jean Addison. "The emails contained the IP addresses and hostnames to a lot of our computer systems, but no one can get to any classified information unless they are physically connected to the internal network. The situation is a black eye for us, but there's little chance that any important data was compromised."

"It looks like the real damage is going to be to Mr. Calloway's career. If he did run the network scan, that's a clear violation of our IT policy and the conditions of his Q," said Brigit Hepworth, referring to the Q security clearance that all Lab employees had from the Department of Energy.

Thinking for a moment, Kyle Samson gave his recommendation. "Let's start a formal investigation on Ken Calloway, but I don't want to approach him just yet. Let's wait and see if he tries to do this again. In the meantime, we need to determine if he's acting alone, or if he's just a pawn for someone else."

●————●

Charles and Becky had finished the delicious Italian dinner and were now sitting on the couch, watching the gas fireplace.

"Charles, I've been flirting with you all night," Becky said, seemingly frustrated. "Don't you like me?"

"I really like you. It's because I like you that I want to take this slowly," Charles lied, using the familiar cliché. "This relationship might have the chance to go somewhere meaningful, and I don't want to screw it up by rushing into anything. I don't want to get burned like I did by my ex-wife," he said in a way that made Becky feel sorry for him. "Besides, I haven't met your boss yet, and I'm still holding out for her permission to date you."

"Well, let's introduce you," Becky said. "What about Monday? We could meet at that same sandwich shop where we had our first date. It would be a fun way to celebrate our one-week anniversary."

"Are you serious?" Charles asked.

"About the lunch or the one-week anniversary?" Becky asked.

Charles laughed. "Both," he said. "Actually, I think that would be a good idea. I'd like to meet your boss. Then I could get all the dirt on you," Charles said jokingly.

"Let's do it," Becky said.

"That sounds good to me. I'll even bring you a little gift," Charles said, leaning in for a passionate kiss. He would give Becky the CD with the hidden rootkit at lunch on Monday.

●————●

The low, rhythmic tones of a bass guitar filled the cabin. Tanner sat on the leather couch, playing his Fender bass and thinking about his next steps. Tweaking Becky's version of the rootkit wouldn't be a big deal, but he was more worried about hacking into her supervisor's smartphone.

"Do you think it's possible to hack her phone?" Magic asked Tanner.

"That's the funny thing with technology. As more and more information is digitized, it becomes easier to steal. Look at what Napster did to the music industry—stealing music became simple. Stealing information off a phone shouldn't be any different."

"I guess the real question then is how long it will take," Larry said, entering the conversation.

"Yes, that's my biggest concern, along with how complicated it will be. It might be something that I can't automate, and I'm not sure if I could train you or anyone else on how to do it," Tanner speculated. He was interrupted by the chirping sound of Larry's secure satphone.

"Hello," Larry answered.

"This is Charles reporting in."

"How did the date go with Becky?"

"It was good, and I have even better news," Charles said. "Becky's boss is coming to lunch with us on Monday at the same sandwich shop where we had our first date. If we want to steal her passwords off her phone, this is going to be our best opportunity."

"Roger that. I'll let Tanner know," Larry said.

"Charles is going to have lunch with Becky and Jodi on Monday. So I'll need you to have the other rootkit ready to go, along with the instructions on how to hack Jodi's phone," Larry told Tanner.

"That's the problem," Tanner said, putting down his bass guitar. "I've never hacked a smartphone before. There are so many factors to consider like phone type, manufacturer, and model . . . They all run different kinds of operating systems, and I can't automate a hack on something that is so vague."

"You've got to figure out a way to do it," Larry said, sounding both encouraging and threatening.

"Let me do some more research and see what I can find. In the IT world, there's always more than one way to skin a cat," Tanner replied.

"Hacking that phone is now your number-one priority. We might only get one shot at this," Larry said.

October 4, Mountain Safe House, New Mexico

Saturday was extremely busy. Tanner woke up at 5:00 a.m. and got an early start. With Larry's deadline looming, everyone was actively involved in helping Tanner. Together they searched all sorts of websites, gleaning information on how to hack a smartphone. By noon Tanner had outlined the basic steps on a white-board and convened a meeting to diagram his game plan.

"As the statement goes, there's good news and bad news," Tanner said, addressing the group. "The good news is that I think I have enough information to launch an organized attack on Dr. McDonald's smart-phone. I just might have your classified information by Monday evening," Tanner said optimistically.

"And what's the bad news?" Larry asked.

"I won't have the smartphone hacking script automated for you to run by Monday, which means that I'll have to make the trip to Los Alamos with you."

"That's out of the question," Larry said curtly.

"Before you slam the door on my idea, let me explain," Tanner countered. "Modern cell phones are designed for convenience and ease of use. Manufacturers have spent so much time on features and functionalities that they've neglected security. Bluetooth is a good example of this. It's a wireless technology that was created to link two phones. To make Blue-tooth compatible with the widest variety of devices, it had to forgo a lot of security controls. That's the irony of information technology. The more open and user-friendly a protocol or application is, the more vulnerable it can be to an attack. If Jodi is using Bluetooth, we might be able to bluesnarf her account information directly off her phone," Tanner explained.

"Bluesnarf? What's that?" Patrick asked.

"It's hacking a wireless device by using the inherent weakness in Bluetooth technology. I wouldn't even need physical access to her phone because it could be done remotely. The wireless range of Bluetooth is about thirty feet, so I'd have to get in close and shadow Jodi long enough to get a good data transfer."

"Could you do it while she was in the restaurant with Charles?" asked Larry.

"Theoretically yes, but since I don't know anything about her phone model or manufacturer, I'd have to hack real-time and try a variety of different techniques to get one to work."

"If we could get you close enough to her phone but still keep you locked up, would that work?" Larry offered.

"If I was in range of her Bluetooth signal, yes, it would," Tanner replied.

"Okay, you work on figuring out how you're going to hack that phone, and I'll figure out how to get you close enough to Jodi without being seen," Larry resolved.

Tanner spent the rest of the day configuring two laptops to digitally eavesdrop on Bluetooth technology. Searching the Internet, he found some premade tools that other people had already developed for bluesnarfing. If he had more time, Tanner would have felt better about writing his own hacking script, but under the deadline, he had to risk using work that someone else had already done.

Tanner worked long into the night, finally stopping at midnight. Larry and Patrick had gone to sleep while Magic and Michael had stayed up to help Tanner. He'd had made some excellent progress, and with what he had learned, he hoped that he could find a way to successfully hack into the smartphone.

"Hey, can you log me into the website so I can play a little music?" Tanner asked Magic. "My brain is starting to cramp up. I need to take a music break."

"As long as you put your headphones on, I'll give you a half hour," Magic said as he brought up the music website.

October 5, Mountain Safe House, New Mexico

Sunday was a great day. Tanner was awake to see the beautiful autumn sun rising in the east. After playing his bass for a while, Tanner had pulled another all-nighter to keep up his momentum rather than getting sleep. Listening to his MP3 and drinking Mountain Dew, Tanner was in the zone as Larry came downstairs for breakfast.

"Did he stay up all night again?" Larry asked Michael.

"Yeah, and he's making great progress, so don't disturb him," Michael said.

"I'm surprised he hasn't slipped into a sleep-deprived coma," Larry said. "If he keeps pushing himself, he might pass out."

"He's never tried hacking a phone before, so maybe he's caught up in the novelty of the idea," Magic said before changing subjects. "So how are we going to get him up to Los Alamos without risking that he'll escape or call for help?"

"Patrick and I were discussing that last night," Larry said. "It's simple actually. We'll handcuff him in the backseat of the Suburban. Patrick will sit next to him so he doesn't cause a commotion. With the tinted windows, nobody will see him. If we can get the Suburban parked close

131

enough to the restaurant, Tanner should be able to do his Bluetooth hack and not even leave the vehicle."

Larry stopped talking as he heard a strange sound coming from Tanner. It started out quiet, but soon he recognized the familiar tune of "Happy Birthday." Tanner finished the song with a smile, singing the final "to you" in an operatic voice that was loud enough to wake Patrick upstairs.

"What was that all about?" Magic asked, an annoyed look on his face.

"The Birthday Paradox," Tanner replied with a tired smile. "That's the key." Larry and his men stared at Tanner with blank looks on their faces.

"The birthday what?" asked Larry.

"The Birthday Paradox—a paradox meaning it isn't what you would expect," Tanner explained. He hobbled over to the kitchen to get something to eat. "It's a concept in probability theory, and the solution to how I'm going to hack that smartphone," Tanner stated before explaining. "Simply put, the Birthday Paradox states that if twenty-three randomly chosen people were put in a room together, there's a 50-percent chance that at least two of them would share the same birthday. This is counterintuitive because, with 365 days in a year, most people would think the group size would have to be larger to get a successful match."

"So how does that relate to computer hacking?" Magic asked.

"Well, a birthday attack exploits the mathematics behind the birthday paradox. By taking a random sample of input values in the Bluetooth network, I can predict the sequential patterns and hack the Bluetooth link."

None of that made any sense to Larry, but he didn't have to understand all the details to see that Tanner was on to something. "How long will it take to get that ready?"

"I should have it finished by the end of the day, but I'm still going to have to make the trip to Los Alamos. The birthday attack is just the approach to hacking the smartphone. I still don't know the exact details of how I'm going to do it," Tanner said. "It's like a football game. I can create a basic game plan, but I need to be on the sideline, trying different options and making adjustments as the game is played."

"Finish up your work, and we'll head out to Los Alamos tomorrow after breakfast," Larry said.

"I will, but first I need to grab a couple hours of sleep," Tanner said, finishing his bowl of cold cereal before crashing on the couch.

October 6, Mountain Safe House, New Mexico

Tanner woke up Monday morning thrilled about the chance to leave his mountain prison. Almost six weeks had passed since his abduction, and now it was the beginning of October. Fall had arrived showcasing its bright autumn colors in patches of forest around the cabin.

Tanner turned his gaze from the bay window. He had been thinking about Sandia Peak, a majestic mountain just east of his home back in Albuquerque. "This weekend is the balloon festival in Albuquerque. You'd like it, Magic, especially the balloon glow on Friday night when they fire up their burners. If you really want an adventure, you should see it from the top of Sandia Peak. From up there it looks like hundreds of fireflies are in the night sky."

"How do you get to the top?" Magic asked, eating his breakfast.

"The best way is the Sandia Peak Tram, but I wouldn't recommend it if you're afraid of heights. The tram has one of the longest spans in the world," Tanner said.

"Time to go," Larry said, ending the casual talk around the kitchen table. Tanner quickly finished the fourth soda he'd had for breakfast and followed his kidnappers outside.

"You first, Tanner, in the back," Larry said, motioning toward the rear seat.

Before getting into the Suburban, Tanner took a moment to study the dirt road as it disappeared off into the distance. But Patrick was in no mood for sightseeing, and he forcefully shoved Tanner inside the vehicle before handcuffing his wrists together. Using an additional set of handcuffs, Patrick then locked Tanner's ankles against the steel supports on the bottom of the seat. The restraints made Tanner feel like Houdini, getting ready for one of his famous magic tricks. Patrick's final touch to the ensemble was the same black canvas bag that had gone over Tanner's head for the trip to the hideout a month ago. Satisfied that Tanner was secured and blindfolded, Patrick, Larry, and Michael piled into the SUV and drove away.

Tanner closed his eyes, focusing his other senses on his surroundings. He would only get one chance at traveling this road, and he had to concentrate. Judging by the bumps and movement of the truck, Tanner estimated they were going about twenty miles per hour. Counting "one-Mississippi, two-Mississippi" in his mind, he timed how long they traveled, and if they deviated from their initial western direction. A few moments passed and he felt the Suburban go over a cattle gate. Making a quick calculation, Tanner determined they were about two miles away from the cabin. The Suburban continued the same direction for another ten minutes before coming to a complete stop. Tanner heard the turn signal blinking and sensed the car as it turned north onto pavement. The SUV accelerated, and Tanner guessed they had driven about five miles on the dirt road and were now on some sort of highway. The Suburban climbed the windy road higher into the mountains. After what seemed about an hour, it finally slowed down and stopped.

"We're here," Patrick announced as he pulled the cloth bag off Tanner's head. Looking out the side window, Tanner got his first glimpse of Los Alamos. They appeared to have entered the city from the west side. Looking up at the traffic light, Tanner verified his assumption when he saw the New Mexico Highway 501 road sign. Across the street, a clock on the side of a credit union flashed 10:10 and 46 degrees. In just a matter of seconds, Tanner confirmed what he had suspected for weeks. His captors' secret hideout was somewhere in the Jemez Mountains, about an hour out of Los Alamos.

Cruising through town on Trinity Drive, Tanner squirmed in the backseat. "I need to go to the bathroom," he said urgently.

"Didn't you go before we left?" asked Larry.

"Yes, but did you see how much Mountain Dew I had for breakfast?"

"Can't you hold it?" asked Patrick.

"What's the point? We've got a few minutes," Tanner said. "Look, there's a McDonald's. Pull in so I can go," he pleaded.

Michael stopped the Suburban, and Larry and Patrick jumped out to get Tanner. With a jacket covering his hand, Patrick pressed the barrel of his gun against Tanner's back, escorting him casually through the side entrance of the building. Fortunately, the breakfast crowd was mostly gone, and there was nobody on their side of the lobby to watch the men moving toward the restrooms.

Relieved to have made it to a toilet in time, Tanner took a deep, relaxing breath. His stomach was turning as adrenaline poured into his blood stream. His actions over the next few minutes had to be executed exactly the way he had envisioned a thousand times in his mind.

"That better be the last of it, because we ain't going to stop again," Patrick said forcefully.

"I'm done, but let me wash my hands first," Tanner said, reaching for some soap. Just outside the restroom door, Larry stood guard, preventing anyone else from coming in and disturbing the other two.

Tanner finished washing his hands and dried them off with a paper towel. He tossed the paper towel toward the trash can, but missed badly because of the handcuffs on his wrist. The paper towel fell to the floor and rolled under the counter. Sighing in frustration, Tanner bent down to pick up the trash, but instead he discreetly grabbed a black metal can that was hidden underneath the sink.

With Patrick momentarily distracted, Tanner made his move. Spinning around in a quick motion, he raised his hands and pointed the can of mace at Patrick, who was busy checking his satphone. Patrick looked up just in time to get a full dose of pepper spray right in his face. Blinded by the mace, Patrick wildly reached out and tried to grab Tanner, but Tanner had already moved to his next surprise. Kicking his right foot forward with all the strength he could muster, Tanner drove his ankle up between Patrick's legs. Patrick buckled over and fell to the floor, squealing in excruciating pain.

Tanner didn't have any time to feel sorry for Patrick. Having heard his partner's guttural scream, Larry burst through the door. But he was unprepared for Tanner's surprise attack. As soon as the pepper spray hit Larry, he swiftly dropped his gun and shielded his eyes. Tanner lunged from his position and drove his shoulder into Larry's chest, forcing him back against a toilet. Larry hit the ground hard, but he still managed to reach out and grab Tanner's leg. Tanner kicked his other foot into Larry's gut, knocking the wind out of him. Tanner jumped back and noticed Larry's satphone on the floor. Grabbing it, Tanner sprinted out the restroom, around the front counter, and into the parking lot on the opposite side of the waiting Suburban.

———●———

Outside in the Suburban, Michael wondered what was taking so long. He jumped out of the SUV and ran inside to check on his partners, but he wasn't prepared for the chaos that greeted him. Larry was hunched over the bathroom counter, trying to catch his breath. Patrick was in worse shape, wriggling in pain on the tile floor.

"Get him!" Larry shouted vehemently, pointing toward the front. Michael quickly turned and ran toward the main entrance of the restaurant. With his gun hidden by his side, he surveyed the confused looks on the employees' faces. One of them mumbled something and pointed toward the exit on the opposite side. Michael burst out into the parking lot just in time to see a maroon Mazda 3 accelerate away. He couldn't get a good look at the driver, but he did manage to catch a glimpse of Tanner in the passenger's seat. Michael momentarily thought about taking a shot, but with so many people around, he decided that would just draw unwanted attention. Instead, he ran back inside to help clean up the mess.

Behind the front counter, the startled employees were just about to call 911. Michael flashed them a fake police badge, saying that he and his partners were chasing a drug suspect. The employees bought the story long enough for Larry and Michael to escape, dragging the semi-conscious Patrick out to the Suburban with them.

———●———

Inside the Mazda 3, Tanner spoke rapidly to the driver. "We don't have much time. Where are the bolt cutters?"

The driver pointed toward the backseat, and Tanner turned around and quickly grabbed the bulky cutting tool. Pulling up his pant leg, he wedged the sharp ends beneath the strap on his ankle monitor and clipped it in one motion, causing a red light to begin flashing wildly. Tanner rolled down the passenger window and chucked the device over a small embankment on the side of the road.

———•———

"What happened?" Michael shouted as the black Suburban sped down the road after the Mazda.

"Not now, just follow the car!" Larry shouted. "Tanner still has that ankle monitor on. If we hurry, we can catch him," he said, rubbing his swollen eyes.

Watching the GPS monitor mounted on the dash of the Suburban, Michael saw that Tanner was about a half mile away, heading east on Trinity Drive. The Suburban shot through a red light and quickly gained on Tanner's location.

"He's up here on the right, just off to the side of the road," Michael said. The black SUV screeched to a stop on the sidewalk. Michael and Larry jumped out and hurried over the grassy embankment, guns drawn at their sides. Reaching the top of the small incline, they found the ankle tether discarded on the ground.

"No! No! No!" Larry shouted out in frustration. Grabbing the monitoring device, he turned around and ran back toward the SUV. "Let's get out of here. We've got to regroup and get Patrick some help. We've clearly underestimated Tanner."

October 6, East Side of Los Alamos, New Mexico

Tanner's magnificent escape seemed to take an eternity, but in reality it only lasted a few moments. He anxiously watched out the rear window for a black Suburban, but he never saw it. After several long minutes, he felt confident that they weren't being followed. He turned around and took a breath, suddenly aware of pain coming from his shin. With the adrenaline rush at the time, he hadn't noticed anything during his escape, but now he could see that he'd accidently cut himself when removing the ankle monitor.

"Are you okay?" the driver asked as Tanner pressed the cuff of his jeans against the wound to stop the bleeding. Looking up at the driver, Tanner expected to see the long brown hair that he had grown accustomed to so many years ago. Instead, she now had blonde hair with loose curls just above the shoulders. Her hair might have changed color, but her soft brown eyes were still the same. It was Megan Holland.

"The pepper spray you hid in the bathroom worked perfectly," he said with a smile. "But these guys won't give up that easily. We've got to get somewhere safe."

Megan didn't respond. She drove the Mazda 3 out of town and down Highway 502. She stared silently at the road ahead. Even though he hadn't seen her in years, Tanner could see that she was angry. It was going to be long drive back to Albuquerque.

—•—

Larry knew there wasn't any point in trying to catch up with Tanner. By discarding his ankle monitor on the side of the road, Tanner had bought precious time for his escape. They couldn't afford to get involved with the local cops by continuing a reckless pursuit. Larry needed to regain control of the situation. He reached for his satphone to call Charles but found his front pocket empty.

"I've lost my phone. It probably fell out when Tanner ambushed me. Let's go back and get it," Larry said, wiping his burning nose and eyes on his shirt.

"What about Patrick?" Michael was clearly concerned about his teammate, who was moaning painfully in the back seat. Larry thought for a moment and decided it was more important to help his injured man.

"Give me your phone," Larry ordered. Michael handed his satphone to Larry, who used it to call Charles.

"Where are you?" Larry asked Charles.

"I just got into Los Alamos. I'm getting ready for my lunch date."

"We've got to abort. Tanner has escaped, and Patrick is hurt. There's a city park just behind the science museum. Grab your trauma kit and meet us over there," ordered Larry.

—•—

Charles didn't waste any time and rendezvoused with the others a few minutes later. "What's wrong with Patrick?" he asked. He opened the rear door of the Suburban and saw Patrick squirming in pain, his face bright red from the mace.

"Tanner ambushed both of us with pepper spray and kicked Patrick in the groin. I'll be okay, but he's really hurting," Larry said.

Charles did a quick field examination. Patrick was in bad shape.

"It's okay, buddy. Take it easy. I'm going to give you something for the pain," Charles said as he prepped a syringe with morphine. Just seconds after he injected the medicine, Patrick relaxed and stopped moaning. Charles then retrieved an instant cold pack and placed it on Patrick's groin.

"How bad is it?" Larry asked.

"He's got a lot of swelling down there. We should probably have a doctor look at it."

"We don't have time for a trip to the ER," Larry said. "What can we do about the pepper spray?"

"Just flush your eyes out with water. It's going to burn for a while, and your nose will run like crazy."

"Here," Michael said, grabbing some bottled water that he had brought from the cabin. Charles and Michael helped Larry and Patrick flush out their eyes. After a few minutes, Larry's eyes looked a little bit better. Charles wished he could say the same for Patrick and his injury. Turning to Michael and Charles, Larry hastily drafted a new game plan.

"Charles, your date is canceled. Call Becky and make some excuse. Let's all head back to the cabin. We've got to stabilize the situation." Pausing for a moment, Larry turned toward Michael. "What about the getaway car?"

"It's a dark red Mazda 3 with New Mexico tags. I wasn't in a good position to get the license plate number."

"Well, at least that's a start. Call Magic and give him that information. Tell him to contact our man at the DMV and see what he can find. This isn't over yet. We still have Tanner's parents as collateral," Larry said with new resolve in his voice.

October 6, Just Outside of Santa Fe, New Mexico

Tanner and Megan sped toward Santa Fe. Tanner wanted to get back to Albuquerque as soon as possible, but Megan had other plans. Just after crossing a bridge over the Rio Grande, she came to a rest stop. She took the exit and pulled the car around behind the back of the buildings, parking out of sight from the passing traffic.

"Hey, what are you doing?" Tanner asked.

"I haven't heard from you in ten years, and suddenly I start getting messages on an old email account that say you're in trouble," Megan frowned. "I'm not going any farther until you tell me what is going on," she demanded. "I want to know everything, starting back when we were in college."

Tanner took a deep breath. It was time to come clean about his illegal past. "Remember my roommate Jeff Kessler?"

"Yes," Megan said with a skeptical look on her face. Tanner knew she had never trusted Jeff.

"He and I started a small business while at school. People paid us to hack into the campus network and change their grades. It was mostly small stuff, but we made some decent money as college kids."

"You were doing this *while* we were dating?"

"Yeah. Nobody knew about it. We kept the whole operation really quiet."

Megan was exasperated. "So basically I was dating a criminal."

Tanner knew how Megan felt about honesty. She'd been a Mormon her entire life and had extremely high ideals. "I became very skilled at hacking. After I graduated, I decided to pursue it full time. I did some shady stuff over the years. I hacked into computers all over the world, but I gave it up several years ago and found a legitimate job," he added.

Megan shook her head in disbelief. Tanner had made sure she'd had no idea about his past. "These mysterious guys kidnapped you and forced you back into hacking?"

Unknown to the Starting Five, Tanner had managed to secretly communicate with Megan while he was under guard at the cabin. His messages were short and cryptic, but he had given Megan the most important details of his capture. He had also provided her with the information necessary to facilitate his escape.

"I'm not sure, but somehow they found out about my past. They needed someone to hack into Los Alamos Labs, and they figured I could do the job," Tanner said.

"What did they want you to steal?"

"The classified plans for a supercomputer."

"Did you do it?" Megan asked.

"I didn't steal anything, I promise," Tanner said. "We were getting really close, but then you came and rescued me."

The information was a lot for Megan to digest. "How am I supposed to react to this?" she asked. "If I hadn't seen that ankle monitor, I'd think you were making the whole thing up."

Tanner empathetically nodded his head. "I wish this was all just a bad dream, but it gets worse. These guys also kidnapped my parents."

"What?" Megan asked. Tanner hadn't said anything in his secret messages about his parents' involvement.

"I was going to visit them in Arizona. When I got there, the kidnappers had gotten to them first," Tanner explained. "Now that I've escaped, I've got to find my parents and rescue them."

"I think you should call the police," Megan said.

"I can't get the police involved. I'll have to explain everything to them, and when they learn about my past hacking, they'll arrest me," Tanner said.

"Maybe not," Megan observed. "You said you haven't done it in a long time."

Tanner was sure that involving the police right now was a waste of valuable time. "The guys that kidnapped me are pros. The police won't be able to track them down. Besides, I know more about these guys than anyone else. I have the best shot at confronting them and freeing my parents."

"How are you going to do that?" Megan asked.

Tanner took Larry's satphone out of his pocket. "With this," he said, showing Megan the device. "It belonged to the main boss. I took it from him during my escape. Now I'm going to use it as leverage to get my parents back."

October 6, Mountain Safe House, New Mexico

On the other side of the Jemez Mountain range, the black Suburban pulled up to the cabin hideout with Tanner's 4Runner close behind. Patrick had fallen asleep from the morphine, so Michael and Charles gently carried him into the house. Larry went straight to the bathroom and put his head under the bathtub faucet. He flushed his face with water for a solid minute. The burning from the pepper spray had subsided, but he still had trouble seeing clearly. Unfortunately, Larry didn't have any more time to waste on his injuries, so he hurriedly dried off and joined the other members of his team. Charles handed Larry a pair of sunglasses as he came into the kitchen. "Put these on. It will make it so you don't have to squint so much."

"Did you cancel your date with Becky?" Larry asked as he took the shades from Charles.

"I told her I had the stomach flu and that I would call her back tomorrow. She was really disappointed, but I think she'll still help us out when the time comes."

"Good," Larry said. He turned toward Magic. "What about the getaway car?"

"I've got our man at the DMV working on it. He said he would get back to us within the hour with a list of all the registered cars like that."

"Okay, that gives us some time to think this through and make a rational decision," Larry said, trying to keep his cool. "We've hit a snag, but we're not backing out of this operation yet."

Charles spoke up, asking the question that was on everybody's mind. "Who helped Tanner escape, and how did he arrange it?"

"That's an excellent question, and it's the key to finding him," Larry said.

•————•

The maroon Mazda 3 zipped across the overpass and onto Interstate 25. Tanner had convinced Megan to resume driving back to Albuquerque while he explained everything that had happened in the past month. As Tanner provided the specific details about his captivity, Megan could see that he was being completely honest. He had been through a lot.

"It seems like the kidnappers were pretty nice to you, considering the circumstances. I mean, they could have made your life really miserable if they wanted," she said.

"I worried about that at first, but then I could see that it wasn't their style. Like I said before, they were all business. They must have figured out that kidnapping my parents would be more motivating than beating me up," Tanner said.

"Do you have any idea where your parents are?" Megan asked.

"I have a gut feeling that it's somewhere close, but I don't have anything solid to go on. That's why I've got to turn the tables and go on the offensive against these guys. It's my best option for finding my parents and getting out of this mess alive."

"How do you know the kidnappers will cooperate with you? Maybe they've already packed up and left," she pointed out.

Megan's question was a good one. "I learned a lot about these guys over the past month. They're getting desperate for those classified documents. They've put a ton of time and money into this operation, and they're not going to pull out without a fight."

"That sounds really dangerous. I still think calling the police is our best option."

Tanner noticed Megan's use of the word *our*. It sounded like she was willing to help him out for the time being. "It is risky, but I don't have time for the police to sort this out. I think these guys will attempt to get their operation back on track, but if things don't work out, they'll kill my parents and leave the state."

Megan paused at the definitiveness of Tanner's statement. She could feel Tanner's anxiousness about his parents. "You said you quit hacking a couple of years ago. Why did you stop?"

"My grandma got scammed by some hackers operating out of Europe. They cleaned out her bank account and left her broke. When that happened, I realized I wasn't any better than those criminals. I couldn't sleep for weeks thinking about all the innocent people I had hurt as a hacker."

"It sounds like you had a change of heart," Megan said.

Tanner took another breath. "There's actually more to the story. I cleaned up my life and joined your church."

Megan was flabbergasted. "You're a Mormon?"

"Ironic, isn't it?"

Megan was so shocked that she almost drove right off the road. "When did this happen?"

"About three years ago. After I quit hacking, I decided I needed some direction in my life. I knew that religion had a positive effect on you, so I started looking into Mormonism," he said.

"I can't believe it. You were practically an atheist in college. How come you never told me that you joined the Church?" she asked.

"I didn't have your number," he answered weakly.

"That's a poor excuse. I'm sure you could have found a way to contact me if you'd wanted to," Megan said.

Tanner paused for a moment and then decided to let go of his pride. "I was worried how you would react if I told you. I said a lot of bad things about religion when we broke up."

Tanner silently recalled the arguments that had ended their relationship. Even after all these years, it was still painful for him. There was an awkward pause in the conversation, and Tanner felt vulnerable about what he had just said. He quickly changed the subject. "So is this your car?"

"No, I thought it would be too risky to use my own car. This belongs to my younger brother. I'm watching it while he's in Afghanistan."

"Is he in the military?"

"Yeah, he's a captain in the Army over there. He's got another year before he comes home," Megan said.

"So do you still live around here?" Tanner asked.

"I moved back to Albuquerque over the summer. I'm house-sitting for my parents while they're on a church mission."

"Where are they?"

"They're in Canada. They won't be home for another year."

"Can we go to your parents' house? We need to find a safe place, but we can't use my house. They'll be watching it guaranteed," Tanner asked.

Megan's emotions were all over the map. She was angry with Tanner for how he had ended their relationship back in college. Part of her wanted to kick him out of the car and leave him stranded on the side of the road. On the other hand, she knew that Tanner was desperate to find his parents, and that he needed her help. The entire situation was chaotic, but Megan's curiosity got the best of her in the end. Tanner seemed to have grown up, and she wanted to find out how different he was.

"Okay, let's head back to my place. We can figure out where to go from there," Megan said.

⸺•⸺

Twenty minutes later, Megan pulled the Mazda into the garage of her parents' home and shut the garage door. The house was in an older but well-kept neighborhood on the east side of Albuquerque. Tanner hoped they would be safe here.

Tanner followed Megan into the kitchen. He noticed that she hadn't aged much since college, and that she still had her slender and athletic figure. He thought about the first time he had met her. They were in the same racquetball class at the University of New Mexico. Megan had surprised him with how fast she moved on the racquetball court. Tanner had thought she might be on an athletic scholarship, but he later found out that she majored in information systems with a minor in music. It had seemed an unusual combination to him at the time. Megan opened up a hall closet and took out a bath towel. "Let's get you cleaned up first," she said. Megan hadn't said anything about Tanner's hygiene in the car, but he smelled like an old gym shoe. It must have been obvious he hadn't showered in days.

Tanner recognized the not-so-subtle hint and headed off toward the bathroom. As he walked down the hall, Megan called out, "I'm going to run down the street and grab you some things. I'll be back in a bit."

⸺•⸺

Megan got in her silver Toyota Camry, deciding to leave the Mazda hidden in the garage since that was the car used in Tanner's escape. As she pulled out of the neighborhood, she reminisced about her year-long romance with Tanner. They've met during spring of their sophomore year. They had started out as friends, but their relationship grew and evolved over the summer. By the time classes had begun that fall they were seriously dating. For the next several months, everything seemed perfect. They had fallen in love, blowing off classes to spend every possible minute together.

Then something had changed the following year. Tanner became quiet and elusive whenever Megan started talking about their future together. After a few heated discussions, she discovered that Tanner didn't ever want to get married. He knew that Megan was a Mormon, and that she would only marry a person of her faith. Megan had tried several times to get Tanner interested in her religion, but he mistook Megan's intentions as a sign that she was trying to fundamentally change him. Tanner pushed back, saying that Megan wasn't accepting him for who he was. They had a huge argument, and Tanner gave Megan an ultimatum—him or her religion. Megan chose the latter.

Megan finished her shopping and returned home thirty minutes later. When she came into the house, she was momentarily startled to see that Tanner had shaved his goatee. With his facial hair gone, she suddenly remembered how handsome she thought he was. She cleared her throat.

"I got you some things. I figured you'd need them." Reaching into the bag, she pulled out a stick of deodorant, a toothbrush, and some other personal items.

"You didn't have to do that," Tanner said.

"Actually, I did. You smelled bad," she said with a laugh.

Tanner chuckled. "They were working me nonstop at the end. I hadn't showered in four days."

Megan handed the personal items to Tanner. "So what's your plan?"

Tanner turned serious. "I've got to figure out a way to contact my kidnappers and let them know that I want to meet with them."

October 6, Mountain Safe House, New Mexico

Just over an hour northwest of Albuquerque, Larry and the other members of the Starting Five brainstormed their next move. It was almost three in the afternoon, and despite all their efforts, they had accumulated little information. To make matters worse, Larry didn't have time to go back and look for his lost satphone. He wondered where it was.

"I got something back from our guy at the DMV," Magic said, reading an email on the computer console. "It's a list of red Mazda 3s registered in New Mexico."

Michael looked at the email on the computer. "Wow, there are 346 people on that list. That's too many."

Larry also looked at the printout. "Narrow the search down and focus only on the cars that are registered in the Albuquerque area."

Magic sorted the list by location. "That takes us down to 127."

"Okay, that's our starting point. Everything we know about Tanner originates in Albuquerque. We'll begin our search there," Larry said. He turned toward Michael and Charles. "You two, take the Suburban and head out for Albuquerque. In the meantime, we'll prioritize this list of Mazda owners and send it to your phones. One of these people helped Tanner escape."

"What if Tanner isn't in Albuquerque? Or what if he's already gone to the cops?" asked Charles.

Larry shook his head. "I've thought about that, and I always come back to the same conclusion. In times of stress, people fall back on what's familiar to them. I'm betting Tanner's back in Albuquerque, but I doubt that he's called the police. He knows he can't get them involved because of his past."

"If he's not going to the cops, then what is he going to do?" Michael asked.

Larry smiled. "I think he's going to try to come after us."

• —————— •

"Are you hungry?" Megan asked. It was getting close to dinnertime and she was looking for something to do. "I could make something to eat."

"That would be great," Tanner said. "I'm sorry if I've been ignoring you, but I'm almost done."

Tanner had been using Megan's laptop for the past two hours, researching information on the Internet. Next to him was a yellow legal pad with five pages of notes, outlining his plan to find his parents.

"I'm not much of a cook, but how about some chicken and rice?" Megan offered.

"I'm sure you're a better cook than I am," Tanner said as he studied Larry's satphone.

Tanner needed to unlock the satphone. It was the only way he could communicate with the Starting Five. He would only have ten attempts to unlock the device before it permanently disabled itself. On the notepad next to him, Tanner had listed fifteen different PINs that he thought might possibly work. Choosing which one to try first was the hard part. Was Larry the type of person who would choose a completely random number, the best for security but the hardest to remember? Or was he like most people, choosing a code that had personal significance?

The first PIN that Tanner tried was "52779," which spelled "Larry" on the phone keypad. The message "incorrect password" displayed on the screen, and Tanner clenched his fist in frustration. He could have kicked himself for his stupidity. Larry wasn't his real name; it was a pseudonym and wouldn't be the password. Tanner had now wasted one of his attempts. Picking the next best option on the list, Tanner typed in "LANL" using the phone's associated numbers. Again, "incorrect password" appeared. This was a lot harder than he thought. He tried four other attempts, each one failing like the previous. Tanner was nervous, and he wished he had his bass guitar. It would be the perfect time to play a song, and allowing his mind to ponder all the possibilities. Suddenly, Tanner remembered when Larry had asked Tanner to play something from the band Rush. Larry had mentioned it was his favorite band. Tanner picked up the phone with new resolve and punched in the number "2112"—the title of Rush's most popular album. The satphone hesitated for a second before displaying "Welcome" on the screen. Tanner's shout of joy startled Megan, who was sautéing the chicken over the stove.

"What's wrong?" she asked.

"I just unlocked the satphone," Tanner said, standing up in his excitement. Successful hacking often required a mix of skill and luck, and Tanner had just gotten his big break. Scrolling through the menus, Tanner could see all of Larry's contacts. There were phone numbers for Patrick, Michael, Magic, and Charles, along with someone named Reagan. There were also a dozen different emails detailing plans for the hacking operation. Tanner had hit the jackpot. There was enough information here to convict Larry on several different charges. Tanner quickly connected the phone to the computer and spent several minutes downloading the valuable information. When he finished, he turned off the phone, making it impossible to track.

Dinner wasn't anything fancy, but it was delicious. Sitting at the table across from Megan, Tanner felt emotions he hadn't experienced in years. He watched Megan cut her chicken, noticing little things like how her hands held the utensils. They were the same elegant hands he remembered gliding across the piano keys when she played.

Megan had always been a gifted musician, and her natural abilities were far superior to Tanner's. When they were dating, Tanner had often asked Megan to serenade him. He would sit for hours and listen to her play classical pieces from Beethoven or Bach. Music was always a common thread in their relationship, and the fact that Tanner used music in his escape from the Starting Five was serendipitous.

"I think I have a general idea of what I want to do," Tanner said. "With the phone unlocked, I can contact Larry and arrange a trade."

"What kind of trade?"

"I'm going to tell Larry that I have his satphone, complete with all his contact numbers and other important information. I'm going to arrange a trade—his satphone for my parents."

"That sounds risky," Megan said, some doubt in her voice.

"I agree, but I've got a couple of surprises they don't know about," Tanner said, and he finished outlining the rest of his plan for Megan.

OCTOBER 6, MOUNTAIN SAFE HOUSE, NEW MEXICO

Larry checked the clock on the wall. It was now 7:00 p.m. They were going too slow—at this pace, it would be morning before they tracked down all the Mazda 3 owners in Albuquerque.

"We can cross off two more people on the list," Magic reported. He had called the owners, pretending to be a detective from the Albuquerque Police Department. They each had legitimate explanations for their whereabouts that morning. "That takes us down to ninety-two," Magic said.

Unfortunately, Larry didn't have time to conduct a more thorough manhunt. He had imposed a twenty-four-hour deadline to find Tanner. If they failed to locate him in that time, they would cancel the whole operation and kill Tanner's parents before retreating back to California.

"Okay, let's keep focused on those names," Larry said. He wanted to be in Albuquerque with Michael and Charles, but he'd decided instead to coordinate the search from the cabin. Besides, he needed to stay and keep an eye on Patrick, who was still lying on the couch in pain. Larry didn't know if Tanner had intentionally planned to take out Patrick or if it had happened in the moment of the fight, but Tanner's well-placed kick had significantly handicapped the entire team.

Magic's satphone rang loudly, echoing in the cabin. Keeping his eyes focused on the computer monitor, Larry instinctively reached for the phone. He was unprepared for the voice he heard on the other end.

"Sorry about Patrick. It was nothing personal, just business," Tanner said, mimicking what he was told after his own toe was broken.

Larry shot up. Checking the caller ID, he immediately recognized the inbound number for his lost satphone. "Hello, Tanner," Larry said, masking his surprise. "I was wondering what happened to my satphone."

"I want to negotiate an exchange," Tanner said.

"Your parents for my phone?" Larry asked mockingly. Next to Larry, Magic listened in on the conversation while proactively starting a trace on the call.

"You should be more careful with your phone, especially with all the information you keep on it. And you thought Jodi McDonald was foolish," Tanner said, goading him.

Larry's face turned white as he remembered all the important data that he had stored on his satphone. He quickly composed himself and jabbed back at Tanner. "You're just a punk kid. If you want to play games with me, I'll crush you."

Tanner was unfazed. "I'll call you tomorrow morning with the details. Bring my parents, and I'll bring your phone. Or I can take it to the police. I'm sure they could find a use for it," Tanner said before ending the call.

"What did he want?" asked Magic as Larry hung up.

"Tanner is challenging us to a battle of the wits," Larry said. He shook his head.

"Maybe that will work to our advantage," Magic said with enthusiasm as he showed Larry the coordinates of the phone call. "Look! Tanner is definitely in Albuquerque. That call just came from the university. Should I send the team to this location?"

"There's no point. He's long gone by now. He's probably just using the phone's tracking device to entice us to come find him," Larry said. He started a fresh batch of coffee. The upcoming intellectual contest would surely go long into the night. He welcomed it.

———•———

Tanner turned off the satphone after disabling its GPS tracking feature. He was counting on Larry to trace the call, hoping it would lure him out of his mountain hideout. But Tanner didn't want to take any extra risks, so he'd had Megan drive down by the University of New Mexico before he made the call.

"Well, I guess I'm committed," Tanner said as Megan drove her silver Toyota Camry up San Mateo Boulevard.

"We're committed," she corrected him.

"I really appreciate all you've done to help, but I don't want you involved anymore. It's too dangerous. If you can loan me some money and your car, I'll check into a motel and get out of your hair," Tanner said. Even though he welcomed Megan's support, he feared for her safety. He was confident that Larry would try to kill him, and that Larry wouldn't hesitate to kill anyone else who might get in the way.

The Camry slowed down and pulled into a grocery store parking lot. Megan put the car in park and turned toward Tanner. "If I didn't want to be involved, I wouldn't have picked you up this morning, I wouldn't have taken you to my house, and I wouldn't have listened to your plans. I'm completely committed, so let's stop wasting time arguing about something that isn't going to change."

Megan's assertiveness might have startled other men, but not Tanner. He had seen it in the past, and it was one of the characteristics he found most appealing about her. Tanner loved how Megan wasn't afraid to speak her mind and have her own opinions.

"Okay. Well, if you're in, let's take a little drive," Tanner said.

"Where do you want to go?"

"Let's head over to the Sandia Peak Tram. I want to go up to the top."

———•———

It was after 9:00 p.m. when Megan and Tanner finally came back down from the summit of the ten-thousand-foot peak. They had spent an hour at the top, surveying the location and preparing for Tanner's rendezvous with the Starting Five. After going over every possible detail, Tanner was confident that the summit would be a suitable location for his rendezvous.

"I just got really tired," Tanner said, yawning as the silver Toyota Camry headed south on Tramway Boulevard.

"Well, it's been a long day," Megan replied. She thought about the sleeping arrangements for tonight. She had already decided to let Tanner stay at her place, but she wasn't sure if Tanner would feel comfortable with that.

"I think we've gone over everything for tomorrow. My plan isn't as good as I wish it was, but we don't have much choice," Tanner said. Megan could see that he still had his perfectionist attitude, even after all these years.

"There's still the option of going to the police," she ventured.

"If we involve the cops, it will scare Larry and the others away. They aren't stupid enough to let themselves get caught. Besides, how can I prove anything to the police in such a short time? We've got to make our move now."

Megan knew Tanner was right. They had debated the idea, and involving the police didn't have the same potential as their current plan. "I guess the hardest part now is just waiting for tomorrow," Megan said. She was a proactive person, and she hated waiting for something to happen.

Megan paused before moving onto another subject. She wanted to make sure that her proposal to stay the night wasn't taken in the wrong context. "Tanner, you're welcome to stay at my place," she said, quickly adding, "I have that extra bedroom you could use."

"That would be nice. Thank you." Tanner was grateful for Megan's offer, and in a way, he felt more comfortable at her house than being alone in a hotel room.

Ten minutes later, Megan pulled into the garage. Tanner was ready to end the day, but first he wanted to watch the weather forecast. "Do you mind if I turn on the TV?" he asked. They walked into the house.

"Go ahead," Megan said. She walked to the fridge, selected two bottles of cold water, and offered one to Tanner. "I figure this is better than caffeine and sugar before bed," she said, handing the bottle to Tanner before taking a seat on the recliner next to him. Tanner made a face, obviously already missing his Mountain Dew, and Megan laughed at his annoyance.

She fell silent as she sat down next to him. All day long Megan had wanted to talk about what had happened between them when they dated. Now, waiting for the weather report, she finally felt the mood was right.

"Can I ask you a question?" she asked hesitantly.

"Sure."

"Why did you change your mind about religion?"

Tanner took a moment to formulate his response. Megan deserved an honest answer, not just because of her help today, but because Tanner

156

had changed his view on religion 180 degrees. He could tell that she was perplexed.

"I was immature back in college. I thought I had all the answers, but then my whole world came crashing down after the fiasco with my grandma. I quit hacking, but I still felt hollow inside. I needed direction in my life. Then I thought about you. You always had a confidence and peace that was different from anyone I had met. You said that your religion was your anchor in life. I needed something to give me hope, so I decided to take an honest look at it. Your example convinced me to find God."

"You said that religion was for losers when we broke up, remember?" Megan said. While she had moved past her failed relationship with Tanner, she was extremely curious about his newfound beliefs.

"I think I was just lashing out at the time. I was hurt that you decided to choose your religion over me," Tanner reluctantly confessed.

"I didn't do that to hurt you. I loved you. I wanted to marry you. But ever since I was a little girl, I've always dreamed of marrying someone of my faith. It was tearing me apart, having to choose between you and my religion," Megan confided, emotion in her eyes.

"I didn't understand the importance of a Mormon marriage at the time, but I do now," Tanner said. "I'm sorry. I acted like a real jerk." For a moment Tanner's apology hung in the air like an ominous storm cloud, but then it dissipated as he let out a soft chuckle. "It wasn't until after I learned more about Mormons that I understood what it was that made you so different."

"What was that?" Megan asked.

"You knew God's plan—the plan of salvation," Tanner said. "You knew there was a purpose for being here on earth, and it reflected in everything you did."

"So how come you're not married? As a Mormon, you understand the importance of eternal families in God's plan," Megan said.

Tanner hesitated a moment. He hadn't planned on revealing so much to Megan, but for some reason the mood was right, and he found it cathartic to finally open up about his past. "Even though I turned my life around, I guess I still feel like nobody would want to marry me because of all the bad stuff I did."

Sensing Tanner's vulnerability, Megan offered him some hope. "That's in the past. You're a different person now. Besides, you don't have to be perfect to be a good husband or father," she said.

"I know, but relationships are hard to maintain. The one relationship that I really cared about I screwed up long ago," Tanner said, looking Megan in the eyes. The intensity of his gaze made her shiver. She shook it off.

"Hey, we were young and foolish back then. We both made some mistakes. Thankfully we're wiser now." Getting out of her seat, Megan walked over to Tanner and gave him a secure embrace. "I'm sorry," she whispered.

"I'm sorry too," Tanner replied. Megan pulled back and noticed that he had tears welling up in his eyes.

"I think we should call it a night. It might sound cliché, but tomorrow's a big day." Megan said. "Are you going to be okay?"

"I will. Thanks again for everything you've done." Tanner gave Megan one final hug. He got up and walked off toward the guest bedroom.

Megan sat alone in the living room, savoring the moment. After taking a few minutes to regain her composure, she turned off the lights and TV before heading off to her own bedroom.

<34>

OCTOBER 7, MOUNTAIN SAFE HOUSE, NEW MEXICO

As Tanner and Megan ended a long day, the Starting Five knew they would have no such luxury. Except for Patrick, who was in a drug-enhanced sleep on the couch, everyone else was working full speed. The unexpected phone call from Tanner energized the kidnappers in their manhunt. Tanner was indeed back in Albuquerque, and with a lot of luck, they just might find him before sunrise.

Going through a list of all the major hotels in Albuquerque, Larry told Magic to call the front desk at each location, asking if he could speak with Tanner Zane. Larry knew it was a long shot—Tanner would be a fool to check in using his real name—but the monotonous task gave Magic something to do while they waited for updates from the search team in Albuquerque.

"He's not at any hotels by the airport," Magic said, turning to Larry. It was 2:15 a.m., and the clock seemed to be going faster than normal.

"The bright spot is that we're down to forty-seven people on this list of Mazda owners," Larry responded without looking up from his laptop. Using a combination of deductive reasoning and intuition, he was narrowing down the list of people who may have helped Tanner escape. "But we've worked on all the easy suspects first, so now we have the hard ones left." Larry stood up. He took a second to stretch before making a call.

159

He had been hunched over his laptop for the past twelve hours, and his shoulders and neck ached from his poor posture.

He called Charles on another secure satphone. "This is Larry. Give me an update."

"We just drove by Tanner's house again. There's no sign of him there," Charles said.

"He would be an idiot to go there, but I thought he might send his accomplice to collect some stuff. Where are you going now?"

"We're heading off to see if we can find this person named Brent Holland from the list of Mazda owners. His address looks like an apartment complex on the south side of town. We should be there in about ten minutes," Charles said. "What about your satphone? Has Tanner used it again?"

Larry sighed in frustration. "No, he hasn't. The phone is probably disabled; we can't find its ID on the network anywhere. Tanner has gone underground."

"We know his email addresses. We could send him a message and see if he's checking his email," Charles suggested.

"We already did, but we haven't got anything back. My gut tells me that Tanner has disappeared until tomorrow. We might just have to wait for him to contact us," Larry said.

"I'll call back after we check on this Brent Holland character," Charles said, ending the conversation.

Larry thought about his next steps. He didn't want to pursue a backup plan yet, but he knew his time was running out. If he didn't find Tanner in the next twelve hours, he'd have to abort the entire operation and eliminate Tanner's parents. Fortunately, New Mexico was a vast and desolate state—perfect for killing two senior citizens and dumping their bodies in some remote location.

———•———

Michael and Charles arrived at the apartment complex listed on the car registration for Brent Holland. It was always risky to wake people up at such an early hour, but neither of them had any choice. Knocking on the door to apartment #1205, Charles took out his fake police ID and got it ready to show to the occupant. Michael stood off to the side with his SIG Sauer gripped firmly in his hand. After a few moments, they heard the sound of somebody working the lock on the other side of the door. The door opened with a crack, but it was still secured by a chain lock.

"Who are you?" said an overweight and angry woman on the other side. She had obviously just woken up.

"I'm sorry to disturb you at such an early hour, ma'am. My name is Detective Charles Smith from the Albuquerque Police Department. We're tracking down a felon named Brent Holland. This apartment was his last known residence."

Charles spoke with a professionalism that added to his credibility. He even held up the fake police badge for the woman to see. He always thought that action was silly because the average citizen didn't have a clue what a real police badge looked like, let alone a fake. But seeing some kind of ID always made people feel better. Charles then held up a 5 x 7 photo of Tanner for the woman to see.

"I don't know him," the woman said, suddenly willing to cooperate.

"How long have you lived here, ma'am?" Charles asked, taking out a notepad and pen for effect. A simple act like that always seemed to enhance his authenticity.

"I've been here for about eight months. He might have lived here before me, but I don't know. You'll have to talk to the manager if you want more information, but she usually doesn't get in until 9 a.m."

"Thank you for your help. I'm sorry to disturb you. Good night," Charles said as the woman closed the door.

"Another dead end," Charles grumbled as they both climbed back into the SUV. It was the hour of the night when the body was the most sleep deprived, and Charles and Michael were dragging.

"Let's update Larry and then find some coffee," Michael said as he pulled away in the Suburban.

● ———— ●

Back at the cabin, Magic and Larry stood up while going about their tasks. They hoped that staying upright would help keep them awake. It was approaching 5:00 a.m., and they waited for their internal body clocks to kick in, signaling the start of Tuesday morning.

"We're down to twenty-three Mazda owners that we can't account for, including this Brent Holland person. Nobody seems to know where he went," Larry said.

"Do you want me to contact our man back east and see what he can dig up? It's almost 7:00 a.m. there, so he should be getting into work. Maybe he can run Brent's name though the system," Magic said.

"Do it," Larry commanded.

Their contact was a junior data clerk at the Pentagon. Larry always liked to use junior people for information gathering. Often the worker-bees felt slighted at not having a job title with more importance. They also thought their small positions didn't allow them access to any secret information, but that was often not the case. Clerks and help desk support agents had access to a tremendous amount of data—they just didn't know it. Larry had learned that with a little guidance and five thousand dollars, such people could often be convinced to look a little harder.

OCTOBER 7, ALBUQUERQUE, NEW MEXICO

The alarm clock buzzed loudly, waking Tanner at 6:00 a.m. He was convinced that the alarm clock manufacturers had all agreed to use the same annoying noise to start the day. It had to be the worst sound in the world.

Tanner put on his jeans and T-shirt before heading out to the kitchen for some breakfast. Opening the door, he was surprised to see Megan up and ready to go running.

"I didn't expect you to be up so early," Megan said, stretching her legs on the floor.

"I woke up an hour ago and couldn't go back to sleep. I guess it's jitters about today," Tanner explained.

"That's why I'm going running. I want to burn off some of my nervous energy. Do you want to come?"

"I should stay out of sight. I'll just stick around here and make sure everything is ready to go."

Megan finished her stretching routine while Tanner ate a couple of bowls of cereal. He wasn't sure if he'd have time for normal meals today, so he decided to eat more breakfast as a precaution. "Be careful out there," Tanner warned Megan before she left. As she turned to walk out the front door, Tanner grabbed the TV remote to check the weather again. The meteorologist said it was going to be cloudy with a 70-percent chance of rain later in the day.

Major General Yang Dao was in no mood for the idealistic rhetoric bantered around the table by his comrades. Of the dozen leaders in the First Technical Reconnaissance Bureau, the general was the only one who had spent significant time outside of China. He had seen the real world, and he knew that the United States wasn't the incompetent giant that his colleagues believed it to be. The United States was a vast nation with more technological resources than his country could imagine. Yang Dao understood what few other socialists in the world did—the United States of America was an intellectual behemoth. *When will the men seated around this table realize that demonizing America isn't anything more than lip service?*

An aide leaned in and handed Yang Dao a note, rescuing him from his thoughts. It was from Reagan. The general quietly excused himself and walked back to his office, where he picked up his desk phone and called a confidential number in America.

"Good evening, General," Reagan said after the call was connected.

"When can I expect the plans for the quantum computer?" the major general asked.

"We were on schedule until yesterday. Then we hit a snag," Reagan said. "My computer hacker escaped. We know his location, and we're closing in on him right now. We'll have him back by the end of the day."

Yang Dao didn't speak for a few moments. When he finally did, his voice wasn't angry, but it conveyed the general's frustration. "I guess asking how he managed to escape is irrelevant. How does this impact the project?"

"Even if we can't find him, there is a good chance we can still get you those plans. We have all his computer programs and notes."

"Is there anything he could tell the authorities that would put me at risk?" the major general asked.

"Not really. The team in New Mexico has done an excellent job keeping our hacker isolated from the public. If he goes to the police, he could only tell them that he had been kidnapped and taken to a remote location."

"What about the FBI?" Yang Dao knew that the FBI was the best investigation unit in the world. It was the FBI, not the local police, that he feared.

"Even with all their resources, the FBI would have a hard time connecting the dots. My man in New Mexico assures me that if he doesn't get our hacker back in the next twenty-four hours, he'll pull out and clean up the whole operation," Reagan said.

"Very well. Call me tomorrow with an update," Yang Dao replied. He hung up the phone and stared at the city lights across the valley. The general was beginning to regret hiring Reagan to steal the classified plans.

•———•———•

When Megan got back from her run, she found Tanner already dressed and working on the computer. Next to him was a stack of notes. Glancing at the top of the stack, she noticed the daily schedule for the Sandia Peak Tram.

"How's it going?" she asked, taking a bottle of water from the fridge.

"It's coming together. I figure it's about time to make another call to Larry."

"Are you going to tell him where to meet you?"

"Not yet. I'm just keeping him on the line, waiting for the right time to pull the hook."

"Is there anything I can do to help?" Megan asked from the kitchen.

"Maybe after you get ready we'll make another trip over to the tram station. Besides that, I think we're ready to go. The weather forecast is calling for clouds and rain this afternoon. That might work to our advantage at the top of the peak. You know how foggy it can get up there when a storm sets in."

Megan watched the morning news with Tanner while she had a breakfast of yogurt, granola, and toast. At 8:30, she headed off to the shower. Tanner was waiting for this moment. As soon as he heard the water turn on, he grabbed the keys to the Mazda and headed out the door.

Tanner drove about five miles from the house and made his phone call to Larry.

"Good morning, Tanner," Larry answered, sarcasm lacing his words. "We've been searching for you all night. You've proven yourself to be quite elusive."

"I hope you're not too tired because it's going to be a busy day," Tanner responded.

"What's the next step in our little game?" Larry asked, annoyed.

"I'm organizing our rendezvous. I'll call you after lunch with the details," Tanner said. He quickly ended the call and disabled the GPS tracking feature once again.

———•———

Larry turned to Magic to see if he had isolated the location. "He's still in Albuquerque," Magic said. "It looks like the call came from the east side of town, on the corner of San Mateo and Montgomery."

"Tanner didn't say much, except that he'll call us back after lunch," Larry said.

"I thought he would have given us more details about what's going on," Magic said.

"That wasn't the point of the phone call," Larry stated. "He wanted us to know that he's preparing for a showdown in Albuquerque."

"That sounds risky. Why would he do that?"

"I imagine that he believes he can beat us, but I think he's getting too confident," Larry said, wondering if he should call Charles and Michael back to prepare for this afternoon. "Did we hear from our man at the Pentagon?" Larry asked Magic.

"Brent Holland is in Afghanistan. He's deployed with the Marines over there. He's not due back until next year."

"Does he have any family or relatives living in Albuquerque?" Larry asked.

"I'm not sure. I'd have to dig some more to see what I can find," Magic replied. "Do you want me to focus on Brent Holland, or should I keep going down this list after the other Mazda 3 owners?"

Larry thought about his strategy for a moment. The search for the mysterious driver of Tanner's escape vehicle had been fruitless. They had wasted enough time trying to track down the owner of the red Mazda 3. Besides, it was pointless to find Tanner now that they had an impending face-to-face meeting with him. "Let's bring everyone back. We'll need some time to come up with a plan for when we meet Tanner," Larry said.

———•———

Tanner headed west on Montgomery toward Wyoming Boulevard before turning north to Paseo Del Norte. Pulling into the parking lot of a small branch of the Bank of Albuquerque, he took a deep breath to calm his nerves. He put on a University of New Mexico baseball hat and dark sunglasses. He then walked into the bank and went toward the only teller. Luckily, the bank had just opened for the day and nobody else was in the lobby.

"Good morning," the young woman said, puzzled that Tanner still kept his sunglasses on. Tanner didn't respond, instead handing the young teller a note and a brown paper sack. She read the note and turned ghostly white. Tanner was robbing her.

October 7, Albuquerque, New Mexico

Bank robberies fall under the jurisdiction of the FBI, and Special Agent Luke Catos happened to be in the area when he got dispatched to the crime scene. *What a great way to start a Tuesday,* Luke thought as he got out of the Ford Crown Victoria with his gourmet coffee in hand. The local police officers had already secured the area with yellow tape, and, as usual, the suspect had fled the crime scene. However, after talking with the other police officers and bank manager, Special Agent Catos realized this wasn't an average bank heist. He decided to call his boss, the Special Agent in Charge of the Albuquerque FBI branch.

Five miles away in the Albuquerque FBI field office, Nicole Green picked up her desk phone on the third ring. Sitting in her corner office on the third floor, she stared out the window at Sandia Peak, wondering when the first snow of the year would appear on the mountain ridge. "This is Nicole," she answered with a yawn in her voice.

"Red, this is Luke. I'm at that bank robbery on the northwest side. You better come and check it out. Something isn't right about this," Agent Catos said. "I know you like to be involved in stuff like this, so it will give you a good excuse to get away from that desk for a while," he added with a laugh.

"Okay, I'm heading over," Nicole said before hanging up the phone. Even though her given name was Nicole, most of her staff called her Red in reference to her short, fiery red hair.

Nicole was the Special Agent in Charge, or SAC, and she had headed up the Albuquerque office of the FBI for almost two years. At forty-four years old, Nicole stood at just five feet four inches tall and weighed 120 pounds. Despite her small frame and friendly personality, she was tough as nails and was well respected in the law enforcement community. Early in her FBI career she had served at smaller field offices in Nebraska and Oregon before being transferred to Houston to work in the financial crimes unit. There she found her true crime-fighting passion, chasing bank robbers and throwing them in jail. To this day, nothing got Nicole's blood flowing like a bank heist, and she wasn't going to let this opportunity pass her up. Grabbing her Glock 23 service pistol, she put on her suit jacket and headed out the door, glad to be free from her desk for the moment.

Speeding up Interstate 25 to the Paseo Del Norte exit, Nicole looked west at the clear blue Albuquerque sky contrasting against the pinkish-tan earth. Originally from Pennsylvania, she had been instantly awestruck by the Southwest landscape when she was first stationed at Kirtland Air Force Base in Albuquerque. After serving her time in the Army, she joined the FBI and secretly hoped that someday she would be assigned back to the area. When the opportunity came to work in the Albuquerque field office, she immediately accepted and was thrilled to come back to what she now considered her desert home.

She put aside her thoughts as she arrived at the Bank of Albuquerque branch. A detective from the local police force immediately recognized Nicole and gave her a friendly smile.

"I'm glad to see you came out for this one, Red," Detective Perry said. As a twenty-three-year vet on the Albuquerque police force, Mark Perry was the only local cop who dared to call Nicole Green by her nickname.

"Good morning, Mark. How're the wife and kids?" Nicole asked with a warm smile.

"Doing well, thanks. My youngest just passed his CPA exam."

"I bet he's excited to be finished."

"He's looking for a gig right now in California. He has an interview with one of the big accounting firms out there next week." Nicole and Mark stopped their conversation short when they heard someone coming out the door of the bank. It was Special Agent Catos.

"Hey, Red. Let me show you what I got," Luke said, and Detective Perry followed both FBI agents into the bank. Inside Nicole saw a tech from the local crime scene unit taking pictures.

"Here's what we know. About 9:03 a.m., just after the bank opened this morning, a white male in his late twenties and approximately six feet tall came in. He was wearing jeans, a gray sweatshirt, a red University of New Mexico baseball hat, and sunglasses. He walked right up to this counter and handed the teller this note." Special Agent Catos held up the note sealed in a plastic bag so Nicole could read it.

Open your drawer and put your money in the bag.

"Short, but to the point," Nicole said. "Did he show anyone a weapon?"

"No, but that's not uncommon. Most of these things only involve a demand note with no weapon to back it up," Luke told her. "But here's where it gets weird. The suspect handed the teller this paper grocery sack and waited for her to fill it up with money. She included a couple of dye packs as instructed in her training. The suspect didn't say anything. He just took the bag and casually walked toward the front door. When he got to the entrance he stopped, shook the bag a couple of times, and dropped it onto the floor before fleeing outside in a red Mazda 3."

"He just left the money?" Nicole was confused.

"Yeah, just dropped it and ran off. Do you think he knew there was a dye pack in it?" Luke asked.

Nicole was familiar with the workings of a dye pack. Invented to help thwart bank robberies, it was common practice to give the robber a stack of money with a dye pack hidden in the middle. Once the thief passed through the entrance of the bank, a radio transmitter hidden in the doorframe activated the dye pack. About ten minutes later the pack would explode, spraying red dye all over, rendering the money useless and the suspect "red-handed."

"It's possible, but why would he take the risk and not the money? Now he's facing time for a felony and still broke," Nicole said. "Did we get any prints?"

"We did. They've already been sent to the office for analysis. We're waiting on word from them," Luke said.

"What about the plates on the Mazda?" Nicole asked.

"Negative. There was something smeared all over the license plates like mud or paint. The security cameras couldn't make it out. He parked the car on the side of the building but kept the engine running for a quick escape."

"Looks like it was amateur hour at the bank," Nicole said. When she was assigned to the financial crimes unit in Houston, Nicole learned firsthand how bank robberies worked. She had seen some good heists and some really boneheaded attempts. This situation looked like it was heading toward the latter.

"Yeah, it was definitely a rookie job. This guy didn't have it all together," Detective Perry agreed. He, too, had seen his fair share of bank robberies over the years.

"But check this out. The detective and I noticed this just before you got here." Holding up the brown grocery sack in a gloved hand, Agent Catos turned it on its side so Red could see nine numbers written on the bottom: 6403 26198.

"What's that?" Nicole asked.

Luke responded. "Not sure. We thought it might be an address or a Social Security number, but we couldn't match it to anything."

Nicole read the numbers out loud, trying to find a pattern, "6-4-0-3, 2-6-1-9-8. Why is there a space between the first four numbers and the rest?"

"Excuse me," said the young teller, who had been involved in the crime. She had been talking with another police officer when she overheard the conversation. "I'm sorry to interrupt, but I think I might know what that is. It sounds like a bank account number."

"A bank account number?" Nicole echoed.

"Yes, most of our accounts start with the four-digit code 6403."

"Are you saying this guy robbed his own bank?" Special Agent Catos asked in disbelief.

"It's possible. Let me get my manager and we can look it up," said the young woman. She appeared a little shaken from her first bank robbery.

Walking back with the teller to the manager's office, Nicole introduced herself to the supervisor and a police officer who were inside. Instructing Luke to hold up the paper bag so the manager could see, Nicole asked, "Does this number look familiar to you? Your employee thinks it could be a bank account number."

"She's right. That 6403 prefix is unique to our branch. Let me look it up for you," the middle-aged manager responded.

"I've seen some stupid things before, but this is way out there. If this really is a bank account number, the perp should get the idiot of the year award," Mark Perry said.

"If that's truly the case, we've got other problems," Nicole replied.

"Problems? How so?" asked Luke.

Nicole explained. "Why would anyone put his own account number on a piece of evidence and intentionally leave that evidence behind for us to find? Even the dumbest criminal would understand the ramifications of that."

"Maybe he was trying to frame someone else. Make it look like he didn't do it," Luke countered.

"Why wouldn't he just shout out the name of the person he was trying to frame? Why go through the effort of putting the account number on this bag? More important, how would the suspect know the bank account number of the person he was trying to frame? If this is a legitimate bank account number, I'll bet you it's his," Nicole concluded in a way that caused everyone in the manager's office to pause for a moment.

"Uh, here's the information. It's definitely an account number," the manager said. "It belongs to a Mr. Tanner Zane. He lives just about a mile from here."

"Mark, will you run everything you have on Tanner Zane? It looks like his DOB is August 10, 1980."

"I'm on it," Detective Perry said. He walked out of the room, already talking into his radio.

Nicole turned her attention back to the bank manager. "May I see?" She looked at the computer monitor, scanning the account information that belonged to Tanner Zane. It was all there—his address, phone number, date of birth, even his Social Security number. He had been a bank member for almost five years with no outstanding credit card balances. Scrolling down the page, Nicole did a double take at the last bit of information on the screen: the balance in Tanner's bank account. "Whoa! It says here he has almost a hundred grand in his account. Is that accurate?"

The bank manager clicked through a few computer screens. "Glancing at his account history, it looks like he's paid very well by his employer. He gets a direct deposit twice a month, and he doesn't seem to spend that much."

Just then, Detective Perry entered the room and rejoined the conversation. "We don't have any priors on Tanner Zane, and the NCIC doesn't show anything either. He's clean. Not even a speeding ticket."

Red paused for a moment before responding, talking to herself as much as to the group assembled in the office. "Why would someone with that much money and no prior record rob a bank?"

"Greed, ego, the adrenaline rush . . . ," the other police officer in the room rattled off.

"I don't think so, not this guy. He doesn't fit the profile. First, he has money in the bank—a lot of it—so he doesn't need any more. Second, he doesn't have a criminal history. Tanner Zane is clean. But the most disturbing fact is that he specifically led us to himself by writing down his own bank account number on this bag. In all my years chasing bank robbers, I've never seen anything so deliberate," Nicole said. She considered her hypothesis. "I think Tanner Zane specifically robbed his own bank to get the Feds involved. He could have committed a hundred other crimes if he just wanted to deal with the local cops. For some reason, he specifically wants the FBI to track him down, and he left us the perfect starting point to find him." Nicole looked around the room. The others in the office looked astonished.

"See? I told you she was the best," Detective Perry whispered to the other police officer in the room.

———————

Tanner arrived back at Megan's house just as she finished getting ready for the day.

"What took you so long?" She knew Tanner was going to make a call to Larry, but he seemed to be gone for an extra-long time.

"I stopped at the store and bought a couple of pre-paid cell phones. We'll need them to communicate with each other today," Tanner said, omitting that he had just committed a felony.

"How did the call go?"

"I told Larry I would call back with instructions for our meeting this afternoon. My guess is he's going to try and get his team together and come up with a contingency plan," Tanner said.

"His plan probably involves killing you and your parents. He'd be a fool to let any of you go," Megan said soberly.

"I know. That's why we have to control the situation and act first," Tanner said. "If you're ready, let's take another trip to the top of the peak. I want to walk the area again before the storm comes in."

———————

Nicole Green jumped in the car with Agent Catos and sped off toward Tanner's home. Following close behind with lights flashing but sirens quiet, Detective Mark Perry joined the pursuit. He quickly updated dispatch with the situation and asked for additional backup.

Arriving at Tanner's house, the FBI agents jumped out of the car with their weapons drawn. Two other police department cruisers blocked off the street to prevent escape. Detective Perry hopped out of his car and signaled that he would go around back to guard the rear exit. Nicole stood off by the garage door and covered Agent Catos as he walked up to the porch. Holding his Glock 22 tightly in his left hand, Luke rang the doorbell and waited for a response. Twenty seconds passed, and he rang the doorbell again. In the background, he could hear additional police cars coming up the road. Nosy neighbors were looking out their windows and even coming out into their yards to witness the commotion. After the third ring, Luke noticeably relaxed. Nicole walked up to join him on the front porch. "Looks like he's not here," Luke said as Detective Perry came around from behind the house.

"The back door is locked and everything is dark inside. I think we missed him," Mark said.

"I'm calling Judge Hernandez and getting a search warrant. We should have something within the hour. In the meantime, let's get SWAT out here and ready to go in once we have the warrant. We've got to figure out what's going on," Nicole said.

———•———

Larry was grateful to have his team back at the cabin but upset that they had failed to locate Tanner. Tanner had moved far past being a nuisance—he was now a full-blown liability. Mentally, Larry scolded himself for letting this happen. They had become too casual with Tanner, and they had instinctively let their guards down. Bringing Tanner to Los Alamos was an obvious blunder, but there were also small things like letting Tanner play his guitar and move unrestricted around the cabin. Larry could see that Tanner had socially engineered them into a false sense of security.

"Our goal this afternoon is to quickly and quietly recapture Tanner and get my phone back," Larry began as he addressed his team in the main room. He didn't have to elaborate. Everyone knew that this was going to be their only chance to salvage the operation.

Larry continued. "We're not sure when or where we're going to rendezvous, so be prepared for anything. Pack all your weapons and gear. We can throw it in the back of the SUV and improvise as needed."

"Wait!" Magic said. He was monitoring the computer console, keeping an eye on the local law enforcement communication to see if anything about Tanner came across the wire. It just had.

"What have you got?" Larry asked.

"It looks like Tanner Zane is the primary suspect in a bank robbery down in Albuquerque."

Larry's jaw dropped. They gathered around Magic's computer. "Now why would he go and do something stupid like that?" Larry asked.

October 7, Albuquerque, New Mexico

A lot had happened in the short time since the FBI arrived at Tanner's home. Two other FBI agents were now helping on scene, and best of all, the SWAT team had taken up defensive positions around the house. With a sniper watching the front door and one guarding the back, Nicole realized the setup was overkill, but she never left anything to chance.

Waiting for the search warrant to be issued, Nicole and the others compiled all the information they could find on Tanner Zane. None of the local databases or the National Interstate Identification Index showed any criminal record. The fingerprints taken off the brown paper bag at the bank had also come back negative. The county had no record of any firearms registered in Tanner Zane's name, and he wasn't the owner of a maroon Mazda 3. Adding to all the inconsistencies, an FBI agent dispatched to check with Tanner's employer reported that Tanner was on sabbatical and wouldn't be back at work for another month.

"Luke, what have you got for family or relatives around the area?" Nicole asked her junior companion.

"Tanner doesn't have any family around. It looks like he's an only child, and his parents live in Arizona. I've contacted the field office there, and they're sending someone over to interview them," Special Agent Catos said.

"Good work," Nicole said. "Once we have the warrant, I want to go in." Waiting for authorization to move was the worst part of the process, but the Constitution was the law of the land, and Nicole respected privacy and due process even if they did slow things down. She always did things by the book so that when the bad guy went to court they could throw the book at him.

Walking to the small communication post they had set up just down the street, Deputy Perry, with a big smile, said, "Good news, guys. We got one of the tellers at the bank to identify Tanner Zane. He's definitely a member of that branch. She saw him in there a month ago. The teller said she couldn't forget a good-looking face like that."

"That is good news. I'll let the judge know when she calls back. With that extra bit of information, she shouldn't have any problem giving us a warrant," Nicole said.

Fifteen minutes later, Nicole got a telephonic search warrant from Judge Maria Hernandez to enter Tanner Zane's home and search for any evidence from the bank robbery.

"Captain," Nicole called out to the leader of the SWAT team. "I got the warrant. I want you guys to go in ASAP."

"Roger that," the captain said, and he hurriedly assembled and informed his men. Donning all their combat gear, the SWAT was ready to go in just a manner of minutes.

"We're ready, ma'am," the captain said.

"Do it," Nicole ordered. She always liked watching the SWAT team in action.

Eight men in black coveralls skillfully moved toward the front door in standard cover formation. The point man rang the doorbell, waiting a small amount of time to give Tanner another chance to respond. With no answer, it was time to break down the door. Another team member came up from the rear of the group with a two-handed battering ram. It took the large and powerful man just two hits to splinter the front door to Tanner's home. The SWAT team spilled in and professionally cleared the building in seconds.

"Nobody's in there," the captain said as he came out of the house. "It looks like it's been vacant for some time, actually."

"Good work, Captain. It's always better to be safe than sorry." Even though Nicole had a gut feeling that Tanner Zane wasn't a significant threat, she couldn't rule out that he might be hiding inside with a shotgun, waiting to take a cheap shot at a cop. Turning to Special Agent Catos and Detective Perry, she planned her next move.

"Let's get the lab guys in there and see what they can find. Maybe we can match a fingerprint to one on the paper bag. Also, I want to see if Tanner has any computer equipment in there that the IT forensics guys can take a look at."

•——•

Tanner wasn't aware of the commotion going on at his house, but he suspected it. He knew it wouldn't be long before the FBI found his account number and followed the trail back to his home, and when the timing was right, he'd lure the FBI into his plan. Tanner also figured the cabin hideout up in the Jemez Mountains was having its share of commotion. Within the hour, he'd call Larry and give him the details for their final encounter.

Standing on the Sandia Peak observation deck overlooking the valley below, Tanner enjoyed the quiet before the storm, both figuratively and literally. His plan would bring unavoidable chaos with it. Looking out toward the western sky, he could literally see the approaching rain clouds.

"Why did you come get me?" Tanner asked.

"You needed help," Megan responded. "You sounded desperate."

"I wasn't sure if you'd even come, seeing how things ended between us back in college."

Megan paused for a moment before responding. She wanted to tell Tanner something important, but she didn't want to risk looking foolish.

"This might sound funny, but about two weeks ago, I had a dream about you. It was a different dream, long ago before we actually met. You and I were childhood friends, playing at the park. In my dream you fell off the teeter-totter and got hurt. I tried to get help, but there was nobody around. It was just you and me."

"Wow, that's weird," Tanner said, wondering why Megan was sharing this story.

"It is weird, considering that I had moved past our relationship. But it left a strong impression on me. I woke up the next morning determined to contact you, but I couldn't find your information anywhere. I finally decided to check that music website we used for our project back at school. I was surprised to see that you had recently posted a song for me."

Tanner let Megan's story sink into his mind. Megan had always been a spiritual person, and it was obvious that she had felt inspired to help Tanner. "It was either inspiration or desperation that convinced me to try and contact you."

Megan laughed. "Maybe it was a little bit of both," she said.

Tanner checked his watch. It was time to get going. "Do you have any thoughts or suggestions before we head back down?" he asked as they waited for the tramcar to depart.

"No, I think we've gone over everything."

"If anything goes wrong, you're supposed to go straight to the FBI and tell them everything you know." Tanner was sure the FBI would be interested in learning about his ordeal, especially since he was now the primary suspect in a bank robbery.

"Tanner," Megan said, turning toward him. "I know we've planned it all out and thought of every last detail, but I'm still worried. I don't want anything to happen to you." He could hear the emotion in her voice.

"I'm worried too, but I was a dead man anyway after I finished the hacking job at Los Alamos. As I see it, this is a better alternative even with the risks."

Megan was flooded with waves of emotion. She felt scared for Tanner and what he was about to do. She also felt sad for all the hardship he had endured. It didn't seem fair that Tanner had been put through so much over the past month. She wished there was something more she could do to help, but she felt inadequate. Instead she just firmly held Tanner's hand as they boarded the tram, hearing the sound of thunder rumbling off in the distance.

———•———

Tanner Zane's house was a beehive of activity. With FBI agents, local police officers, and crime scene techs running around, it was amazing that anything got done. But Nicole was an experienced investigator, and she had everyone working in unison. By all accounts, Tanner's home was unremarkable, and in line with what the SWAT team had reported: it looked like the home had been vacant for several weeks. The good news was that Tanner had three computers, all of which would be analyzed by the IT geeks in the forensics lab for details regarding the bank robbery.

"Nicole, come over here and take a look at this," one of the crime scene technicians said. They had been working for almost forty minutes to find a good fingerprint to match to the one from the paper sack at the bank.

"What ya got, Scotty?"

Scott Reinhold was a young pup compared to the rest of the group on site, but he was very good at his job. Nicole was confident he would discover something.

"Look at what I found on the alarm keypad. We got a match. It looks like an index finger."

"Excellent work, Scotty. Let's double check and verify the results. I want this case to be rock solid," she responded. Nicole had never seen a crime solved in less than an hour, as was so commonly portrayed on TV dramas. But even the FBI was entitled to a lucky break now and then.

"Uh, Red, you better check this out," Agent Luke Catos said in a way that made the smile on Nicole's face quickly disappear. Maybe she had celebrated too soon. Luke was standing down the hall next to a stepladder. Standard procedure for a search warrant was to check everywhere in the house, including the attic, for hidden items like guns or money. "Look at what we found up here," Luke said, motioning to the opening in the ceiling.

Red quickly ascended the ladder and shined her flashlight into the dark void. At first, all she could see was pink insulation and dust, but her light beam soon stopped on a black box with a dozen wires coming out of it. Moving in for a better look, she pulled on a wire, tracing it down the wood beam to where it disappeared into the ceiling below. Coming back down the ladder, she walked over to the smoke detector that was directly above the main computer desk in the living room. She took a barstool from the kitchen, climbed on top of it, and removed the smoke alarm housing from its base. Looking up into the recess of the mount, Nicole saw a miniaturized fiber optic camera.

•———•

It was hard for Tanner to hide his anxiety. With so many different people and variables involved, it was impossible to remove all the uncertainty in their preparation. All they could do was try to minimize the risk.

"It's time to make the call," Tanner said as Megan and he walked back to Megan's car.

Larry answered the phone. "Okay, Tanner. What's your plan?"

"Bring my parents down to Albuquerque and meet me on the top of Sandia Peak tonight," Tanner demanded.

"Your parents are dead. We killed them last night," Larry lied.

Tanner swallowed hard, trying to keep his emotions in check. "I doubt that. My parents are the only leverage you have. If you killed them, then why did you even bother answering the phone?" Tanner asked.

Larry sounded startled. Tanner wasn't backing down. "Okay, that's too soon for us to get your parents. As you know, they aren't here at the cabin."

"I imagine you can find them quickly. My guess is they're close by," Tanner said with confidence.

"So, I bring your parents, we make the exchange, and everything is forgiven and forgotten?"

Tanner had to be careful about what he said next. He knew that the Starting Five wouldn't go quietly into the night. "Look, I don't want to prolong this mess any more than you do. I've already given you enough information so that you could finish the hacking job yourself. You don't need me anymore, so let's end it civilly and be done." Tanner hoped Larry would buy it.

"How do I know you won't involve the cops?" Larry asked.

"I believe you've been keeping close tabs on police radios. If so, you'll understand that going to the cops would be counterproductive right now."

Larry knew exactly what Tanner was inferring. By robbing the bank this morning, Tanner made himself a wanted man and therefore eliminated the option of involving the police. It was an effective way for Tanner to guarantee to Larry that the cops wouldn't be at the rendezvous.

"Tell me your plan," Larry said.

"There's a tram that goes from the east side of Albuquerque up to Sandia Peak. Take the 6:30 p.m. tramcar to the top of the mountain. It's about a fifteen-minute ride. I'll call halfway up to speak with my parents and make sure they're okay. After I talk to my parents, I'll give you further instructions." Tanner wasn't a pro, but he knew that by rendezvousing at the top of an isolated mountain peak, he could watch and see who was coming up on the tram.

"We'll be there," Larry said.

"I'll see you at the top of the mountain. By the way, I hope you're not afraid of heights," Tanner said before hanging up.

———•———

Nicole Green was rethinking her assumptions. An hour ago, she had a solid suspect in the bank robbery, but now it wasn't all that clear. Finding the surveillance equipment hidden throughout Tanner's house was unnerving. Either Tanner was obsessed with home security or someone was spying on him. As soon as she found the security gear, she called the field office and dispatched an IT techie to the crime scene. Eric Adams wasn't an FBI agent, but he was part of the technical support staff that was critical to many of the Bureau's investigations.

Eric looked over the surveillance equipment collected around Tanner's house. "Wow, this is hi-tech stuff," he said. "I mean, this is top-of-the-line gear. It rivals the stuff we've got. The miniaturization of the fiber optics is especially good."

"Is this something available to the public?" Nicole asked. She was afraid of the answer and the path it would lead her down.

"No, I don't think so. It's the type of stuff only available to governments," Eric said.

"How sure are you about that?"

"I'm pretty sure, but I'll take some pictures and send the information to the technology folks back at headquarters. They'll give us the official answer," he said. "But this is the part that concerns me. There's no serial number, model number, or brand name on this equipment. It's an anonymous black box."

"Thanks for your help, Eric. Stick around here and see what you can find on those computers," Nicole responded. Then, taking out her cell phone, she made her own call to FBI headquarters in Washington, DC. She was confident that someone besides Tanner was involved in this drama.

October 7, Albuquerque, New Mexico

Larry's carefully organized and deliberately executed project had rapidly morphed into a chaotic mess. In less than twenty-four hours, he had lost his computer hacker, his secure satphone, and his composure. Tanner seemed to be running the show, which infuriated Larry to no end. He couldn't let Tanner outsmart him.

Tanner's latest call had thrown the group of kidnappers into an all-out frenzy. With little time to prepare, Larry and his team had packed their gear and headed off to rendezvous with Karl and his men in Santa Fe. The black Suburban carrying Larry, Charles, and the others sped down Interstate 25, followed closely by a red Jeep Cherokee. Inside that second vehicle, Karl and his two grunts rode with Gordon and Carla Zane, who an hour ago were shoved into the back of the Cherokee and told to sit still and remain silent.

"Magic, what intel do you have on this location? We can't go in there blind," Larry said. The caravan was less than thirty minutes out from the designated meeting spot, and they lacked a solid plan of attack.

"It looks like the tram was built in 1966 by a Swiss company," Magic said, reading off his laptop screen. "It's the longest passenger tramway in the world. There are two support towers. The first one is two hundred feet tall, and the second one is eighty feet tall. Two tramcars alternate going up and down and are suspended almost one thousand feet in the air. Each car can carry about fifty passengers. The trip up takes about fifteen minutes and ascends almost four thousand feet to the top of Sandia Peak. At the top there's a restaurant and observation deck overlooking the city. The opposite side of the mountain has a ski resort, and it looks like a single road comes up the back side."

Tanner had chosen this spot wisely. With the tram coming up the front side of the mountain and only one road up from the back, Tanner would be able to spot anyone arriving.

"What's around the base of the tram station? Is there an open area about a mile away where we can park?" Larry asked, thinking of a plan.

Magic rapidly pulled up Google Maps to check out the area. Switching to satellite view, he looked for an isolated staging point. "It says a large portion of the mountain is in the Sandia Mountain Wilderness. The satellite view shows a small subdivision just to the northwest of the tram," he reported. He zoomed in a little further. "Wait! There's a picnic area just next to that subdivision. It's about two miles out from the tram station. That's probably the best we can do."

"Okay, that's our staging point. Charles, keep your eyes open for a road to the picnic site just before we get to the tram station," Larry said. He then called the men following in the Cherokee behind them. "Karl, this is Larry. I'm working on a plan, so hang tight. Just follow us for now, but take note of the exit off Interstate 25 that goes around the north side of the mountain. I'm thinking of splitting up later and having you drive around the back side to ambush Tanner."

———•———

Tanner was lost in his thoughts as he drove the maroon Mazda 3 up the back side of Sandia Peak. He couldn't believe it was just yesterday that Megan had helped him escape from Los Alamos. This was turning out to be one of the longest days of his life.

The weather was turning colder. As Tanner approached the small parking lot at the summit, he noticed a faint mist starting to collect on the windshield. The elevation up here was over ten thousand feet, which meant the weather could be completely different than on the valley floor. Tanner checked his watch and saw that it was after 4:30 p.m. Dialing up a number on his pre-paid cell phone, he called Megan, who was at her house, waiting to hear from Tanner before heading over to the tram. "I just got to the top. I'm going to scout out the area and get ready for Larry and the others."

"Okay, I'm leaving for the base station in a moment. I'll call or text you when I see the black Suburban," she said.

"Trust your instincts. If something doesn't seem right, get out of there and call the FBI," he said. He had programmed the FBI's local hotline number into Megan's phone before leaving.

"Okay. I'll call you when I get to the tram. Be careful."

"You too," Tanner replied as he hung up the phone. At the top of the mountain, the wind was blowing steadily as it often did. It was beginning to rain softly, and Tanner hoped the weather would remain poor. With the wind and rain coming down, no one was likely to wander around the observation deck and disrupt his rendezvous with the Starting Five.

•———•

The black Suburban exited Interstate 25 and headed west on Tramway Road. In the distance, Larry could see the ominous mountain peak rising up from the desert floor. *Too bad we had to leave Patrick back at the cabin,* Larry thought. *We could really use his skills right now.* Not that the other three men weren't good. Each was well trained, but Patrick had special training in spy operations that would have provided an extra edge in this situation.

"Looks like the turnoff to the picnic area is coming up," Charles said, breaking the silence. A moment later, the black SUV slowed and turned left onto Forest Road 333 with the red Cherokee following. As Charles navigated the several sharp turns, Larry noticed the granite rocks and Prickly Pear cacti that littered the landscape.

"There's a trail called the Tramway Trail up ahead. It goes from this picnic area along the base of the mountain over to the tram station," Magic said as they pulled into the isolated park.

Grabbing a pair of binoculars from his field bag, Larry got out of the car first, followed by the others.

"This will do," he said, looking around at the vacant park. It wasn't really a park—more of a wilderness spot. Except for a few picnic tables, the area was in its natural state, with Piñon pines and Juniper trees scattered all around. Larry focused his binoculars toward the tram station. He could see a blue-and-white tramcar ascending the mountain right now. "How high did you say those towers on the tramway were?"

"The bottom one is just over two hundred feet tall. The other is eighty, but that one is two-thirds up the mountain," Magic replied.

Karl got out of the Cherokee and joined the group as they surveyed the area. The other two men remained in the car to guard the Zanes. "What's the plan, boss?" he asked.

Larry turned west, looking out over the valley toward the dormant volcanoes in the distance. Through the thick clouds, he could tell the sun was starting its descent. "The plan is first recapture Tanner. If we can get him back to the cabin, I'll break every last bone in his body until he finishes the hacking job."

"And if we can't take him back?" Charles asked.

"Then we rid ourselves of Tanner and his parents tonight," Larry said.

"What about your satphone?"

"This little exercise was never just about my satphone," Larry explained. "It was also about showing Tanner that he can't mess with me."

Charles nodded his head, but he didn't quite agree. He felt that Larry was getting too emotionally involved in his sparring match with Tanner. He thought about suggesting to Larry to stand down and rethink the situation, but he decided that wouldn't make a difference. Larry was the boss, and he had clearly decided to proceed with the rendezvous.

Larry finished scoping out the terrain. He turned and addressed his group of mercenaries. "Tanner knows that he can identify the four of us," he said, motioning to the rest of the Starting Five, "but he hasn't seen Karl or his team. That's a huge advantage that we can use in our favor," Larry said. "Charles, Michael, and I will ride up in the tram with Tanner's parents. Magic will drop us off and wait back here." Larry turned and spoke to Karl. "I want you and your boys to drive around the mountain and head up the back side. You'll be our little surprise for Tanner. We'll recapture Tanner at the top, and then you'll drive back to the cabin with him and his parents."

Karl nodded and quickly headed off to the Jeep. After moving the Zanes from his vehicle into the back of the Suburban, Karl drove away with his two henchmen.

Watching the red Cherokee leave, Larry addressed the rest of the Starting Five. "Charles and Michael, get your field packs with your night vision goggles, climbing gear, and extra rope. We're going to rappel out of that tramcar on the way back down and hike along that trail back here to regroup with Magic. We can't risk taking the tram all the way back to the station. I'm sure Tanner is planning to have the cops waiting for us at the bottom." Larry didn't have to tell his men to take their guns and extra ammo. A gun with lots of bullets always helped balance the odds when walking blind into a situation.

< 39 >

OCTOBER 7, SANDIA PEAK, NEW MEXICO

The black Suburban was parked in the nearly
empty tram station parking lot. It was just after 6:00 p.m., and
all across the Rio Grande Valley, the city sparkled with the faint
orange glow of sunset. However, gray storm clouds covered the top of
Sandia Peak. It was as though the earth was aware of the showdown that
was about to happen.

Michael, Magic, and the Zanes waited in the Suburban at the base
station while Charles bought tram tickets for the group. Larry was standing alone in the parking lot, getting an update from Karl. His second
team had driven around the back side of Sandia Peak and was now
taking the winding road up the mountain.

"When you get there, split up and search the area for Tanner.
You know what he looks like, but he won't recognize you. When you
find him, take him back to the Cherokee. I don't care if you have to
rough him up in the process, but keep him alive and secure until we
get up there."

Larry ended the call and climbed back into the Suburban's passenger
seat, then turned toward Gordon and Carla. "Take off their blindfolds,"
he said to Michael, who reached over the backseat and removed the dark
cloth bags from the parents' heads. Shielding their eyes against the setting sun's light, Gordon and Carla looked around at their environment.

188

It took them a second to get their bearings, but then it dawned on them that they were in Albuquerque.

"Mr. and Mrs. Zane, today is your lucky day. Your son has finished his work and is waiting for you. You'll be rendezvousing with him at the top of Sandia Peak."

Carla spoke out. "The top of the mountain? Why up there?"

"That's all you need to know. If you cooperate, you'll live and see your son. If not, you'll be killed," Larry said bluntly.

Glancing out the window, Larry could see Charles hustling back down the path from the tram station, flashing a thumbs-up. Opening the driver's door, he got in and spoke. "It's all set. I got tickets for us, and the operator even guaranteed our own private car. I told him we have our parents with us and that one of them is scared of heights. He seemed okay with the request after I slipped him an extra fifty bucks. He said it's really slow for a Tuesday night."

"Okay, let's get them ready," Larry said. Going around to the back of the vehicle, Larry opened up the tailgate, took out two wheelchairs, and set them up on the far side of the Suburban, out of view of anyone in the tram station. Then, opening the back passenger door, he motioned for Gordon and Carla to get out of the vehicle. "These are for you to ride in. We'll wait until the last second to board the tram. As you heard, Charles arranged for our own private car, so you won't be talking to anyone. Do you understand?"

Both Gordon and Carla nodded.

Carefully helping the couple get out of the Suburban, Larry and Michael guided each parent to a wheelchair. Once seated, Larry took out a pair of handcuffs and threaded them around the base of the wheelchair, locking each leg in place. He then repeated the same process with their arms. Satisfied the elderly couple was adequately restrained, he wrapped a large flannel blanket around each of his captives, concealing their handcuffs. The final touch was a baseball cap on Gordon's head and a scarf wrapped around Carla's neck for added obscurity.

"Just in case you try to get brave, we'll have one of these pointed at your back the entire time," Larry said. He showed them his black SIG Sauer pistol.

Magic started up the Suburban and headed off for the picnic area. Larry turned to Michael and Charles. "Hide your field packs in the storage area underneath the wheelchairs. Let's go."

Michael got behind Gordon's wheelchair and, with his pistol pointing at the vinyl back of the seat, pushed Gordon up the hill. Larry did the same with Carla while Charles ran ahead to let the operator know they were ready to go. Fortunately, nobody else had arrived to ride the tram on this drizzly October night.

●━━━●

A Toyota Camry sat in the opposite corner of the parking lot where the Suburban had just unloaded its passengers. The owner wasn't in the car but, rather, hiding in a small grove of trees just to the south. Through a small pair of binoculars, she saw the entire sequence of events. With Larry and his group around the corner of the building and safely out of view, Megan made her phone call.

"This is Megan. I just saw them leave for the tram. Both your parents look okay, but they're handcuffed to wheelchairs."

"Wheelchairs?" Tanner repeated. The wind was blowing hard, making it difficult for him to hear.

"Yeah. It looked like they did it to keep your parents from escaping," Megan said. Tanner thought about it for a second. "It's an ideal way to keep my parents restrained yet mobile enough to get them on the tram. Can you tell if they're getting on the 6:30 tram?" he asked.

"I can't from my point of view, but I'll head up there in just a bit to make sure," Megan said. "One more thing—they all have guns."

"Excellent work. Call me when you know if they got on the tram," Tanner said before disconnecting the call.

Megan's stomach was turning. All day long she had been nervous about the situation, but seeing the bad guys up close put her over the edge. Despite Tanner's confidence that everything would be okay, she was panicked. Not sure what else she could do, she pressed the speed dial button for the FBI hotline.

"FBI, Albuquerque Office. How may I direct your call?" asked the friendly operator on the other phone.

"I have some information about Tanner Zane," Megan said, just as Tanner had instructed her.

"One moment please," replied the operator.

<40>

OCTOBER 7, ALBUQUERQUE, NEW MEXICO

As soon as Megan mentioned Tanner's name to the operator, a preplanned sequence of events went into motion. First, the operator recorded the conversation and started a trace on the phone call to determine its origin. Then the operator patched the call through to the SAC, who had asked to be notified immediately should anyone call about Tanner Zane.

"This is Special Agent in Charge Nicole Green. How can I help you?"

"I need help. I'm calling about Tanner Zane. He's in trouble, and he told me to call the FBI," Megan began.

"Thank you for calling," Nicole said, motioning for Special Agent Catos to pay attention. "What do you know about Tanner Zane?"

"Someone kidnapped him and forced him to hack into Los Alamos National Labs, but he escaped and now he's trying to rescue his parents."

"Where is Mr. Zane right now?" asked Nicole.

"He's at the top of Sandia Peak, waiting for the terrorists to bring his parents," Megan replied.

The word *terrorists* added immediate urgency to the situation. "Thank you for contacting us. It was the right thing to do," Nicole said. Swiftly turning to Luke, she covered the receiver with her hand and spoke.

"Tanner is at the top of Sandia Peak. Find out if we can get someone up there ASAP. Go!"

Returning to her phone call, she spoke to the frightened woman. "I need you to tell me everything you know."

⎯⎯•⎯⎯

On the back side of Sandia Peak, Deputy Ryan Neagle of the Bernallio County Sheriff's Department started his ascent up the mountain as fast as the winding roads would let him. This wasn't like his other leisurely fall trips up to the summit. The phone call he'd received five minutes ago had jump-started him into action. It wasn't often that he got a call directly from the FBI. Something was happening at the summit, and he was the only cop within a half hour's drive that could respond. Glancing at his laptop, he waited for the picture of Tanner Zane to download. Tanner was the primary suspect in a bank robbery attempt earlier that day, and all indications showed that he was at the top of the peak.

⎯⎯•⎯⎯

Further along on the same mountain road, Karl and his men approached the summit.

"Listen up, you guys," Karl said to his grunts. "We need to find Tanner and isolate him until Larry gets here. There's bound to be people eating in the restaurant or strolling around the observation deck, so we need to be as discreet as possible. Check your weapons and make sure you're locked and loaded." He pulled into the far end of the parking lot at the top.

⎯⎯•⎯⎯

At the base station on the opposite side of the mountain, the blue-and-white tramcar was ready to go.

"It's going to be cold up there," the tram operator said through the window of his booth. Charles turned and looked at the twenty-something man with white headphones attached to his ears like hearing aids.

"What did you say?" Charles asked, keeping a watch out of the corner of his eye for his teammates' arrival.

"Up there on the top. The wind is always blowing, and it's usually twenty degrees colder up there. You should have brought a heavier coat," the operator replied. Charles was just about to respond when he saw his team pushing the wheelchairs up the ramp.

"Here comes my mom and dad. Thanks for your help," Charles said to the operator. He hurried down the ramp to assist the others. Walking between the wheelchairs and the operator's booth, Charles effectively blocked the young man from getting a good look at the Zanes as they came up the ramp.

Pushing Mr. and Mrs. Zane into the tramcar, Larry, Michael, and Charles quickly found their seats as the operator started the tramcar's steep ascent. Larry called Karl on the satphone. "Where are you?"

"We just pulled into the parking lot at the top. There are a dozen or so cars parked up here. It looks like there are some people in the restaurant but not many strolling about," he said.

"We just got on the tram and are on the way up. It's a fifteen-minute ride to the top. Check out the area and see what you find. Call me immediately if you find Tanner, got it?"

"Roger that, I'll give you a buzz. Over and out," Karl said.

———•———

Inside the restaurant at the summit, Tanner anxiously sat at the bar, sipping a Coke. The restaurant didn't have his favorite drink, which annoyed him, but that wasn't his primary concern right now. Larry and the others should have just gotten on the tram. Using his pre-paid cell phone, Tanner punched the speed dial that connected him to the tram ticket booth down at the base of the mountain.

"Sandia Peak Tram," a warm female voice said with a slight Spanish accent.

"Yes, I was going to meet my family and go up on the 6:30 tram, but I'm running late. Can you tell me if an older couple has recently gone up?"

"Oh, I'm sorry. I just saw them board the tram. They're already on their way."

"That's okay. I'll be there in a couple of minutes, and I'll hop on the next car. Thanks," Tanner said, relieved that Larry and the others were following his instructions.

The young lady in the ticket office had barely hung up when the phone rang again. She answered in the same friendly voice, "Sandia Peak Tram. How can I help you?"

"This is Nicole Green of the FBI. We're chasing a bank robbery suspect that we believe might have taken the tram up the mountain. Our suspect is a white male, thirty years old, six-two, and weighing approximately 190 pounds. He has brown hair and blue eyes. Have you seen anyone by that description?"

"No, I haven't, but it sounds like I wish I had," the ticket girl said. "Actually, it's been a slow night with the bad weather and all. The only people that went up in the past hour were three men and their parents in wheelchairs."

"Can you describe them?" asked Nicole. The ticket girl gave a vague description of Tanner's parents and the other men. Nicole listened and visualized in her mind the photos she had seen earlier in the day of Mr. and Mrs. Zane.

"Okay, thanks for your help. The local police are on their way. Please be ready to assist them," Nicole said before hanging up the phone. Turning to Agent Catos, she spoke. "We might have a possible ID on Tanner's parents. The girl at the ticket counter said she saw two people matching their description heading up the mountain with three other men, but none of them were Tanner."

"What's the ETA for that county sheriff going up the back side?" Luke asked.

"He said he should be at the top in ten minutes. I wish we could get the chopper up there, but the pilot said it's too stormy at the top," Nicole answered, staring out the window at the cloudy summit.

Today had been an unusual day for Nicole. Starting out with the mysterious and failed bank robbery attempt, the situation had become more intriguing when they searched Tanner's home and found hidden surveillance equipment. Then, when the field agents out of the Phoenix office couldn't get a response at Gordon and Carla Zane's house, Nicole started to get the uneasy feeling that experienced agents get when they know something is wrong.

"I guess we'll just have to take the tram," Luke said. He turned right onto Tramway Drive. The Ford Crown Victoria sped east along the road with lights flashing and siren wailing. Going almost 90 miles per hour, they quickly approached the base station for the Sandia Peak Tram just as two police cruisers arrived on the scene.

<41>

OCTOBER 7, SANDIA PEAK, NEW MEXICO

The tramcar carrying Tanner's parents was at the halfway point and suspended almost one thousand feet in the air. Larry wasn't afraid of heights, but being up this high and hanging by just a few steel cables made his hands and feet sweat. Picking up Charles's phone, he dialed the number to his own secure satphone. Tanner answered it on the first ring.

"Okay, Tanner, we're at the halfway point," Larry said.

"Let me talk to my parents—both of them. I want to know they're each alive," Tanner quickly replied.

Larry turned and held the phone to Gordon Zane's ear. "Tanner, is that you?" the older man said.

"Yeah, Dad. Are you okay?" Tanner asked.

"Yes, your mother and I are both fine considering the situation."

"Listen up, Dad. I'm getting us out of here. Do exactly as I say when you get off the tram at the top."

"Tanner, they have your mother and I handcuffed to wheelchairs. We can't do much—"

Larry ripped away the phone and put it to Carla's ear.

"Tanner, are you okay?" his mother asked.

"Mom, it will be fine. Just keep your ears open and listen to me when you get up here. I—"

"Okay, Tanner," Larry interrupted. "You got your time to talk. Now what do you want me to do?"

"When you get to the top, take an immediate left to the observation deck and wait there for further instructions," Tanner said, hanging up the phone. Tanner had moved from the bar, and he was now standing in the corner of the restaurant by the bathrooms. Quietly, he stepped out the back door, unaware that Karl and his two henchmen had just come in through the front.

———•———•———

On the back side of the mountain, Deputy Ryan Neagle sped toward the summit. It was dark outside, and he strained to see what was up ahead beyond the headlight's beam. Ryan killed his blue-and-red police lights in anticipation of his arrival at the summit. He didn't want to scare off the bank robbery suspect.

Despite his frantic rush up the mountain, Deputy Neagle took the entire event in stride. He had seen worse during his time as a cop in LA years ago. It didn't matter what the news said, the cops and citizens of Southern California were losing the war on gangs. Violence, drugs, and guns were rampant in the Golden State. After fourteen years of chasing gangs, Ryan had seen enough and transferred to New Mexico. The pay wasn't as good here, but the job was significantly less stressful. In addition, the quality of life was a lot better for his wife and three kids. In New Mexico he could even afford to own a home on a cop's salary—something that was impossible to do in Southern California.

Navigating the last switchback before the summit, Deputy Neagle slowed down his Ford Explorer and casually drove though the parking lot. His first task was to locate a maroon Mazda 3 that matched the car used in the robbery earlier that day. He had barely entered the parking lot when we saw it down at the far end, parked beneath a huge Ponderosa pine. *That's going to make it a little interesting*, Ryan thought, pulling behind the car. The license plate was dirty, but he wiped it off and radioed the plate number back to police dispatch. He then took a moment to call the FBI and give them an update.

"Agent Green, this is Deputy Ryan Neagle from the Bernalillo County Sheriff's Department. I just arrived at the summit. I located a maroon Mazda 3 that fits the basic description of the vehicle used in the bank robbery this morning. I'm going to do a quick visual inspection of the vehicle before I patrol the grounds. I have the license plate informa-tion for you," he said.

"Excellent. Please keep us informed. We have further reason to believe the suspect's parents are on the way up in the tramcar on the other side." Nicole paused. "Deputy, I'm going to get you some help. The bad weather at the summit prevents us from landing a helicopter, and I don't want you walking into this situation alone."

"That sounds good. I'll follow up with additional information as it arrives." Ryan got out of his cruiser and looked at the Mazda. Shining his flashlight in the windows, he didn't notice anything out of the ordinary. The interior of the car was clean and well maintained with no signs of weapons or narcotics. Turning off his flashlight, he walked up toward the restaurant just as the tramcar approached its stop at the top of the mountain.

●———————●

Down at the base station, Nicole relayed the information she got from the county sheriff's dispatch. "The Mazda is registered to Brent Holland. That corresponds to what Megan told us on the phone. She's been watch-ing it while he's deployed in Afghanistan."

Luke Catos nodded his head. "So Tanner borrowed the car without Megan's knowledge and robbed the bank. Good thinking on his part. That keeps her out of the loop and prevents her from being charged as an accomplice," he said as they prepared to take the next tramcar to the top.

●———————●

Tanner stood in the shadows of the restaurant between some tall pine trees. His dark jacket blended into the landscape. He watched the tram-car arrive and carefully looked for signs of his parents. The doors opened, and Larry came off first, followed closely by Michael and Charles, who were pushing two wheelchairs that held Tanner's parents. Tanner was relieved to see they were still alive. The small group casually moved over to the observation deck where they waited for Tanner's final phone call.

●———————●

Inside the restaurant, Karl and his two henchmen finished their search for Tanner. Unable to find him, they decided to split up and search outside. Karl came out the front door while the other two used the rear. They would sweep the outside of the building, circling back toward the observation deck where Larry and the others waited.

"What's that?" The shorter of the two men pointed at something as they came out the back entrance. Looking toward the parking lot, they noticed a county sheriff's SUV parked next to their red Cherokee. Karl and his two henchmen weren't professionals like Larry and the others. They were just ordinary street thugs hired on at the last second with the promise of easy money for babysitting some senior citizens. Seeing the patrol car parked by their Cherokee spooked them, and they quickly went back inside the restaurant to escape through the front door.

●———●

At that very same moment, Deputy Neagle came up the stairs from the parking lot. Looking ahead he noticed a group at the observation deck, including two people in wheelchairs. *Cold night to be looking at the city lights . . . they must be the suspect's parents,* Ryan thought. Slowing his approach, he unsnapped the holster on his sidearm and cautiously moved toward the group just as Karl's two henchmen came out the adjacent door. Coincidentally, one of the thugs stood about six feet tall and was roughly the same build as the suspect Tanner Zane.

"Stop right there!" Officer Neagle shouted, shining his bright flashlight and trying to determine if one of the men was the robbery suspect.

The darkness and wind only exacerbated the edgy situation, resulting in the first mistake of the night. One of the undisciplined street criminals drew his weapon from behind his back and spun toward the bright flashlight. Larry shouted, "No!" from the observation platform, but it was already too late.

With fourteen years' experience as a hardened LA street cop, Ryan Neagle instantly recognized the outline of the Smith and Wesson handgun. Deputy Neagle's training and experience took over in a reflexive manner. "Drop your weapon!" he shouted, moving sideways and taking cover behind a short wall constructed of granite rocks. The henchman, blinded by the powerful flashlight, took a wild shot that ricocheted off the gravel path nowhere near Deputy Neagle. Aiming his 9mm with expert skill, Deputy Neagle rapidly returned fire with two rounds, hitting the man in the chest.

The sound of the pistol shots was deafening to everyone in the immediate area. Inside the restaurant, patrons screamed as they ducked for cover. On the far side of the restaurant, Tanner was just about to call Larry when he heard the sudden, unmistakable sound of gunfire. Tanner quickly dove for cover behind a large tree trunk.

Resolving not to go down without a fight, the other hooligan wildly reached for his large handgun, pointing it toward the cop, who had turned off his flashlight and disappeared into the darkness. The thug took several wild shots that ricocheted off the stone wall in various directions, but he wasn't prepared for the recoil of the powerful .45 caliber weapon, which kicked back and up toward his face. The steel-plated top of the pistol smashed with tremendous force into his forehead, cutting a two-inch gash just above his right eye.

Lying on his stomach to reduce his profile, Deputy Neagle didn't have time to deliberately plan his next move. In just a manner of seconds, he analyzed the new threat and responded. Aiming his weapon toward the man, who was now holding his hand above his right eye, Ryan took another two shots, dropping the second gunman just a few feet from the first.

———•———

The sudden eruption of a gunfight turned the scene outside the restaurant to turn into complete pandemonium. Larry, Charles, and Michael tried to make sense of the chaotic situation. Fearing they had walked into an ambush, they drew their weapons and searched for defensive cover from the firefight. However, with nothing to offer significant protection in front of them and the large drop off behind, they hurriedly jumped back into the waiting tramcar, abandoning Tanner's parents on the observation deck. Larry was the last one to duck for cover. He felt a sharp pain followed by a burning sensation on the inside of his upper thigh as he rolled into the tram. "I'm hit!" he called out to Michael and Charles, who responded by firing their guns indiscriminately toward the unknown attacker. Ironically, the shot that hit Larry wasn't from Deputy Neagle—it was one of the wild shots taken by the second street thug, which ricocheted off the stone wall and, in a moment of dumb luck, struck Larry in the upper part of his thigh.

"I'm taking fire! I'm taking fire!" Ryan Neagle screamed into his radio as he rolled further behind the rock wall, looking for protection.

"What did he say?" Special Agent Catos asked. He was listening into the conversation on his radio down at the tram's base station.

"Someone's shooting at him!" Nicole yelled. Turning to the tram operator, she shouted, "Get this car moving! We've got to get up there, now!" Immediately, the tram operator started the process of sending the tramcar up to the top while bringing the other tramcar at the summit back down.

"We don't have time to wait for the SWAT team. Get on the tramcar!" she said, yelling at Luke and the other two Albuquerque Police Department cops with her.

———•———

At the top of the mountain, Larry, Charles, and Michael were surprised that the tramcar suddenly started its descent. Karl, who had been lying on the ground next to the restaurant, also heard the motor start on the tramcar pulley. Realizing that this might be his only option for escape, he hurriedly jumped up and ran toward the tramcar as it pulled away from the station. "Don't shoot!" Karl shouted as he jumped off the platform into the departing tramcar. Michael and Charles pulled Karl aboard and then hurriedly bent down to assess Larry's condition.

"How bad is it?" Larry asked through clenched teeth. He was beginning to look pale.

"I think I can take care of it. Lie back and sit still while I patch you up," Charles said. Grabbing the trauma kit from his field bag, Charles took out a pair of scissors and cut away Larry's pant leg to expose the bullet wound. Only then did Charles realize the extent of the damage. The femoral artery, one of the largest arteries in the body, had been ripped apart by the bullet. Despite Charles's attempt to stop the bleeding, the bright red liquid continued spurting out every time Larry's heart pumped. With his limited first aid kit and no surgical options, Charles knew it was hopeless. Larry was going to die before they reached the bottom.

He took a syringe from his bag and injected a large dose of morphine into Larry's forearm. "This will help with the pain," Charles said.

October 7, Sandia Summit, New Mexico

Tanner watched in shock as the frenzied events unfolded at the top of the mountain. The entire ordeal seemed to last an eternity, but in reality it took less than twenty seconds. The unexpected gunshots, followed by a return volley, had paralyzed Tanner with fear. Still hiding in the trees about one hundred feet away from the observation deck, he realized that something had gone terribly wrong with his plan. He had been hoping to have the FBI waiting for the Starting Five at the bottom of the mountain after he had successfully exchanged the satphone for his parents. Now, watching helplessly as the tramcar pulled away from the summit, Tanner had the sick feeling that Larry and the others were getting away.

———•———

"What's taking so long?" Nicole shouted impatiently as the tramcar slowly ascended up the mountain. The situation had turned into a total mess. Up top, there was a shoot-out going on with one or more bad guys against a single county deputy. He wouldn't last long with those odds. Two more cops were now heading up the back side of the mountain, but they wouldn't reach the top for another ten minutes—an eternity in a gunfight.

At the summit, Deputy Neagle carefully assessed the situation. Two minutes had passed since the last shots were fired. Crawling on his stomach, he managed to follow the rock wall around to the edge of the parking lot. He was now almost fifty feet away from where he had taken his first shots. Facing north, he could see both the tram station and the front entrance to the restaurant. *But where was the blue-and-white tramcar?* Straining his eyes, he could make out the silhouettes of two people in wheelchairs by the observation deck. Deputy Neagle wanted to go out and assist the elderly couple, but his first priority had to be his own safety. He was significantly outnumbered, and until his backup arrived, he didn't dare risk endangering any more lives.

The mood on the descending tramcar turned somber. Despite his best efforts, Charles couldn't stop the massive bleeding from Larry's wound. As they passed the upper tower, Larry took his final breath.

At least he was relaxed, Charles thought. He had given Larry a large dose of morphine to help ease his transition into death. Michael and Karl watched passively as their comrade passed on. They quietly observed a moment of silence for their friend, but as was the case in all battles, they didn't have time for anything else.

"Now what?" Karl asked, breaking the silence. With Larry dead and Patrick still at the cabin, they weren't sure what to do. Neither Michael nor Charles had clear seniority, and Karl was junior to both of them.

"We get out of here," Michael stated bluntly. "There's going to be a ton of cops waiting for us at the bottom. We execute Larry's escape plan and rendezvous with Magic back at the picnic area. Let's get our ropes and harnesses ready." Turning toward Karl, he said, "You can use Larry's gear."

"I've never done any mountain climbing," Karl protested.

"Don't worry. We ain't going to be climbing. We're rappelling," Charles said. He reached up and smashed out the overhead lights with his pistol, darkening the cabin's interior before he could see Karl's face turn white with fear.

Back at the top of Sandia Peak, Deputy Neagle heard the panicked screams of the patrons in the restaurant. Glancing over the rock wall, he had to make a decision. If he remained behind his protective cover, he might risk the suspects fleeing with the restaurant patrons, who were now starting to come out the back door. On the other hand, if he secured the situation, he might risk his own safety in the process. It didn't take long to come to his conclusion. Quickly jumping to his feet, he ran toward the two men who had been shot. With his Glock 17 drawn and pointed at the bodies, he kicked away the guns still gripped in their hands. Then, grabbing his handcuffs, he rapidly secured the arms of each man. Even though he knew these guys were dead, he still followed procedure, making sure they were secured. Without wasting any time, he swiftly moved around the back of the restaurant toward the fleeing patrons. Shining his flashlight at the crowd, he yelled out, "Police! Stay where you are! Remain calm!"

Far off in the distance, he heard the sounds of sirens coming up the road.

⸻

Nicole willed the tramcar to go faster as they approached the halfway mark. Up in the distance, she could see the other tramcar as it descended down on the opposite side.

"Red, the backup just arrived at the top of the peak," Agent Catos reported.

"I hope they're not too late," Nicole said.

⸻

In the descending tramcar, Michael, Charles, and Karl got ready. Putting on their climbing harnesses, they avoided looking at Larry's corpse lying on the floor. Michael had been first to finish securing his harness, and he was now helping Karl with his.

"I can't do this, man," Karl quietly said.

"You can wait for the cops at the bottom if you want, but we're getting out before that," Charles said. He took three long, black ropes out of the gear bags. Moving to the end of the tram, he threaded the ropes around the steel support bars, securing them in a classic figure-eight knot.

"Looks like that other tramcar is coming. We better get out of sight in case someone is looking for us," Michael pointed out. All three men quickly lay flat beneath the window's ledge out of sight of the approaching tramcar.

———•———•

"Here comes the other tramcar," Luke Catos told the group.

"Why is it all dark?" asked one of the local cops.

"Maybe the lights got shot out during the gun fight," the other offered.

"Or it could be carrying suspects down to the base," Nicole said as she drew her weapon and secured a firing position. Following her lead, Luke and the two police officers aimed their guns at the oncoming tramcar.

"I can't see anything inside. It's too dark," Luke said. The oncoming tramcar was just fifty feet away.

"Be prepared for anything," Nicole whispered to the others. They patiently waited for the exact moment when the two tramcars would be adjacent to each other.

"Just a couple more seconds," Luke said. Tensing up, all four of the law enforcement officers prepared for an ambush—but it never happened. The other tramcar passed by quietly without incident.

"Did you see anything?" Nicole asked the group.

"Negative, it was too dark. I couldn't see over the edge onto the floor of the tramcar," Luke responded.

"I only noticed a couple of shot-out windows," one of the police officers said. Nicole grabbed her radio and called down to the lone police officer waiting at the base station.

"A tramcar is heading down your way. It's dark inside, and we can't see if anyone is in there. You'd better take precautions when it gets there," she said.

———•———•

Ryan Neagle didn't have time to relax. Swiftly calling out to the backup that had just arrived, he directed them to secure the witnesses in the restaurant. Unaware of who might be hiding in the area, Deputy Neagle ran to the observation deck and checked on the elderly couple in wheelchairs.

"Come on, we've got to get you out of here!" he shouted, trying to lift the female out of the wheelchair. As he lifted her, the wheelchair came off the ground. Ryan threw back the blanket covering her lap, revealing the handcuffs on her wrists and ankles.

"We were kidnapped. The bad guys are getting away!" Carla shouted over the wind.

"Who?" Ryan asked, puzzled.

"The bad guys. They escaped in the tram heading down."

"How many were there?"

"Three or four."

"They fired off a couple of shots and then jumped on the tram," Gordon said.

"Did you get shot? Are you okay?" Ryan asked. He quickly looked over the edge of the observation point, trying to determine how far the tramcar had gone. It looked like it had just passed the halfway mark.

"We're okay," Tanner's mother replied.

"I've got to warn the others." Crouching down to minimize his profile in case there were other shooters, Ryan grabbed his two-way radio. "This is Deputy Neagle. I have two dead men up here. Witnesses say there could be three or four more suspects hiding in the tramcar on its way down. They are armed and dangerous."

●————————●

"They just passed us!" Nicole shouted as she listened in on the radio conversation, but there wasn't anything she could do. Her tramcar was heading in the opposite direction and would be at the top in just a few more minutes.

●————————●

"Okay, let's go," Deputy Neagle said. He started to wheel the woman inside the building. Looking up, he saw a man jump out from behind the trees, coming across the far side of the patio with his arms raised in the air.

"Police! Get down on the ground and put your hands behind your back!" Ryan ordered as he drew his weapon for the second time tonight.

"Tanner!" Carla screamed as the man complied with the officer's demand, getting down on his knees. Tanner knew tonight wasn't the time to experiment with civil disobedience.

"He's innocent! Don't hurt him!" Gordon called out as one of the other police officers ran out of the restaurant, aiming his gun at Tanner. With the help of Deputy Neagle, the two police officers handcuffed

Tanner and searched him for weapons, but they only found two cell phones.

"What's your name, son?" the other police officer asked.

"Tanner, sir," he replied.

"Tanner Zane?" Deputy Neagle asked with surprise. He had assumed that Tanner had fled with the others on the tram.

"Yes, sir."

"Well, Tanner Zane, you're under arrest."

OCTOBER 7, SANDIA PEAK, NEW MEXICO

The descending tramcar approached the last support tower. Michael, Charles, and Karl put on their night vision goggles, turning the outside world into pale shades of green. Michael forced open the door and stood on the edge of the tram, looking down two hundred feet to the ground.

"I can't do this!" Karl screamed above the wind.

"I don't care," Michael said as he threaded the rope through his figure-eight descender, securing it to his harness with a locking carabineer.

"Remember, we're moving, so you'll have to cut the rope just as you get near the ground or you'll be dragged across the rocks below," Michael reminded the others.

Rappelling wasn't a difficult task once learned. However, rappelling at night from a moving tramcar two hundred feet in the air was insane. Looking off into the distance, Michael and the others could make out the flashing lights of numerous police cars flooding the parking lot below. They had to escape in the cover of darkness or face a very unpleasant encounter.

"See you at the bottom!" Michael shouted. He clenched his hunting knife in his teeth and took a giant leap backward, pushing himself out of the tram into the dark night. The wind was less pronounced near the bottom of the mountain, but it still pushed Michael slightly to the side as he slid down the rope. Even with leather gloves, his brake hand heated up from the friction of the rope. Looking up briefly, Michael saw Charles jump out of the tram next, gliding down on his own rope.

Up in the tramcar, Karl suddenly felt alone. Closing his eyes, he forced himself to take the first frightening step backward. Panic gripped his mind as he felt like he was free falling, but the rope immediately caught him, and he found himself suspended about three feet below the tram deck.

Michael was almost done with his descent. Squeezing his brake hand, he slowed down until he stopped just a couple of feet from the ground. With his free hand he grabbed the knife from his clenched teeth and, in one quick swipe, cut the rope and landed on the desert floor with a hard bump. Fortunately, with his night vision goggles on, he was able to anticipate a landing free of any cacti or sharp rocks. Seconds later, Charles joined Michael on the ground. Done with their rappel, both men looked up toward Karl, gauging his progress.

"He's not going to make it," Charles said casually. Neither of them knew Karl very well, and his safety took a backseat to their own.

"We can't wait. The tram is almost to the bottom. Let's double time it out of here," Michael said. They grabbed their backpacks and sprinted along the trail at the base of the mountain toward the picnic area.

Karl wasn't experienced in rappelling, and he was having a difficult time controlling his descent. Alternating between free-falling and jerky stops, he had barely descended twenty-five feet by the time the tram started its final approach to the base station.

• ———— •

"What's that?" asked an FBI agent. He could see the tram up in the distance with something dangling over the side.

"It looks like someone is hanging up there," the other FBI special agent said, squinting. A total of six local cops and two FBI agents were waiting for the tram's arrival at the base station. All of them had taken up defensive positions with their weapons drawn.

"Stop the tram!" yelled the senior FBI agent. The tramcar came to a stop just short of the station. Suspended on the rope just twenty feet off the ground, Karl hung like a piñata waiting for its first hit.

"Stay where you are! We have you surrounded!" shouted the FBI agent through a loudspeaker. Three different floodlights illumined Karl's awkward situation as he dangled hopelessly in midair.

"Just get me down! I'll cooperate, I promise!" Karl shouted.

In the other tramcar, Nicole swore out loud. "What's going on now? Why did we stop?"

"It sounds like they're having trouble down at the station. They stopped the tramcar short of its ending point," Luke said, listening to the developing situation on his radio.

Nicole shook her head and sat down in frustration. It had been years since anything like this happened to the Albuquerque field office, and Nicole had spent the entire night on the sidelines. Sitting like mice trapped in a cage, Nicole and the others waited helplessly just a dozen yards from their destination at the summit.

Just over a quarter mile away, Michael and Charles stopped their retreat. They found a hiding position behind a large outcrop of rocks. Looking back at the situation with their binoculars, they had to make a decision.

"What do we do about that idiot? He'll tell the cops everything," Charles said.

"We've got to take him out," Michael said. Karl's ineptitude had prevented him from escaping, and now he was a huge liability.

"Can you take a shot from here?" Charles asked.

Michael was a trained sniper. His target was approximately five football field lengths away. "I've made shots longer than that."

Michael quickly assembled his SIG Sauer SSG 3000 sniper rifle. Lying prone on a flat section of ground, he aimed the rifle's sights toward Karl, hanging off in the distance. It was fortunate the cops had their spotlights directed on Karl because it helped illuminate Michael's target on the stormy night.

Charles sat next to Michael with the spotter's scope, calculating the distance and elevation change. "Range is 482 meters. The wind is northwest at about five miles per house," he called out to Michael. Fortunately, the impact from the wind was negligible at this lower elevation.

Charles wasn't worried about the outcome. Adjusting for the environmental factors, Michael was ready. Letting out a slow exhale, he held his breath and pulled the trigger.

The sniper bullet traveled faster than the speed of sound, reaching its target before the shot rang out from the rifle. The .308 caliber round hit Karl squarely in the chest. The first sign of anything wrong was a sickening "sludge" sound followed by Karl going limp at the end of the rope. The two FBI agents at the tram station looked confused, wondering if their suspect had passed out when the sound of a gunshot echoed off the mountainside.

"Get down! Someone's shooting!" an agent yelled. Already in defensive positions behind their cars, the law enforcement agents hunkered further down, listening for additional gunshots to get a fix on the shooter. The shots never came. Quietly swinging back and forth at the end of the rope, Karl's corpse looked like a lifeless piñata.

As a trained sniper, Michael would never take a second shot and risk exposing his position. As soon as he pulled the trigger, he began breaking down his sniper's rifle.

"You got him," whispered Charles as he squinted through his spotter's scope. Confident that Karl wouldn't divulge any secrets of their operation, the two men packed up and moved out. Having lived at an altitude over seven thousand feet for the past six weeks, they had the added benefit of being aerobically conditioned. They sprinted along the trail, covering the rest of the distance in fifteen minutes. By the time the FBI learned of the extra rappelling ropes hanging from the tramcar, Michael and Charles were approaching the picnic area.

"What happened? Where's Larry?" Magic asked as the two men climbed into the waiting Suburban.

"Dead," Michael said tersely. "Get us out of here. The cops are all over the place." Not taking any time to argue, Magic started up the black Suburban and drove off in the opposite direction of the crime scene.

⸻

Nicole Green and the others in her tramcar arrived at the summit with little fanfare. The ordeal was already over. Extra police officers had already driven up, and they now had the situation under control. Two dozen witnesses, including Mr. and Mrs. Zane, were isolated in the restaurant, enjoying complimentary soft drinks while being interviewed by the sheriff's deputies. The paramedics had also arrived and were ready to load the dead bodies into the ambulance.

"Welcome to Sandia Peak," Deputy Ryan Neagle said, extending his hand to Nicole as she got off the tram.

"Looks like we got here too late," Nicole apologized.

"It's not your fault. It's been a crazy night for all of us," Deputy Neagle responded. He had already briefed Nicole over the radio while she waited for the tramcar to finish its ascent. Nicole knew about the two dead bodies, the men who had escaped going down, and the arrest of Tanner Zane. With the situation at the top stabilized, she wanted to speak with the man who had started the whole fiasco twelve hours before. Walking over to a sheriff's patrol car, she opened the back door and spoke.

"Tanner Zane, I'm Special Agent in Charge Nicole Green of the FBI. Where do we begin?"

OCTOBER 7, NORTH OF ALBUQUERQUE, NEW MEXICO

The black Suburban headed north on Interstate 25 back to the cabin in the Jemez Mountains. With Larry dead, Michael and the others searched for leadership.

"What do we do now?" Magic asked.

"It's over. The project failed. There's nothing we can do," Charles responded gloomily.

"Let's call Patrick," Michael said, dialing a number on his satphone. Michael let it ring six times before it went to voice mail. He hung up and dialed the number again, and this time Patrick answered on the fourth ring.

"This is Patrick," he said. He had obviously just awakened.

"This is Michael. We've got major problems. Larry is dead, and we couldn't find Tanner. The cops showed up and the whole thing turned into a catastrophe."

"Where are you now?" Patrick asked, sounding more awake.

"Magic, Charles, and I are heading back toward Santa Fe. Larry died in the tramcar from a massive gunshot wound to his leg. We couldn't save him," Michael said.

"Was it an ambush?"

"We can't tell. A gunfight erupted just after we got to the top. Before we knew it, we were jumping back into the tram for cover. We also lost Karl and his two men."

There was silence from Patrick. Then he said, "Okay, get back up here, but don't draw any attention to yourselves. We're going to clean up this place and fall back to California. What's the condition of the safe house in Las Vegas?"

"I don't know, but we're going to have to sanitize it too. Some of our gear is still there, including everything that belonged to Tanner's parents."

"We probably have some time to do this right. It would be impossible for Tanner or his parents to determine the location of either safe house tonight," Patrick said. He laid out the team's strategy. "First thing, ditch the Suburban and get another car when you hit Santa Fe. The cops will be looking for a black Suburban. Then go straight to the safe house in Las Vegas and clean it up. Work all night if you have to, but take everything out of there. Then get back over here. I'll need your help to sanitize this place," Patrick ordered.

"Roger that. We'll keep in touch," Michael said.

It was after 10:00 p.m., and Tanner still felt on edge. It had been nearly two hours since the FBI had brought him and his parents in separate cars down from the top of Sandia Peak to the FBI field office. Handcuffed and sitting in an interrogation room, Tanner was alone except for an FBI agent, standing at the far end of the room.

Tanner wondered where his parents were. He hadn't seen or spoken to them since his arrest. Tanner was sure the FBI was keeping them separated until they got the full story from both sources. That was standard police protocol, but Tanner didn't care. His parents were alive and so was he. His six-week nightmare was ending.

Tanner was surprised and relieved by the FBI agent who was running the show. Nicole Green was a pro. The way she acted and she spoke to the other agents confirmed that Tanner was lucky to have her on the case. During the hour-long drive down the mountain, Tanner told Nicole Green everything. He didn't care if he had a lawyer present or not. Tanner was an honest person, and he believed that telling the truth was always best. Besides, he had nothing to hide. With a competent leader like Agent Green calling the shots, Tanner was confident she would sort everything out. That was why he had robbed the bank that morning. Tanner had needed to bring in the FBI because they had the best resources and skills to investigate and solve his kidnapping.

The story of what had happened on Sandia Peak became clear when the FBI showed Tanner the photos of the crime scene. He confirmed that one of the dead corpses was the ringleader named Larry, but he couldn't identify the other three dead men. Unknown to Tanner, his parents had already positively identified Karl and his henchmen as the guards who held them captive at their safe house. When Nicole told Tanner that his home had been bugged, he'd assumed the case was pretty much solved. But that was over an hour ago, and he was still isolated in the interrogation room. *What else are they waiting for?* Tanner thought. Finally, he heard someone coming down the hallway.

The door to the interrogation room opened and Nicole Green entered with two new people. One was the local FBI computer specialist, and the other a psychologist who contracted with the Bureau. In Nicole's hand was a can of Mountain Dew. Handing the soda to Tanner, she took a seat across from her suspect. In spite of his handcuffs, Tanner swiftly opened the soda and took a drink.

"I thought you weren't supposed to drink that stuff," Nicole said to Tanner.

"What?" Tanner asked, a little bewildered. The stress of the day was starting to take a toll on his mental alertness.

"Caffeine. I thought Mormons didn't drink it," she said.

Tanner was momentarily taken aback. He didn't recall mentioning his religion during his questioning. However, this was the FBI, and Tanner wasn't really surprised that they knew about his religious beliefs. A good investigation would certainly uncover that piece of information. "Yeah, that's a common misconception. It depends on how you define it. Mormons aren't supposed to drink coffee or tea, and some people extend that to anything with caffeine," he answered.

Agent Green accepted the brief explanation, nodding her head in a "whatever-you-say" motion. "Okay, Tanner, explain to me again how you managed to escape from the 'Starting Five,' as you call them," she said, removing her suit jacket and hanging it on the back of her chair.

"It goes back to a computer encryption class that Megan and I took in college," Tanner began. "Our final for the class was to create a simple encryption algorithm that would allow secret communication between two people."

Tanner didn't know it at the time, but Megan sat just ten feet away from him on the other side of a two-way mirror. In the company of two

FBI agents, she hadn't been arrested, although she had been escorted to the field office to substantiate Tanner's story. Nicole listened intently to Tanner as he explained how they coordinated his escape using musical theory.

"Megan and I decided to take a different approach for our final project. Most of the other students created their own computer code, but since I play the bass guitar and Megan is an exceptional pianist, we decided to use musical notes instead. Using just the notes in the bass clef, we developed our own encoding system."

"Explain how that worked," the computer specialist asked.

"Okay. Do any of you understand music?" Tanner asked the group.

The psychologist raised her hand. "I played the cello when I was in high school, but that was a long time ago."

"That's fine, you'll understand this. In the bass clef for music, there are seven basic notes—A, B, C, D, E, F, and G. If you include sharps and flats, there are more notes but not quite double the amount because a C sharp is also a D flat and so forth."

"That's right," the psychologist agreed.

"Megan and I chose to use sharps, which allowed us to use twelve notes in all—A, A#, B, C, C#, D, D#, E, F, F#, G, and G#." The group in the conference was starting to look confused. "Can you get me some paper?" Tanner asked.

The junior FBI agent left the room and quickly came back with a sheet of paper. Tanner began drawing out his explanation with a pen. "Okay, here's the A, A#, B, C, C#, D, D#, E, F, F#, G, and G#. The primary notes A, B, C, D, E, F, and G all represent the same letters in the alphabet, while the sharps of those notes correlate with H, I, J, K, and L. Played as eighth notes, this sequence gives me the first twelve letters of the alphabet. Then, if I play the same thing using quarter notes, it represents the rest of the alphabet. For example, an 'A' played as an eighth note equals an 'A' in the alphabet, but played as a quarter note it's an 'M.' Using this scheme, Megan and I were able to communicate using the twenty-four most common letters of the alphabet—everything except Q and Z. We used a quarter rest note for a space between words, and a half note marked the end of a sentence."

Watching how Tanner diagramed the basic encryption method, the psychologist nodded her head. "I can see how that would work. It wouldn't sound like fluid music when you played it, but the hidden message would still get across."

"That's right," Tanner said. "For instance, the word *help* would translate to A#, E, G# all played as eighth notes, and D played as a quarter note, followed by a rest note for the space. Then a B played as an quarter note and an E played as an eighth note would be the word *me*."

"But how did you communicate with Megan when you were locked away in that hidden cabin?" asked the IT specialist.

"Like I said, I posted the music to a website that we used for our project. Larry and the others didn't know that I was secretly communicating with someone. They thought I was just playing music."

"So Megan read the musical score you posted, which contained an encrypted message, and responded back to you in the same manner?" asked the psychologist.

"Yes. We went back and forth for almost two weeks planning my escape. The process was tedious, but that's how we coordinated the escape location. It's also how she told me where to find the can of mace in the bathroom."

"That's a fantastic story, Tanner. I'd have a hard time making up one like that myself," Nicole said with some doubt.

"Don't you believe me? I've done everything you've asked. I've cooperated fully. What more can I prove to you?" Tanner asked.

"Easy there, Tanner. I didn't say we don't believe you, but how can we substantiate a story like this? It's so far-fetched," Nicole said.

In reality, Nicole did believe Tanner. She had received the exact same story from Megan. Nicole just wanted to see if Tanner would change his story under pressure.

Tanner continued his defense. "I can show you the website if you want. There's a record of all the communications on there, and I've just told you how to decrypt the music. But right now you should be looking for the bad guys! These guys are pros. They've probably already closed up shop and moved out of the cabin. Quit wasting your time with me and find them. I'm not going anywhere!"

Nicole decided there wasn't much point in pressing him further. "Okay, Tanner, if you're telling us the truth, how do we locate these guys?" she asked.

Sitting back in his chair, Tanner relaxed a bit. "I've been thinking about that for hours. All I know is that they're somewhere in the Jemez Mountains, about an hour's drive south of Los Alamos," Tanner said.

"Maybe I can help," the psychologist responded before introducing herself. "I'm Dr. Erin Haskell, and I'm going to guide you through a visualization process. I want to see if I can pull anything out of your subconscious that could give us a clue to where the cabin is."

———•——•———

Michael, Charles, and Magic arrived at the safe house location in Las Vegas, New Mexico. It took them longer than expected to rent the white Ford van and abandon the Suburban in the parking lot of a twenty-four-hour grocery store. Despite the early morning hour, all three men were far from sleep. The events of the past five hours had pumped so much adrenaline into their bodies that it would be a long time before they felt tired.

Walking through the front door of the cabin, Michael and the others examined the safe house where Mr. and Mrs. Zane had lived for six weeks. "Patrick wants everything taken out—clothes, food, everything. There has to be no sign of anyone living here. We want the place to be as clean and organized as it was the day Karl got here," Michael commanded.

October 8, FBI Office, Albuquerque, New Mexico

Tanner was sound asleep. After he'd spent almost an hour working with the psychologist, Nicole escorted him to a private holding cell with a cot around 2:00 a.m. Tanner was asleep, but the FBI staff remained awake, pressing forward on the bizarre case. With the coffee machine working overtime, they gathered in a large conference room on the second floor to plan their next moves.

"Okay, we've been working all the angles, but we still have a long way to go," Nicole said. She had been awake for almost twenty hours, yet she still appeared fresh, and her clothes looked clean and pressed.

"Our two guys in Los Alamos just called me with an update," Special Agent Catos said. He had been up most of the day too, but he didn't look as good as the SAC. Luke continued, "They finished interviewing Ken Calloway. His family didn't like being woken up in the middle of the night, but after a few minutes of gentle persuasion, Ken told them everything. It all checks out, including the money problems and extortion by a mysterious man named Patrick. Ken told them about the CD with the secret program that he ran at work, but he didn't get his money. Now he's worried that he might lose his job."

"That should be the least of his concerns. He's going to be facing time in federal prison for espionage," Nicole said before changing directions. "What about Becky?"

"We got similar information from her," another FBI agent responded on the far side of the table. "She met a good-looking man named Charles on a dating website. They went out several times, but her last contact was a couple of days ago. She and her boss were supposed to meet Charles for lunch, but he didn't show up."

"And her boss is Dr. Jodi McDonald, the one who's running the quantum computer project at the lab?" Nicole asked.

"Yes, that's correct," the field agent said.

"How did Dr. McDonald take the news when she heard that her computer was the target of the hacking operation?"

"Not very well. She's been up most of the night working with the IT staff at the lab to make sure her data is secure. From what they can tell, the kidnappers were very close to stealing the plans for her quantum computer."

Luke jumped into the exchange. "It was interesting what Dr. McDonald said about using the quantum computer to crack encrypted communications. She said that was a big concern for her team, but I bet you can't guess who confidentially provided most of the funding for her project?"

"The NSA, I would imagine," Nicole guessed.

"Bingo," Luke said. "It looks like our friends over at the NSA also understand the value of quantum computers. With a high-tech system like that, they could crack any country's data encryption."

"Which explains why other nations would be interested in getting that technology first," said the junior agent next to Luke Catos.

"Speaking of the NSA, I sent over the photos of the surveillance gear we found in Tanner's house for their opinion. They agreed with our folks back in DC. The gear is all state-of-the-art stuff. You can't buy it off the shelf. That type of spy equipment would come from a nation-state," Nicole said. Her words sent chills up everyone's spine.

"What about that secure satphone that Tanner had? What do we know about that?" asked the computer technician.

"It's made by a German company that specializes in satellite communications and reconnaissance. We gave them the serial number to see if they could track it down. The phone was stolen from a warehouse in southern California along with five others several months ago. I asked the folks out of the LA office to track down that lead, but so far we haven't heard anything from them," Nicole said.

The agents in the room let out a sighs of frustration. The satphone was one of their most promising leads, and even though they got a list of the contact numbers off the phone, calls to all of the numbers went unanswered.

"So," Luke said with a yawn, "Tanner's parents confirmed the kidnapping. Ken Calloway and Rebecca Lewis both told us they were the targets of a social engineering plot, even though Rebecca didn't know it at the time. We know LANL has a super-secret computer that can crack even the strongest data encryption. And the two corpses at the top of the mountain were ex-cons who had done time in California for armed robbery," he summed up.

"I've gotta hand it to Tanner," Nicole said. "He's one smart guy. Getting the FBI involved by faking a bank robbery was brilliant, and because he didn't take the money or use a weapon during the robbery, he faces a lesser charge," Nicole said. She shook her head in amazement.

"But we still don't know where the real bad guys are hiding, and that's the information we need right now. The folks at the Department of Energy are screaming their lungs out, demanding any information we have on the guys who hacked into their lab," Luke said.

"Dr. Haskell, do you have anything else that could help us track down the location of the secret mountain hideout?" Nicole asked, looking across the table at the psychologist.

"Unfortunately, I don't. Tanner has an exceptional memory. He has the unusual ability to recall the smallest details. Usually I can glean additional information with my techniques, but Tanner had already told us everything he knew about it."

"Which is somewhere in the Jemez Mountains an hour south of Los Alamos. That's good info, but it doesn't narrow anything down." Nicole fiddled with her pencil. She was frustrated.

Just then the door to the conference room opened and an office clerk came in, handing a sheet of paper to Nicole. She studied the information for a moment before responding. "We got the fingerprint reports back from one of the dead men on the tram. The man who was shot on the end of the rappelling rope was David Rosenberger. He's a forty-eight-year-old with several arrests. He did three years for armed robbery."

"What about the other guy who ran the entire operation? The one identified as Larry?" asked Luke.

"Nothing," the SAC said. "We've sent his prints over to Interpol, and they couldn't find anything either."

"That's unsettling, to say the least," Luke replied.

"Yes, it is. And that brings us back to our primary theory. All the facts point to a foreign government enlisting the Starting Five to hack into Los Alamos National Labs."

"Yes, but which government? That's the million-dollar question," Luke said.

The conference room door opened again, and the FBI agent assigned to watch Tanner came bursting through the entrance.

"Red, Tanner's been awake for the past five minutes asking for you. He says he knows how to find the hideout."

October 8, Santa Fe, New Mexico

It was 6:30 in the morning, and the eastern horizon was starting to glow. Exhausted from cleaning all night at the safe house, Michael, Charles, and Magic were on their way back to their primary hideout. Michael decided to stop for a quick coffee in Santa Fe.

"Maybe we should call Patrick and give him the heads up that we'll be there in a bit," Charles said as they walked out of Starbucks. Getting back into the white van, they headed northwest on US Highway 84.

"Hello," Patrick said on the second ring.

"This is Michael. We've cleaned out the safe house, and we're now leaving Santa Fe. We should be there in an hour."

"Good. Any sign of trouble?"

"Nope. We ditched the Suburban in a grocery store parking lot. It will be a while before anyone finds it. We're now in a white Ford van."

"Okay, see you in an hour," Patrick said.

• — •

An FBI agent escorted Tanner out of his holding cell and into a conference room where Nicole Green and the others waited. Tanner sat down at the table. He still had his handcuffs on.

"Luke, take those cuffs off. We don't need those anymore," Nicole said. "Okay, Tanner, what's this idea you have to find the cabin's location?"

"I need a computer with an Internet connection," he said. "I think I have a simple way to narrow down the location."

"What are you going to do?" Nicole asked as Luke came back into the conference room with a laptop.

"Use Google—or more specifically, Google Maps," Tanner responded. "They have a neat feature that shows the satellite view of a map location. I don't know the exact address of the cabin hideout, but I can probably recognize the structure from the air. I was trying to think of a way to do this from a helicopter, but then I realized we don't have to. Google already put all that stuff on their website." Tanner pulled up Google Maps and searched for Los Alamos, New Mexico. "I'll use Los Alamos as my starting point and move out from there."

The group in the conference room listened intently. Continuing his thought process, Tanner said, "I know that I was held somewhere within an hour's drive of the city, and Los Alamos only has two major roads leading away from it. One comes in from the east by Santa Fe; the other comes in from the west though Jemez Springs. If memory serves me right," he said, navigating through the screens on the laptop, "I remember seeing a street sign that indicated we came in from the Jemez Springs side. I'll bet you a million dollars the cabin is a few miles off that main highway somewhere."

———•———

The shoot-out at Sandia Peak made the national news. Reagan watched the report in horror from the comfort of his plush home in California. A pit formed in his stomach. It had been almost twenty-four hours since Larry had called with an update. Seeing the news footage of the crime scene at the top of Sandia Peak, Reagan had the awful feeling that something had gone terribly wrong.

Fortunately, Reagan was adequately isolated from the operation in New Mexico, and it would be extremely difficult to trace anything back to him. Reagan wondered if it was time to just cut his losses. He thought about pulling the plug on the entire project and walking away. He had a fail-safe mechanism to do just that, but first he had to follow up and see exactly what had happened. Since Larry had lost his satphone, Reagan decided to call Patrick instead.

"This is Reagan," he began. "I need to talk with Larry. I saw the news this morning, and I want to know what's going on."

"Larry's dead. I'm in charge of the team now," Patrick said.

There was a long pause on the line. "What happened?"

"We aren't quite sure. Larry died from a gunshot, and a few of our extra men are also gone."

"Was it a trap?" Reagan asked.

"We don't believe it was an ambush. As a matter of fact, everything was going according to plan, but someone unexpectedly fired a shot, and it escalated into an all-out gunfight," Patrick said.

Reagan's temper started to boil. "We've got nothing now. The whole thing is blown!"

"Not necessarily," Patrick said. "We still have all the work Tanner did. He was really close to stealing the information about the quantum diamond. With a little more time, we might be able to find another hacker and finish the job."

"A little more time?" Reagan responded sarcastically. "What makes you think there's anything left to salvage? Larry is dead. The story is all over the news. The FBI is fully involved. It's only a matter of time before they find you and then find me!" Reagan spat into his phone.

"What do you want us to do?" Patrick asked.

Reagan decided it was time to bury the failed operation. Working to regain his composure, he took on a more professional tone. "How long will it take you to clean up and get out of there?"

"If we hurry, we can be out of here tonight," Patrick said.

"Get to work. I'll figure out a plan to regroup and call you back after lunch," Reagan lied.

OCTOBER 8, ALBUQUERQUE, NEW MEXICO

Tanner began his search for the Starting Five's hideout with the hunch that New Mexico Highway 4 was the right place to focus. It just felt right. Switching between the map and satellite view on the Google website, Tanner zoomed in on all the side roads that came off the main highway. The FBI agents in the room watched as Tanner rapidly navigated around the website. "Can you do this while we're on the road?" Nicole asked.

"Yeah." Tanner kept his eyes on the laptop. With a pen and notebook by his side, he jotted down notes of places to further investigate while crossing other areas off the list.

Looking at the clock on the wall, Nicole saw it was 7:15 a.m. "Let's mobilize a task group. I want three Suburbans and a half-dozen agents ready to go in fifteen minutes. Tanner, you'll ride with me and guide us to our location."

The team in the conference room split up and quickly went to work. Fifteen minutes later, Tanner was in the backseat of another black SUV. Special Agent Luke Catos sat to his side. In the front passenger seat, Nicole Green led the group like a general into battle.

"Start out by heading up Interstate 25," Tanner said as he connected the laptop to the cellular network. The Internet speed wasn't as fast as the network link back in the office, but it would do.

The convoy of FBI SUVs headed out of the FBI complex on the Pan American Frontage Road, but before merging on to Interstate 25, Nicole told the driver to make a quick stop at a convenience store. "I'm running in to get some snacks for us and a Mountain Dew for Tanner," she said as she jumped out the door. She had known Tanner for less than a day, yet Nicole was impressed with the young man's wisdom. He had proven to be extremely resourceful, and with a little bit of luck, she hoped he would find where the bad guys were hiding.

Tanner opened his drink and ate a donut as the Suburbans zoomed out of Albuquerque. Taking the exit at the small town of Bernalillo, the convoy of three vehicles cruised up US Highway 550. Tanner continued his feverish work in the backseat.

"We can cross this entire section off the map," he said, pointing to an area just west of Los Alamos where Highway 4 separated from Highway 126. "I can't find anything on the satellite view that looks like a cabin with a green metal roof in the middle of a meadow."

"Keep looking. I'm going to call out the helicopter and send them up ahead," Nicole responded.

———•———

At the cabin, the mood was subdued. Everyone realized their retreat to California was inevitable. Still immobilized from Tanner's well-placed kick, Patrick directed the team's activities from his spot on the couch.

"I just spoke to Reagan, and he wasn't pleased. After defusing the situation, I got him to agree to let us move the operation back to California to see if we can rescue this project," Patrick told the remaining members of the team.

"Can we do that without inside help from Ken or Becky? I'm sure the cops are on to them by now," Charles said.

"I doubt it, but we might get lucky. In the meantime, Reagan wants us out of this place by tonight. So that gives us about ten hours to clean up. Michael, head upstairs and start packing all our stuff. Charles, you take care of the main floor. Start in the kitchen and pack up all the food. You can load everything into the back of the van," Patrick instructed. Both men headed in opposite directions to begin their work.

"Magic, I need you to start breaking down the computer equipment. Pull out all the hard drives and stack them in the back of the 4Runner. We probably won't have time to get any of the other hardware packed up, so our first priority has to be safeguarding the data on those disk drives," Patrick said.

Magic took his orders and headed out into the garage to begin collecting the disk drives. A few moments later, he got the anonymous text message he thought might be coming.

Pull the plug, the message said cryptically.

Looking around to make sure he wasn't being watched, Magic stopped working on the computer gear and began following his new orders.

———•———

The convoy of FBI Suburbans moved up Highway 4 into the Jemez Mountains. Tanner's search routine wasn't as thorough as he would have liked, but he was still making good progress. Using educated guesses and assumptions, he narrowed down his search to the area around the small town of Jemez Springs.

"I keep going over all the scenarios in my head, and I always come back to Jemez Springs," Tanner told the group of FBI agents in the leading Suburban.

"Why do you think that's the location?" asked Special Agent Luke Catos.

"Logistically, it's the only place that makes sense. Even with the blindfold on the day I left the cabin, I was still able to get a sense of my surroundings. We traveled about four or five miles on a dirt road before turning onto pavement. We were on that paved road for almost an hour until we arrived at Los Alamos. Extrapolating the distance from those estimates, I have to put my starting point around Jemez Springs."

"Let's head up that direction," responded Nicole. She too had made some rough estimates of where to narrow down their search. In her own mind she had come to the same conclusion. Jemez Springs would be the most likely epicenter. Looking at the clock on the dashboard, Nicole saw that it was now 8:15 a.m. They would be at Jemez Springs in about twenty minutes.

OCTOBER 8, SAN DIEGO, CALIFORNIA

Reagan had had enough. From his point of view, the project was a catastrophic failure. That's why he'd decided to issue the abort command. He just hoped that Magic would be able to quickly and quietly pull the plug on the operation before fleeing the area.

When Reagan had agreed to get the quantum computer information for the Chinese, he knew that he was taking a big risk. In everything he did, he made sure to have an adequate escape plan. That was why he'd insisted that Larry and the others let Magic be part of the Starting Five. Reagan needed to have his own man on the inside for just this contingency, and with luck, the entire mess would be sealed shut by tonight.

●————●

Magic went about his tasks efficiently. First, he gently pulled back a shelf in the garage, exposing a hidden panel in the sheet rock. Reaching inside, he cut the surveillance cable that went to all the monitoring equipment around the cabin. Then, he opened a valve that released propane from the 500-gallon storage tank on the side of the house into the crawl space beneath him. As the explosive gas started filling the foundation under the cabin, Magic activated a timer for five minutes. He then carefully moved the shelf back into place and walked inside for the last time.

"I've got to grab a couple of things from the barn," he told Patrick, who took no thought of Magic's actions as he casually went out the back door toward the small building one hundred yards away. When Magic reached the barn, he retrieved a hiking backpack hidden beneath a pile of hay and continued his journey away from the cabin.

Inside the house, Patrick was the first and only one to notice the rotten egg odor from the ethanethiol infused into the propane. His first instinct was to look toward the kitchen and see if someone was cooking, but nobody was there. Turning toward Michael, who was coming down the stairs, Patrick started to ask him if he smelled anything funny. He never got the chance to finish his sentence.

The hidden timer in the garage finished its five-minute countdown, forcing the furnace into a heating cycle. As soon as the igniter on the furnace started to glow orange, it detonated the deadly cloud of propane gas that had collected in the crawl space. The wooden floor of the cabin heaved up for a microsecond before a yellow and orange fireball burst out, consuming Patrick, Charles, and Michael. Chasing the source of the fuel, the flame quickly shot toward the exterior storage tank. The ensuing explosion shattered the tank, sending out a thousand pieces of shrapnel in every direction.

Magic was three hundred yards away in the safety of the trees when the explosion happened. He quickly took cover behind a large pine, watching as the shock wave of compressed air expanded outward followed by a large flame that erupted into the sky. Even at this distance, he could feel the heat from the blast. Confident that nobody could have survived that explosion, Magic turned and disappeared into the forest. He had a long walk to Santa Fe.

The driver of the lead Suburban saw a cloud of smoke rising over the horizon. "What's that?" he asked. The FBI convoy had just turned off at Jemez Springs and was now heading up the forest service road toward the safe house.

"That can't be good," said Nicole. "Step on it!" she shouted to the driver, who pushed the accelerator to the floor, zipping up the dirt road at almost fifty miles per hour.

The fiery scene that greeted the FBI agents just a few moments later was overwhelming.

"Get some fire trucks up here! Call everyone!" Nicole shouted, but she knew it was too late.

"This is the right place, but what happened?" Tanner asked. The surrounding meadow looked the same, but the cabin was fully engulfed in flames.

"Looks like some kind of explosion," Luke Catos said.

"Tanner, what kind of fuel was stored around here?" Nicole asked, trying to determine the cause of the inferno.

"I know there was a propane tank for heating and cooking, and diesel fuel for the generator."

The procession of FBI cars stopped about two hundred yards from the fire. "There's a small fire station back at Jemez Springs, and they're on the way. The next closest fire department is at Los Alamos," Luke said.

"You'd better get them up here too. If there's diesel fuel contamination, we're going to need some kind of hazmat crew. Call up Los Alamos and see if there's a hazmat team we can borrow from the lab," Nicole ordered as she helplessly watched the flames.

<49>

OCTOBER 8, JEMEZ MOUNTAINS, NEW MEXICO

The blaze burned longer than anyone expected.
The small fire engine and volunteer crew that first responded from Jemez Springs weren't equipped for an inferno like this, and preventing the fire from spreading into the surrounding forest had been the best they could do. Fortunately, the builder of the cabin had cleared a large area around the foundation as a precaution against forest fires. It wasn't until an hour after the larger fire trucks arrived from Los Alamos that the fire was finally extinguished.

Nicole Green waited for word from the hazmat crew chief that it was safe to sift through the rubble. In the meantime, the surrounding meadow was filling with a contingent of law enforcement officials ranging from the local cops to a couple of ATF agents from Albuquerque. On the far edge of the clearing, a white sheriff's helicopter completed the law enforcement ensemble.

Taking charge of the situation, Nicole commandeered a mobile command center from the county sheriff's department. The command center was a decked-out RV with an impressive amount of equipment. Radios, LCD TVs, and DVD players lined the wall, and computer laptops and high-speed communications gear sat on makeshift tables. The trailer even had a small kitchenette and a bathroom. With over a dozen different agencies involved in the investigation, it was a chaotic yet remarkably effective production.

"It appears the cabin was built three years ago by a health-care executive in Albuquerque but was sold recently to a real estate investment company in California," Catos told Nicole as she sipped a hot cup of coffee. Fortunately, this mobile command post included an instant coffee machine, which was a valuable resource right now. "I've got the FBI office in San Diego looking into it," he concluded, hearing an approaching noise.

The door to the command center opened and a man in a fire suit came in, removing his protective head covering. "Agent Green, the area is safe now. Let me show you what we've got," said the chief. The hazmat team was a great asset to have on site. Coming from Los Alamos, they had extra training and equipment to deal with the sorts of chemical fires and radioactive contamination that might happen at a scientific facility like LANL.

"Tanner, you stay here," Nicole said as she hurried out the door with Luke. Tanner remained in the command center with another FBI agent and a technician who was monitoring the communication gear. With nothing else to do, Tanner sat down in a chair and rested his head against the wall. In thirty seconds he was asleep.

Outside the command center, the middle-aged hazmat chief spoke to the small group of law enforcement officials. "Sorry it took so long. There was an underground fuel tank we had to let burn out before we could fully contain the fire. Fortunately, it didn't appear to have too much diesel fuel in it when the blaze started."

Leading the group past the smoldering debris of the burned out structure, the chief explained his theory. "From what I can tell, this used to be a storage tank of some sort. I would guess it was for propane because the fragments we found included thick steel, suggesting it held a compressed fuel," he explained to the group.

"Did the fire start here?" asked Nicole.

"I don't think so. It seems there were a couple of explosions from the rubble field in the area. If you look, you can see two debris rings, each one suggesting a different origin. It appears the house itself exploded first," the chief said, leading the group around the concrete foundation of the cabin.

"How would that happen?" the ATF agent asked.

"It could be from a variety of things, but from my e
like a classic compression explosion."

Nicole shook her head, confused. "Explain that, please."

The chief continued. "Remember the Cerro Grande Fire we had back in 2000? It started as a controlled burn, but it got out of hand and destroyed four hundred homes in Los Alamos. It shut down the lab for several days." Some of the agents in the group nodded their heads, remembering the destruction. "We had a couple of remote buildings at the Lab that used propane. When the fire engulfed those, they exploded, leaving similar debris patterns."

"Okay, what about the victims? I have a witness who said there could have been four people in there when it blew up," Nicole said.

"That's harder to tell. I'm not a forensics expert, but you probably have more training in that area than I do. We did find some human remains, but nothing that would give us a clue to the identity of the victims. The fire destroyed anything the blasts didn't get. I can show you some of the remains if you want," the chief offered.

Moving through the blast area, he showed the small group the remains of charred human flesh. The gruesome sight caused one of the junior sheriff deputies to vomit.

"You can see this large mass here appears to be a part of a leg or an arm. It's hard to tell because the flesh is so badly damaged. If you look near this spot, you can see other bits and pieces, but I can't tell what parts of the body they belong to," the chief said, his voice as sterile as an operating room.

"Do you think the explosions were deliberate?" Nicole asked, believing it was too coincidental that the explosion happened just as the FBI arrived on the scene.

"I doubt it. We won't know for sure until the crime scene technicians search for explosive residue, but I think it was just an accident."

"Thanks for your help. I really appreciate it," Nicole said. She turned toward Agent Catos, who was just ending a conversation on his radio.

"The forensics and crime scene folks are on their final approach," Luke said.

Looking over a tree-covered peak to the south, Nicole saw a small black dot in the clear blue sky. As the object grew larger, she could tell it was the FBI's helicopter coming back with her crime scene technicians from Albuquerque. Today, Nicole wanted her best people on this case.

October 8, Jemez Mountains, New Mexico

A **firm hand shook Tanner awake. Luke Catos,** who had changed from his dress shirt and dark slacks into blue jeans, a T-shirt, sneakers, and a baseball cap with "FBI" embroidered across the front, smiled down at him. Tanner was momentarily confused until he realized that he had fallen asleep inside the mobile command center. Looking at the clock on the wall, he saw that it was 12:44 p.m. He had been asleep for almost two hours.

"Here, you might like this," Luke said, handing Tanner a turkey and cheese sandwich with a cold soda. "It's not much, but I can get you another sandwich if you want."

"Thanks," Tanner responded, rubbing his eyes and standing up to stretch. There were three other people in the mobile command center besides Luke. Two agents busily worked on laptops while another quietly talked via satellite phone link back to FBI headquarters.

Luke waited a few moments for Tanner to get his bearings before speaking. "The boss is coming back in. She wants to talk with you." Almost on cue, Nicole Green opened the door to the trailer, bringing her simple lunch with her. Her navy blue suit coat, white blouse, and slacks were gone, replaced by a polo shirt, jeans, and a dark-colored windbreaker with "FBI" written on it. With her red hair pulled up and sunglasses on, Tanner didn't think she looked like an FBI agent, but then he noticed the semi-automatic pistol fastened to her hip.

"Hey, Tanner, did you have a good rest? I sure could use one right now," Nicole said with a weary smile. She didn't give Tanner a chance to respond before continuing. "There's been a lot of activity over the past couple of hours. Apparently the cabin was rented out back in August, but all our efforts to track down anyone through the rental agreement lead to an anonymous PO Box in San Diego."

Nicole paused and took a drink of her cold soda. Letting the fizzy liquid trickle down her throat, she cleared her mind before continuing. "We've interviewed everyone in Jemez Springs, but nobody even knew the cabin up here was occupied. Larry and the others must have been extremely discreet."

"They were," Tanner confirmed. "The food and equipment was already here when I arrived. Nobody left except to visit Los Alamos. I know Larry and the others stayed a couple of nights in a motel up there. You might try and see if anyone up there can identify them."

"We've already got half a dozen cops doing that right now. The only photo we have of any of your kidnappers is Larry after he died on the tram. One of the motel staff recognized him from that picture, but she said that Larry always paid cash and registered under an alias. It's one dead end after another."

"What about Ken Calloway and Rebecca Lewis? Can they give you any more information?" Tanner asked, searching for other clues.

"They can only confirm what you told us. It's the same story, full of pseudonyms and fake addresses," Nicole said. She took a seat and closed her eyes to rest for a moment.

"What did you find out about the fire?" Tanner asked. It looked like Nicole was beginning to fall asleep.

She started. "Oh, it looks like natural gas or a propane leak caused the blast," she said. "The crime scene techs are sifting through the rubble, trying to find any evidence of explosives. We should have confirmation any moment. Unfortunately, the explosion and fire killed everyone inside. Wait—*killed* is probably too soft of a word," Nicole said, retracting her statement. "I think *disintegrated* or *obliterated* is more appropriate. There are no fingerprints or dental work to identify any of the victims. We might get something from the DNA samples we took on the charred remains, but that's only useful if the DNA was previously taken and stored in CODIS. That's our national DNA database," Nicole explained. She took another bite of her sandwich. Tanner was surprised how Nicole could talk about disintegrated bodies and charred flesh while eating a ham sandwich. He got a queasy stomach every time he got his blood drawn.

The door to the command center opened, and an unfamiliar woman stepped in and handed a paper to Nicole. "Here's the analysis from the explosion," she said. "It's negative on everything—no plastic explosives, dynamite, gunpowder, or ammonium sulfate. We can probably rule out foul play. I think it was just a bad accident."

"Bad luck for them and for us," Nicole said. The intensity and length of the investigation suddenly seemed to take a toll on her. "Tanner, what's your opinion on these guys? You lived with them for a month. Step back and give me a view of the big picture."

Taking a drink of his soda, Tanner gathered his thoughts. "What sticks out most to me is how the Starting Five operated. From day one they were—proficient. I mean, just look at how these guys worked. They were well trained and well funded, and they operated completely in the shadows. Everything about them shouted ex-military, but I don't think they were from the United States. My best guess is that Larry and the others were foreigners hired to steal technological secrets from the Lab."

"Nothing more than hired mercenaries," Luke pointed out.

"Okay, so where were these mercenaries from?" Nicole asked.

"My gut says they were from some former communist country, like Russia or Yugoslavia," Tanner said.

"So someone over there wants a quantum computer?" Luke asked.

"I don't think so," Tanner said. "I thought about that while I was locked up. These guys were hacking into a lab that is filled with nuclear secrets, but they weren't going after a bomb. They wanted a high-tech computer. Whoever hired them must not need nuclear secrets because they already have them."

Nicole nodded her head in agreement. "Makes sense. So who hired them?"

"I think it was China."

Nicole looked impressed. Tanner didn't have any formal training in criminal investigations, but his mind weaved the facts together like a seasoned detective. Of course, Nicole had already determined that another government orchestrated and funded this crime. Hardly any private organization in the world had the resources or ego to attempt a job of this magnitude. This case had the momentum to go down as one of the biggest investigations in the past decade, but without anyone to prosecute, it might end the same way.

"I think you're on to something," she said. "Our folks back at headquarters are looking into the China angle right now, but how will we ever know for sure? With everyone dead and the evidence destroyed, we only have one lead left. It's this mysterious Reagan character listed on Larry's cell phone." Nicole took the satphone out of the side pocket of her windbreaker. "We've made several attempts to call him, but he won't answer the phone."

"And he probably never will. For all we know, the phone has been destroyed by now," Luke said gloomily.

CNN reported on the explosion in the Jemez Mountains just after lunch. Jeff Kessler instantly recognized the mountainous landscape from the time he visited the property before signing the rental lease. Watching the news feed, he could see a burned-out crater where the cabin once stood. It was highly unlikely that anyone had survived.

With Larry and the others dead, the last link back to Jeff was the secure satphone that he had just destroyed. After driving to a remote city park, he took out a hammer and smashed the satphone into oblivion. He threw all the shattered pieces in the trash. It would take a miracle to trace the device back to him.

Jeff sat motionless on an isolated park bench, thinking about what had happened to his perfect plan. Everything had gone so well, beginning in Chicago when he had quietly recruited Larry, Patrick, Michael, and Charles. The unemployed military commandos trained by the former Soviet Union, spoke English fluently without any accent and were completely anonymous without any criminal records. He couldn't have picked a better group of mercenaries to help carry out his plans. Yet somehow the operation had imploded at the end.

Jeff Kessler, aka Reagan, had failed. Jeff knew from the beginning that this was an extremely risky job, but he desperately need the millions of dollars that the Chinese had promised in exchange for the classified plans to the quantum computer. Jeff didn't have the skill set to hack into Los Alamos, but he had known that his former roommate could do it. He figured that Tanner would eventually agree to do the hacking once he learned that his parents were being held as collateral. The operation had been laid out perfectly, but Larry and his team had underestimated Tanner and his ability to screw things up. In the end, Jeff didn't regret eliminating them for their incompetence.

Now Jeff feared for his own life. The Chinese general had given Jeff a two million dollar advance, and a stern warning that failure carried extreme consequences. Jeff had no way to pay back the major general, and he knew that the Chinese were notorious for holding a grudge. He was a wanted man, and Jeff knew that he had to disappear for a while. Soaking up the warm California sun for the last time, he got in his rental car and fled the state that he had grown to love.

•————•

Tanner watched the sun go down behind the mountains as dusk settled in at the crime scene. With a few high clouds above, everything was lined up for a spectacular New Mexican sunset. The crime scene had evolved from the frantic chaos of the morning into a slow and methodical investigation. A few news crews still hung around, but most of the other spectators had gone home to their families or on to other newsworthy events. Small pools of artificial light appeared as the FBI illumined the meadow, signaling that the investigation would continue throughout the night.

"Tanner, how would you like to ride back with us in the helicopter?" Nicole asked, walking up to Tanner with Special Agent Catos in tow. Both FBI officials looked haggard and worn.

"Aren't you going to stay?" Tanner asked.

"The investigation will go on for some time, but there are good people up here to continue the work so we can get some rest," she said. "You've had a long couple of days, and I bet you're ready to go home." Nicole smiled as she led Tanner toward the FBI helicopter.

"Go home? I thought I was going to jail," Tanner said, surprised.

"You'll still have to answer for that stunt you pulled at the bank, but I'm sure the district attorney and the judge will work something out, seeing how you've cooperated in the investigation," Nicole said. "Maybe we could even get them to dismiss the charges if you'd be willing to help us out in the future."

Tanner was astonished. "Are you serious?"

"Sure. With your background in computer hacking, you'd be an extremely valuable asset to the federal government," Nicole said.

Tanner couldn't believe what Nicole was telling him. He was so excited about the prospect of working with the FBI that he almost forgot about his mom and dad. "What about my parents? Can I see them?"

"They're waiting for us back at the office, and Megan Holland too. She's a sweet girl. You two should give it another chance."

"You think so?" Tanner asked.

"I'm a trained detective, but I don't need any special investigative techniques to see that you still have feelings for each other," Nicole said. She gave Tanner a wink and a smile before leading him onto the helicopter.

OCTOBER 9, ALBUQUERQUE, NEW MEXICO

Tanner woke up late after enjoying a good night's rest. The FBI had put Tanner and his parents up in a hotel suite about a mile from the Albuquerque field office. The FBI's nice gesture allowed Tanner and his parents a little comfort from the rough weeks they had experienced, but they weren't off the hook yet. They were still the primary witnesses in a bizarre criminal case. Nicole Green wanted the family isolated and protected for a couple of days while she continued to debrief them, and the hotel provided a perfect location to accomplish that task. The FBI had a special arrangement with the hotel manager for such purposes. All the staff had been instructed not to disturb the FBI agent guarding the door to the Zanes' suite or the other agent loitering in the lobby.

"Good morning," Tanner's parents said in unison as he joined them in the kitchen area of the suite. They were already enjoying a hearty breakfast at the table. Tanner and his parents had stayed up late last night talking, crying, and laughing. It was good to be together again, even though this wasn't their planned trip along the west coast. Tanner wished Megan was there, but the FBI had taken her home last night. Fortunately, they had stationed a local police car outside her house for extra security.

Tanner gave each of his parents a hug and sat down to eat. On the table were pancakes, eggs, sausage, orange juice, and a two-liter bottle of Mountain Dew with a note on it: *Thanks for your help!* It was signed by Nicole Green. Tanner smiled as he opened the bottle and poured himself a glass.

"It's going to be a busy day," his father said, "but I've got to admit, this is still better than being held against your will." Nicole had said she would pick everyone up around noon and take them back to the FBI offices for additional interviews.

"At least we're all together." Carla put her hand on Tanner's. "Too bad Megan isn't here. I had such a good time with her last night." Megan had stayed with the family at the FBI office until midnight, when Tanner and his parents had finally left for the hotel. Tanner had tried to give Megan a warm hug and a quick kiss on the cheek before leaving, but she grabbed onto Tanner and gave him a full, passionate kiss good night instead. Tanner could still see her smiling face looking back at him as the FBI agent drove her home.

"She's a nice girl, Tanner, and you're not getting any younger, if you know what I mean," Carla added.

"I know. I shouldn't have let her go the first time. I won't make the same mistake again," he said. Walking over to the large window, holding his favorite drink, Tanner looked east toward Sandia Peak. With the bright October sun radiating over the city, Tanner knew everything was going to be okay.

EPILOGUE

Yang **Dao was frustrated but not entirely sur-**
prised at the outcome of the hacking operation in New Mexico.
The Chinese military could have stolen the plans for the quantum computer themselves, but the major general decided against using his own team for the job. A Chinese-led operation of that magnitude was too precarious. After what happened in 1999 with his spy at Los Alamos, Yang Dao couldn't risk having any more Chinese espionage activities discussed on the front pages of American newspapers.

Yang Dao finished his afternoon tea before putting on his gray military jacket. He now had the unpleasant task of reporting the project's failure to the intelligence council. Fortunately, the major general had developed enough credibility with the council over the years that he wasn't worried about the final outcome. There would be other chances for success.

Stealing the classified plans was just one aspect of a greater cyberattack against America. Yang Dao was a skillful tactician, and he always had multiple options on the table. With the other phases of his grand initiative already in the works, the major general was absolutely certain that China would soon rule the digital world.

DISCUSSION QUESTIONS

1. If you could have an eight-week sabbatical from work, how would you choose to spend it?

2. Tanner is kidnapped and forced to do something he promised he would never do again. How would you react in a similar situation?

3. In this era of the Internet and social media, how can we safeguard our personal information?

4. As human beings, why are we so susceptible to social engineering techniques?

5. Throughout the book, Tanner consistently relies on his wits to make sense of his precarious situation. What are some of the exact things Tanner does to keep one step ahead of his abductors?

6. Tanner decided to end his relationship with Megan over a disagreement. How do you think people can maintain a relationship when they have vastly different opinions on an important subject?

7. Given all the recent media coverage about the National Security Agency and its spying programs, how do you feel about the government eavesdropping on our lives?

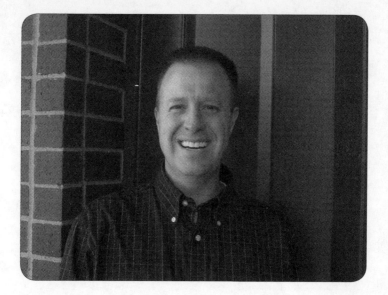

Few people understand the terrifying yet realistic threat of computer hacking like Denver Acey. Denver has spent his entire professional career in the information technology industry, where he has witnessed and even thwarted actual cyber-crime. From his top-secret job working for the US government to securing computer networks at Fortune 500 companies, Denver is personally familiar with hackers and their unscrupulous activities.

But over the years, Denver has become increasingly frustrated with Hollywood's inaccurate portrayal of cyber-crime. Hackers are more intelligent and more sophisticated than simple teenagers who guzzle down Mountain Dew while playing video games. Cyber-crime is a billion-dollar business that encompasses organized crime and foreign governments. For these elite hackers, the fruits of success are iconic trademarks, innovative patents, and government secrets.

Because of his unique background, Denver decided to write a book to dispel hacking myths while highlighting the tenacity of cyber-criminals. Utilizing actual computer hacking concepts and scenarios that he has experienced firsthand, Denver illustrates—in a simple way for even the non-techie to understand—how vulnerable we all are to cyber-crime.